MORNING GLORY

By Allison Blanchard

Martin Sisters Publishing

Published by
Martin Sisters Publishing, LLC
www. martinsisterspublishing. com
Copyright © 2013 Allison Blanchard
Martin Sisters Publishing, LLC, Kentucky.
ISBN: 978-1-62553-058-5

Printed in the United States of America
Martin Sisters Publishing, LLC

Dedication

For my Mom who never stopped believing in me. I love you.

Acknowledgements

So many people to thank for this amazing journey and blessing. First and foremost, I must thank the lover of my soul, Jesus Christ for loving me and blessing me beyond my wildest dreams. Second, I must also thank my mom, Tonya, and my Nana, Brenda, for always being there for me and encouraging me to continue to reach for the stars.

A special thank you must go to my very best friend, Kelly, for laughing with me, crying with me, supporting me, and celebrating with me throughout this journey of publication. She loves Cole and Adeline as much as I do and maybe even more. Well, especially Dylan.

Thank you to Hannah, my sweet sister in Christ who supported me and this series from day one. You are an angel and I am honored to call you my sister.

I must also thank my idol, fellow writer, and friend, Marianne Curley, who has been so supportive of my characters and me. Thank you, sweet friend. Your words of encouragement have meant the absolute world to me.

I also owe a lot to my beautiful sisters in Christ and in my sorority for supporting me, reading my books, and loving my characters as much as I do. Your support means the world to me.

Last but certainly not least, I must thank Martin Sisters Publishing for giving me a chance and supporting me throughout this whole process. Thank you to the moon and back.

PART ONE

To be nobody but yourself – in a world which is doing its best, night and day, to make you everybody else means to fight the hardest battle which any human being can fight and never stop fighting.

E.E. Cummings

PROLOGUE

I had always been afraid of death, ever since my parents died. I lived in fear that one day it would take me as well, or someone else who was more precious to me than my own life; I just never imagined that it would happen so early in my life, before I had even begun truly living.

I watched helplessly as his body fell to the ground. In those moments, all of our memories collided and crashed inside of me, slowly suffocating me. Living without him was not an option. Suddenly, death seemed kind; kind, only if it was to take me as well.

His body hit the ground with a sickening, bone breaking noise. I ran to him and fell next to his broken and battered body. If his heart stopped beating then, likewise, mine would as well. I closed my eyes and allowed the darkness to swallow me.

ONE

Yesterday was the last day of school. I was one more year closer to freedom from the public education system. The last place I would ever imagine myself on the first day of my summer was a bridal salon. Yet, here I was.

I sat in the corner of the dressing room, trying not to breathe in the stale perfume while waiting impatiently for Emma to emerge in her next dress.

The bridal consultant made an appearance first, before Emma. "I think this is the one," She mouthed to me. She was just as exhausted as I was.

I threw the magazine I had been flipping through to the small table and waited anxiously for Emma. She walked out carefully, as to not step on her flowing dress. It was refreshingly different from the others. No ruffles or sparkles in odd places. It was a clean-cut, white satin gown that flowed to the ground. She looked like she was floating. She was smiling widely while walking over to look into the mirror.

"Oh Adeline," she breathed when she saw her reflection.

I walked over to her showing my enthusiasm. "It's perfect Em."

"It is, isn't it?" she asked fixing the veil.

"Yep."

"Do you think Henry will like it?" Emma asked, looking at me through the mirror.

I tried not to cringe at the sound of his name. Henry wasn't a bad guy; I just wasn't too thrilled with the idea of him becoming my brother-in-law.

Henry had asked Emma about a month prior taking her to dinner, getting down on one knee, the whole nine yards. Of course she said yes, and I had then been appointed maid of honor.

I smiled, "Yeah Em. He's gonna love it."

She squealed in response, jumping up and down. I sat back down in my chair while Emma and the bridal consultant, Trisha, began talking about fittings and such. I zoned out immediately. I wanted to get out of there already – someone was waiting for me.

"Now about the dress for the maid of honor," Emma began. "I saw some in the front of the store and I want Adeline to try a few on." I groaned in response.

"Emma, I have to be somewhere," I protested as I stood, following her into her dressing room. Trisha went to bring the other dresses.

"Where do you need to go in such a hurry?" she asked trying to unclip her dress.

I rolled my eyes as I helped her out of the dress. "Cole is picking me up at the house in about ten minutes," I replied. "I already told you this."

"Well, as you can see, I've been busy. Planning a wedding and all," She replied slipping back into her jeans and pulling her blouse over her head.

I sighed as I hung the dress back onto the hanger. "I know Em. I just don't want to keep him waiting."

Emma ignored me, quickly walking out of the dressing room to ensure that Trisha was getting the right dresses. I sighed as I followed her, afraid of what Emma might have in mind for her maid of honor.

I caught a glimpse of Emma taking dress after dress off the racks and laying them in Trisha's arms. I cringed at the thought of trying on each one.

Emma's cell phone vibrated in her purse and I quickly answered it for Bridezillla.

"Hello?"

"Hey Sexy. What'cha up to?"

"Um . . . this is Adeline," I replied awkwardly.

"Well I'll be darn. You sound just like your sister Addie!" Henry exclaimed, trying to laugh off the uncomfortable situation.

"Let me get Em," I trotted over to Emma and handed her the phone.

"It's Henry," I mouthed. Her face broke out into a grin.

"That's him," she muttered to Trisha before taking the phone.

Trisha nodded and smiled while taking the mountain of dresses to the dressing room. I didn't think I would ever leave.

I looked to my wristwatch and sighed heavily when I saw I only had five minutes to get home to meet Cole. I might as well forget it.

Emma was twirling her hair while walking aimlessly around the bridal salon, still on the phone. I rolled my eyes at my older sister. Wasn't I supposed to be the one that spent annoyingly long hours on the phone?

"Okay, I'll talk to you later. Love you too," Emma said before she hung up the phone.

She walked briskly to my side, smiling.

"So, can I go?"

I knew the actual chance of Emma letting me go instead of helping her plan her wedding were slim to nothing, but I had to at least try.

"Sure. We can do this another time," she sighed dreamily.

I stared after her as she went to talk to Trisha. Did I hear her correctly?

"Really?"

"Yeah! Have fun and be home around eleven," she waved back to me while getting Trisha's attention to plan another appointment.

I walked out of the boutique taking in a much needed perfume-free breath. The air tasted sweeter.

I walked down the sidewalk, hoping Cole hadn't given up and gone home. We had made a point to see each other every day, but with Emma's wedding and Cole's tribe needing him, we had to really plan out the time when we wanted to see each other. There never seemed to be enough hours in the day.

I wasn't aware of someone following me until I heard a chuckle. It was a low husky sound that surprised me so much that it almost caused me to trip. I turned around feeling my heart skip a beat when my eyes landed on him.

He was a few feet away, leaning against one of the brick buildings that made up the street. He had his arms folded across his chest, his eyes glancing down to his feet. He was fighting back a smile.

I slowly, carefully walked up to him. It was still strange to see him like this, so beautiful and seemingly unattainable. It was as if he was a mirage that, at any moment, would disappear.

He never looked up to me, but kept his eyes to the ground.

I stopped when I was a foot away, waiting for him to move, to speak, to do anything. I watched him warily, analyzing him.

He finally looked up, or rather down, to me with a smile tugging at the corner of his mouth. I smiled up to him. I opened my mouth to speak, but nothing came out. My mouth was dry and my thoughts hazy.

His blue eyes held me and I realized that no words were needed. Everything we were both trying to say was within them.

"Hey," he said roughly. "You're late."

I rolled my eyes, trying to break his gaze.

"I know. You have Emma to blame."

He leaned away from the wall, towering over me, smirking.

"Doesn't matter, you're here now."

Suddenly, copper arms pulled me in and I saw nothing but him. He was all I needed.

"I missed you," he whispered into my hair, breathing deeply.

His arms tightened around me.

"I missed you too. I love you Cole . . . " I added the last part quickly. I was still afraid that he was a dream that would be gone in a second. It had happened once.

He sighed and tilted his head to look at me. "And I love you. Don't ever forget it."

I gulped and nodded.

He smiled, looking breathtaking. "How's your ankle?"

I glanced down to my braced foot. I had broken my left ankle about six weeks ago and just recently had the cast removed, but I still had to wear a very annoying brace. Cole constantly teased me about it, seeing that it hindered me more than it helped. My balance was shot now that I had to lean most of my weight to the right foot. I stumbled more than I walked.

"Fine," I muttered.

He laughed to himself, shaking his head at the tone in my voice.

"What would you like to do today?" He asked, lacing his fingers through mine, walking me down the street. "Dinner and a movie?"

"You know what I want to do," I shook my head. He knew that a movie wasn't going to cut it for me. I wanted to go see the Chosen. It felt like weeks had passed since I last saw any of them.

He rolled his eyes dramatically, "Can't we be normal for one day?"

"I'm the one who has to be normal 24/7. I want to do something fun."

"Being normal can be fun," Cole countered.

"Nope. I still want to go with you to see *the Chosen*," I said unwavering.

He shook his head, but didn't object. He walked me to his parked black, GMC truck. He opened the door for me and I quickly slid in.

He smoothly pulled out of his parallel spot without a moment's hesitation. We drove in comfortable silence. I was faintly aware of the world outside; I was focusing on his breathing, trying to sync mine to his as his hand intertwined with mine.

"How is everyone? I feel like I haven't seen any of them in forever," I asked, my thoughts suddenly focusing on the eight other Native Americans that had helped save my life.

Cole smirked, "They're good. Ava and Olivia won't stop asking about you. I think Chenoa is rubbing off on them."

I smiled at the memory of Ava and Olivia. They were two of the Chosen, part of a legend that has come to life. Both are able to transform into an eagle, the tribe's spirit warrior. Not only were they both gifted and beautiful, but they were both unbelievably kind to me. They were the two that welcomed me the most, besides Cole and Chenoa of course.

"What about Ella, Dylan, and Elan?"

Cole hesitated and sighed before replying.

"Ella is still herself. Doesn't talk much besides to Elsu. Elan is good. He's gotten better at his flying. And Dylan . . . he's about the same; still having trouble with shifting comfortably."

I frowned. Ella never liked me, so that wasn't news to me. But ever since the Chosen last battled the Rebels, when they saved me, Dylan got hurt and has had trouble shifting from his human form to his eagle. I knew it was entirely my fault, but Dylan was quick to disregard my guilt, always saying he should have been more careful. The truth is, I should have been more careful.

"Oh," I replied quietly. "That's good for Elan. I can only imagine how happy he must feel."

"Don't worry about the others Adeline. They'll come around," Cole said, somehow knowing I was worried about Ella and Elsu.

I nodded, glancing to Cole, and then looked back out the window.

I jumped out of the truck as soon as it was in park. I walked around the truck, my eyes scanning the sky and the clearing.

"Where are they?" I asked eagerly.

Cole chuckled, "They'll be here."

I restlessly looked up and down the empty clearing, wondering what was taking them so long. Cole laughed again at my impatience.

Finally, the sound of an eagle shrieking caught our attention. I looked up to the sky and gasped at the sight of them. I didn't think I would ever get used to them.

There were eight of them, all flying in sync with one another. Their bodies moved with such grace, even with their large size. I stared in wonder, completely hypnotized by their flight patterns.

They finally landed in a circle in the middle of the clearing, about ten yards from Cole and I. I took a step toward them, but Cole grabbed my elbow.

"Wait," he whispered. Something magical was about to happen. I could feel it.

I looked back to the group of larger than life eagles and waited. They all sat motionless, like statues. Suddenly, the wind changed, causing my hair to fly around my face, blocking my vision. By the time the wind died down and I could look back to the circle of eagles, they were gone.

I looked up to Cole, confusion clouding my eyes. He smiled.

"It's a little trick we made up. We've put Dylan and Jacy's gift of wind control to good use. "

"I thought you were supposed to be training," I replied dryly.

"We are," He replied tucking a strand of hair behind my ear. "Besides that wind control is how Jacy is teaching Dylan to spellbind like him. It's one of our tribe's defense strategies. It worked on you." He began laughing at the memory and before I could slap him, the others began running towards us.

"Hey Adeline!" Ava yelled as she ran toward me from the forest edge. Apparently their vanishing act gave them the time and privacy to change. I never completely understood the entire transformation that the Chosen had to go through, but I should have known that they couldn't phase with their clothes on. Likewise, when they phased back into their human forms, they weren't exactly dressed. That's one of the reasons they kept very small satchels with them wherever they went – they always held a change of clothes.

Ava threw her arms around me, causing me to stumble backwards from the impact. Cole caught me, sending a warning look in Ava's direction.

"Oh calm down Cole. She's not made of glass or anything," Ava replied, squeezing me tighter as if to prove her point.

I swear I heard a growl from Cole, but I was too busy trying to breathe to really pay attention.

"Adeline!" Olivia yelled as she ran towards Ava and I.

Another scorching body collided with mine and I almost winced at the extreme heat. Another part about being Chosen were the side effects that went along with it. Apparently, extreme body temperature was necessary as well as eating more than one would consider normal. Cole's answers to my questions had only left me more amazed. He was very wary about telling me the whole truth, afraid that I would have heard too much and would run away. I didn't need to be a mind reader to see his concern. It was written across his face.

Olivia and Ava finally let go, allowing me to inhale a much needed breath. Both laughed at my expression and I blushed.

Cole took my hand and held me close as Ella, Elsu, Dylan, Chenoa, and Elan came into view. I wanted to crawl back into the truck when Ella and Chenoa walked towards us. All the Chosen girls made me want to crawl into a hole and hide. They were all so beautiful that it almost seemed not human. No one could be that striking.

I cowered when Ella walked by me, not paying Cole or me a glance. I sighed, relieved. I couldn't stand to look at her anymore, not with Cole near. Maybe he would realize how much better he could do and leave me. I shuddered at the thought.

"Hey Addie!" Chenoa exclaimed as I was pulled into yet another bear hug. Cole kept his arm around my waist, almost afraid of letting me go.

"Hey," I replied quietly as I was released.

"How's Emma?"

"Good. I think she found her dress," I replied.

Chenoa squealed. I flinched at the high pitch sound.

"And what about your dress?" she asked, suddenly concerned. "The maid of honor must have her dress by now."

"Emma's working on it," I cringed. The thought of all the dresses I would have to try on did not sit well with me.

"I swear Adeline, sometimes I doubt that you are even a girl," Chenoa rolled her eyes.

Dylan and Elan laughed to themselves, but Elsu only sighed heavily, looking very uncomfortable.

"Are we finished here?" Elsu asked Cole, his voice tense.

"Wait, you're done?" I asked the others. I was too late to watch. Watching the Chosen train was the highlight of my week. Watching their eagle bodies transform and fly through the sky effortlessly never ceased to amaze me.

"Yes," Elsu answered quickly, not looking me in the eyes.

Cole glanced at Elsu, debating on whether or not to force him to continue.

"I'm sorry Adeline," Cole finally said. "I guess we are too late."

A rare smile tugged at Elsu's lips.

"However," Cole continued, "we will meet back here tomorrow before the festival."

Elsu's face fell, "What?"

"You have got to be kidding me," I heard Ella walk back to the circle, her sweet voice suddenly turning hard and furious.

"No. Meet back here at five A.M," Cole replied, his voice equally threatening.

Ella began shaking violently. Cole pulled me behind himself to shield me, but as quickly as Ella began losing control, she regained it.

She closed her eyes and took a deep breath. She looked to Cole again and said with gritted teeth, "Yes, sir. Of course."

Cole sighed heavily as Ella and Elsu turned and walked away angrily.

"We'll see you tomorrow boss," Dylan said, patting Cole on his shoulder. "See ya later Adeline."

"Bye Dylan," I waved.

"See ya chief," Elan added as he walked away with Dylan. "Ava, Olivia, you guys coming?"

"Yeah!" Ava replied. "You guys go ahead. We'll catch up."

Ava and Olivia turned to me and smiled. I tried to smile in return, but it probably looked more like a grimace.

"Don't worry about Ella," Olivia began, "she just needs more time to adjust."

"Yeah!" Ava agreed. "She'll come around."

I nodded in response; too afraid my voice would give away my true feelings.

They both turned and ran to catch up with Dylan and Elan. Cole pulled me into his arms and held me tightly.

"Really Adeline," Chenoa said, patting my back, "she will come around. She has to."

I nodded into Cole's chest. This afternoon had not turned out how I had hoped.

After Chenoa had left, Cole decided to take me to my new favorite place; a place that, once, he had only told me about. A place I had always imagined, but as usual my imagination didn't give it justice; the waterfall.

It was dusk when we arrived. The setting sun bounced off the water giving the whole place an ethereal atmosphere. He led me to the tree next the water's edge and we sat down. He leaned against the tree and I leaned against him, safe in his arms. We watched the sun set and the stars come to life. I almost fell asleep, but I fought to stay awake. I wasn't going to miss this moment.

The sounds of the waterfall and the crickets sounded like nature's lullaby; a beautiful symphony, just for Cole and I to enjoy. I had another lullaby though, one that was much more important and much more beautiful – the sound of Cole's heart beating. It was the most important sound in my life. My world revolved around it.

I decided that this must be what heaven is like. I was so content by simply laying in Cole's arms, my head buried into his chest, listening to the gentle yet strong beating of his heart.

"Adeline," he whispered.

I turned my head toward him and became captivated by his blue eyes.

"Yes?" I murmured, suddenly breathless.

He caressed my cheek, then my eyelids, then my lips. I gulped. He bent his head and leaned towards me. He gently kissed me, holding my face with both of his rough, calloused hands. My heart felt like a marching band on steroids.

When he finally released me, he whispered, "I love you."

I gasped for air, my head spinning.

"I love you too," I finally replied, my voice sounding slurred.

He chuckled, holding me tightly to himself.

"Cole?"

"Yes?" He mumbled sleepily. He was exhausted. I should have let him sleep, but I was curious.

"The festival tomorrow . . . what's it about exactly? You've been so busy with training, and I've been so caught up with Emma and the wedding that I've sort of let it slip my mind."

"The festival is a celebration for defeating the Rebels," Cole whispered. He didn't sound as excited as I thought he would.

"Is that bad?" I asked.

"No," he answered, "no, of course not. It's just . . . "

"Just what?"

"It's just that it's not over. It will never be over." He suddenly sounded defeated, like we had already lost.

"Yes it will," I said looking up to him. "We'll fight this and we'll win."

"Adeline," he said, his voice almost breaking. "They won't ever stop. We will have to annihilate them all to ensure your safety, but I will do anything to keep you safe."

I was shocked. I knew war was inevitable, but annihilation?

"What about Tyler? And others like him? What if others join our side?" I asked sitting up, the hope in my voice causing me to sound like a small child.

"Tyler is a special case, however he is just now being released from being debriefed by the elders. It takes weeks to ensure we are not allowing a spy into our tribe. We can't trust every Rebel that comes swearing peace," Cole explained as he sat up with me.

I looked down to my hands, which were intertwined with Cole's. He lifted his hand and tilted my chin to make me look into his eyes.

"Don't worry, Adeline. No matter how long it takes, I will make you safe again or I'll die trying. You have my word," he said with passion and fervor echoing through each word.

My breath caught in my throat and tears stung the back of my eyes. I gulped for air, but my head was dizzy. I couldn't see straight.

"Adeline!" Cole exclaimed. He took me in his arms and rubbed my face with his hands. "Adeline, what's wrong?"

Death? Was that inevitable too?

Life without Cole was not an option. I had tried that once and I definitely didn't call that living. That was barely existing, but to live in a world where Cole no longer breathed, walked, laughed, cried . . . that was worse. That was hell.

"Adeline," Cole said again, his voice tense.

"You're gonna die?" I asked tears now freely falling.

He sighed and pulled me into his arms. I sobbed into his shoulder and he held me tightly. He whispered in my ear, telling me how much he loved me, but not once did he deny the fact that he could die.

"You . . . you can't d-die," I sobbed. "Wh-what will I-I-do?"

"You have nothing to worry about. I will be okay. Don't worry sweetheart. Please, don't cry," he murmured.

I tried to regain control of my emotions, but I was failing miserably. My mind wouldn't, couldn't wrap around the very real fact that Cole and the others could die. A very real and terrifying truth, but maybe I could change that. Maybe I could save him even while being a feeble, useless human with not much to give.

"You love me." It wasn't a question.

"More than my own life."

"Then promise me something," I took his face in my hands, forcing him to look at me.

"Anything."

"Come back to me," I looked up to him and found undying

love and trust. "Do whatever it takes to come back to me."

He sighed and I began to think that would be one promise he couldn't keep.

"I promise I will keep you safe," he began.

"That's not what I asked," I interrupted. "I couldn't care less about myself. I want you to come back to me. I need you to live. A world where you don't live isn't worth anything."

"And a world without you is a world I refuse to live in," he interrupted me this time. "Adeline Connor Jasely, you are my first and only priority."

"And you are mine," I challenged.

He sighed, rolling his eyes, "Please. Let's not get into a fight about who means more to the other."

"You're right," I agreed, "because I would win."

He laughed, "You compare a raindrop to the ocean."

I sighed. There was no way I would be able to convince him, at least not tonight.

"Please Cole," I begged. "Please, be careful."

He rubbed my cheek with his thumb, wiping away stray tears I didn't even realize I had cried.

"Okay," he agreed before placing another gentle kiss on my lips.

He walked me to the front porch, our hands intertwined. The light turned on once we made it to the porch. Emma had been waiting.

Usually, I would walk into a dark house, finding Emma either sprawled on her bed or in the kitchen with wedding magazines and notepads filled with plans.

Cole chuckled, "Guess I better go."

"You don't have to," I protested. Emma could wait.

"And keep you away from bonding over cake toppers and flower arrangements? Never!" Cole smirked.

I moaned. She probably brought home ten different bridesmaid dresses and wanted me to try on each and every one of them for her. This was going to be a long night.

Cole chuckled again as he kissed my forehead, "Goodnight

Adeline."

"I'll see you tomorrow," I whispered breathless. "You'll come pick me up, right?"

"I'll come get you right after training. Just in time for the festival," he agreed.

"What time?"

He laughed again, "What time will you be up?"

"Probably five."

He sighed, "You need to sleep."

"No, I'm fine." I mumbled as a yawn overcame me.

"Goodnight Adeline," he kissed me before I could protest again. "I'll pick you up around nine."

"Mkay," I mumbled incoherently.

I watched him as he walked back to his truck and drove away. I opened the door and walked into the kitchen where Emma was sitting at the table. Strangely, there were no bridal magazines or notepads full of wedding plans. Instead, she was sitting with her hands neatly folded on top of the wooden table. Something was wrong.

"Emma?" I asked as I walked in. I set my bag on the floor and came to stand next to the table.

Emma took a sip of her tea and then set her cup down on the saucer again.

"Em?" I repeated. "What's up?"

"I have great news," she began smiling. "I booked a chapel and reception hall for the wedding."

"That's great Em," I replied, "but don't you need a set date before you book anything?"

"I have," she took another sip of her tea.

"Okay. When?" I asked, finally taking a seat.

"June twentieth."

"This June twentieth? As in, the wedding is in three weeks? Where did you find a chapel and reception hall this late in Great Falls? I already looked and nothing is available till next year!" I couldn't believe this. There was no way Emma found a place.

"It's not in Great Falls, Adeline," Emma replied calmly.

My heart dropped to the floor.

"Not in Great Falls?"

She nodded.

"Then where?"

"Beaufort, South Carolina is the cutest town. The perfect place for a wedding," she began to gush. "You'll love it there. The beaches are so beautiful and Henry's family is so excited to meet us."

"South Carolina?" I shouted. She bit her lips, trying to control herself. "Beaufort, South Carolina?" I repeated. "You can't be serious."

"I am."

"What about here?" I almost screamed. "What about people here who want to see you commit yourself to another human being?"

"Henry has more family than we do. You know that," Emma defended. "His aunts are old and don't need to take a six hour flight to Montana."

I tried to calm myself down. It would only be for a few days, and Cole would be there. He would come.

"Well, I need to let Cole and Chenoa know. They need to book tickets . . . " I began when Emma interrupted me.

"Sweetie, that's something else we need to talk about," I tried not to cringe at the use of the name "sweetie." She was becoming more and more like Henry each day.

"What's there to talk about?"

"Well, Henry and I have been talking and we feel that Cole and Chenoa should stay here in Great Falls. Henry doesn't really know them and feels comfortable with them coming . . . "

I stopped her by slamming my hands on the table. She was shocked, but so was I.

"You don't understand," I began. Tears were beginning to overflow. "You can't keep us away. He is just as much a part of this family as Henry."

"I have to respect Henry's wishes."

"So this is about Henry?" I sobbed. "What about your only

sister? Do you even know how much Cole and I mean to each other?"

Emma rolled her eyes. She was getting annoyed.

"Adeline, please. Henry and I are committed to each other for life."

"You don't know the first thing about commitment." I argued as I was shaking. "I see the way you and Henry are around each other. It's all superficial. He calls you sweetie and you call him babe and you just believe it is love."

"Now stop it!" Emma shouted. "We are going to Beaufort and I am getting married and you are going to be happy for me."

I sat silent. There was nothing to say. I had lost.

"When do we leave?" I asked with no feeling left in me.

"Next Monday."

My eyes widened and my heart took another blow. I had a little over a week to tell Cole goodbye. Sure, it was only for a wedding, but being apart for any amount of time was going to be difficult.

"I'm sorry Adeline," Emma whispered while pulling me into a hug. "Things just worked out this way."

"I just don't understand why Cole can't come," I pleaded. She owed me a better reason.

"Henry wants strictly family." She replied.

"Cole is family."

She sighed, "Maybe you should go to bed now."

I stood and walked to my room. I didn't remember taking a shower or even changing into my pajamas. I do remember grabbing Cole's jacket from my bed, pulling it on, and breathing in his scent. I didn't know how I was going to explain to Cole that I was leaving.

I fell into my bed exhausted, but sleep wouldn't come.

TWO

It was a dark, stormy day. The furious waves were beating against the sand violently. The rain was falling forcefully and there was nowhere for me to run. Besides the obvious storm swirling around me, I knew something bad was going to happen. Something sinister was approaching.

It was in those moments that I saw him appear. My heart fell to my knees.

Chandler Phalcon stalked towards me, his long black hair flowing behind him. He wanted to kill me. He wanted revenge for his dead comrades that had failed to take care of me in the first place.

I blinked and he was gone. I turned to look for him, but couldn't find him. It wasn't until I saw him standing over a dead body a few yards from me that I realized he had been holding a bloody knife.

My eyes fell to the lifeless form at Chandler's feet. Realization slowly hit me.

No . . .

I fell to my knees before Chandler and at the side of my Cole.

My dead, lifeless, no longer breathing, Cole. I gasped for air, for reason, for anything.

"Cole," I began shaking him, trying to wake him up. "Cole . . . "

My mind couldn't wrap around the fact that he was dead until I noticed his still warm blood staining my hands.

Chandler leaned down and snatched my hair, pulling my head up to look at him.

"You're next beautiful."

I woke up screaming.

I woke up with a jolt at quarter of six. I sat up slowly in my bed, trying to calm myself down. My heart was racing and my head was pounding. I didn't have any ordinary dream. It felt more like a premonition, a vision of some sort.

I lay in the bed, staring at the ceiling. Sleep was out of the question, and I was still shivering.

What was even stranger was that this wasn't the first premonition like dream I had. After the Rebels had kidnapped and almost killed me, I started having strange dreams. Not every night, but often. Usually, I would see the same angel figure I saw when I almost lost my life. Her name was Ogin and she was so beautiful and ethereal. In my dreams, she would simply stare at me, not saying anything. At first, it was frightening, terrifying even, but gradually, as the dream became more consistent, I became used to the disturbing angel figure. I would merely sit in the dream as we stared at each other. It even started to become boring. It was only very recently that my dreams turned into nightmares; dark nightmares of my greatest fears, of my own personal hell.

I never told anyone about those dreams, not even Cole. He was worried enough as it was. Besides, they were nothing but silly dreams from an over active imagination. They didn't mean anything.

After an hour of staring at the ceiling, I carefully got out of bed, getting ready for the day. I was planning on driving to see Cole and explain Emma's new plans. My anger towards Emma had not died down overnight. If anything it intensified.

I walked into the kitchen and left a note for Emma, letting her know that I took the jeep and would be back later. I drove to the reservation, but headed toward the place where the Chosen trained.

I needed Cole more than ever, not only because of Emma, but also because of my nightmare. I couldn't seem to shake the eerie feeling that Chandler and the Rebels were becoming stronger, or at least were still a threat.

Finally coming up to the clearing, I pulled to the side and parked the jeep. I got out, but couldn't see anything through the darkness. I looked to my watch. Had they finished training already?

I felt a gust of wind and the sound of nine eagles shrieking above me. I looked up and found them all in formation, with Cole in the lead. They flew above me awhile longer and then came to land in the middle of the clearing, surrounding me. They easily towered over me, their enormous bodies making me feel so small in comparison. And they were all beautiful, especially Cole. Cole's feathers were jet black with lines of lighter brown and white swirling from head to the tail.

Cole's eagle's spirit was Onida. Each Chosen was given the eagle spirit that their ancestors had used. Now all nine of the Chosen were surrounding me, staring at me with curiosity, worry, and annoyance in their eyes.

A silence descended as they sat staring at me.

"Hi . . . " I started. I thought I saw Dylan, the solid brown eagle, and Elan, the gray eagle with white specks, laugh. I turned to look at Cole. His blue gaze was filled with worry. "Can I talk to you?"

He nodded once and looked towards Dylan. Suddenly, the wind changed again and my hair blew all around me. When the wind died down, the Chosen were gone. I waited and soon enough Cole came running towards me from the edge of the woods, where he must have changed.

"What are you doing here? Is everything okay?" He asked his voice filled with anxiety and worry.

I opened my mouth to say something, anything, but no words formed. Instead, I threw myself into his open arms and held him tightly.

"Adeline," he began again. "What's wrong?"

I took another deep breath, trying to buy myself some time.

"Emma finally found a chapel and set a date," I whispered, trying to shake the sinister nightmare from my thoughts, and instead focusing on the situation with Emma.

I looked up at him and he waited for me to continue.

"She found a place in South Carolina and . . . "

He kept quiet, still waiting.

I shook my head, tears beginning to blur my eyes.

"And what? So I will have to buy some plane tickets. That's nothing to be upset about."

"No," I interrupted him. "No, she and Henry . . . they don't want you to come."

Recognition slowly spread across his face. His smile fell into a frown.

"I see. Well, that's not a big deal," he lied. "We still have the summer together."

"I'm leaving next Monday for two weeks," I finished.

Cole sighed heavily and pulled me into him again.

"It's okay. We'll be okay." His voice was shaking. So I wasn't the only one who thought two weeks was a ridiculously long time.

"Hey you two. What's wrong?" I heard Chenoa walk up. "Adeline?"

"It seems that Emma has set a date and the wedding will be in Beaufort, South Carolina," Cole began.

"The beach?" Chenoa interrupted excitedly. "I love the beach!"

"We are not invited Chenoa," Cole finished. "It seems to be Emma and Henry's wish that only family are allowed to attend."

Chenoa recoiled back as if she had been slapped. Guilt and a new wave of tears threatened to overcome me.

"And we're not family?" Chenoa asked, her voice cracking.

Before Cole or I could say anything, Chenoa turned and ran towards the woods. The sound of an explosion let me know she had phased and was flying away.

ALLISON BLANCHARD

"I'm so sorry," I muttered into Cole's chest.

"Don't be. This isn't your fault. I'm just going to have to make other arrangements."

"What 'other arrangements?'"

The other Chosen were making their way towards us when Cole whispered, "Don't worry about it."

I let our conversation drop as Elsu stormed his way over, anger and frustration seeping through him.

"What the hell is she doing here?" he bellowed. I jumped back in surprise.

Cole pushed me behind him, towering over Elsu by a few inches. If I didn't know any better I would say Cole was the older brother.

"You said we needed to train to become stronger to protect her," he glanced my way indignantly. "How are we supposed to do that if she keeps interrupting training?"

"Calm down," Cole gritted his teeth as he forcefully pushed Elsu back.

"Or what?" by this point, the other Chosen had made a circle around Elsu and Cole. Dylan gently pulled me to the outside.

"I'm not asking you big brother," Cole continued. "I'm telling you. Calm down."

Elsu began shaking violently. It was only a matter of moments before he phased, and Cole could get hurt.

"Cole," I tried to yell. It came out more as a shaky whisper. "Stop."

No one listened to me. They all stood and watched, waiting to see which Dyami boy would make the first move. Long silence followed as we watched both Cole and Elsu stare each other down. Finally, the sound of Jacy screeching in the sky above seemed to calm everyone. Jacy was the one hundred and fifty year old shape shifter that has remained in his eagle form since he lost his family in a battle against the Rebels. I considered him my guardian angel.

Elsu ultimately walked away, pushing Elan and Dylan out of his way in his fury. Cole made his way towards me.

31

Everyone began to scatter as Cole pulled me into his arms. I took in the scent of his bare skin, trying to memorize it. How could I leave him with a possible battle looming on the horizon, and almost getting into a fight with his own brother?

"See you at the festival Cole!" Olivia called as she and Ava started leaving.

"Bye guys. Good work today," Cole replied half-heartedly.

Ella merely glared in response, rolling her eyes once she glanced at me. I buried my head into his chest.

"I ruin everything," I whispered.

He kissed my forehead before murmuring, "No you don't. Elsu ruins everything."

"But he's right," I pulled away, looking into Cole's eyes. "I'm not helping. I shouldn't have come. Maybe it's a good thing that the wedding is not in Great Falls."

"Don't say that," he replied harshly. "Although I am happy for Emma, being without you is going to be difficult at best and arduous at worst."

I nodded, not really believing his words. Suddenly, his lips crashed onto mine, leaving me breathless. I'm not exactly sure how long we stood there, expressing the things we needed to say, to hear, without actually speaking. I never wanted to stop.

"You look beautiful," Cole smiled as he drove me to the festival.

I rolled my eyes playfully, "Whatever."

"I'm serious. You always take my breath away."

I breathed in deeply. He really needed to stop saying things like that. Emma's whole destination wedding that was about two thousand miles away was still hanging over my head.

"What are you thinking about?" Cole asked as we parked along the street. The festival was already underway. I could hear the music, see the different vendors of food, and watch the people dancing, talking, and laughing, without a care in the world. Lucky them.

"Do you think I could skip Emma's wedding?" I asked seriously. "I mean, who's to say that this will be the last?"

Cole laughed loudly as he and I got out of the truck and started walking towards the center of the party. "I don't think she will let you off the hook so easily miss maid of honor." He placed his arm around my waist.

I cringed, "Ugh. Don't remind me."

"Adeline!" Someone yelled. Cole and I looked to the person who called my name. I smiled widely when I saw Kai. I embraced her immediately, relieved to see her again.

"It has been too long my dear," Kai grinned. "How have you been? I hope you have been having good dreams. My dream catcher still works now, doesn't it?"

I was at a loss for words for a few moments. I felt Cole's gaze on me and noticed Kai's grin faltering a bit when I didn't answer immediately.

I forced a smile, "I'm doing well! And yes, the dream catcher is great. Thank you again."

If Kai noticed my hesitation she didn't voice it, but Cole did and pointed it out as soon as we walked away.

"Is something wrong?" he said while concern clouded his eyes.

"No, of course not," I lied.

"You can tell me anything, you know that, right?" Cole pleaded. He could read me so well. But I wasn't going to concern him with a few nightmares. He had too much on his shoulders as it was and I was supposed to help him bear his load, not add to it. No, he didn't need anything else worrying him.

"Of course, and the same goes for you," I urged. Cole never really talked to me about the stresses of being Chosen, let alone the Delsin. I tried to coax it out of him, help relieve the pressure that seemed to always be on the forefront of his mind. Cole never wanted this responsibility and I was the reason as to why he had to bear it.

He smiled weakly, fatigue covering his features, "Thank you." He was about to kiss me when someone pulled me out of Cole's arms. I thought heard Cole growl.

"Have you forgotten about me?" Chenoa scolded as she hugged me. I knew she was still hurt about Emma's news.

"Never," I proclaimed, hugging Chenoa tightly. She was truly a sister to me. "Do you forgive me?"

"You're not the one who needs my forgiveness," she quipped pulling me towards another vendor with a slightly frustrated Cole trailing us. "Just know, I better be invited to your wedding."

My cheeks immediately flared. We had a long while before even thinking about marriage. I was just trying to make it through my own sister's wedding. Cole merely chuckled as came up beside me and laced his fingers through mine.

We continued walking through the festival, laughing and talking. For a few moments I felt normal again, like the first time Cole ever took me to his reservation to show me around. Of course, the people were still vigilant around Cole and I, but in that moment I didn't care. I wasn't consumed with thoughts of the Rebel tribe or Emma's wedding. It was just Cole and I enjoying a beautiful day. From an outsider's perspective, there was nothing unusual or strange about us.

"Adeline!" Another voice broke through the barrier of noise, the hum of voices. It sounded strained, panicked, and familiar.

I turned to see Enola, an older member of the tribe, running towards Cole and I. Her gray hair was in its usual two long braids and her feet were bare. Her ancient eyes shone fear. Something was wrong.

For as long as I had known Enola, she had never left her cabin. She lived on the reservation, in a cabin deep in the woods. She wasn't exactly thought of highly in the tribe, and she preferred to be alone. Chenoa and I had made a few visits since my kidnapping. She usually seemed calm, still a bit eccentric, but nothing too out of the ordinary.

But now, as Enola pushed people out of the way, making her way toward me, a horrible feeling took root in my stomach, spreading throughout my body. I quietly pulled away from Cole who, along with all the other people standing around, simply stared as Enola made her way towards me, continually screaming my name. It occurred to me that no one in the tribe had probably spoken to Enola before now, or at least in a very, very long time.

"Enola . . . " I started as she finally made it to me, grabbing my arms tightly. "What are you doing here?"

I glanced around, mortified to find all eyes on the tribe's local nut case and me.

"Adeline," She bellowed tensely. "I have been dreaming."

Her words instantly caught my attention, but I couldn't discuss this. Not now, not here.

"Let's talk somewhere else," I began as I tried to lead her away from the crowd of people.

"No," Enola interrupted. "It cannot wait. Have you been dreaming too?"

I sighed quietly, "Yes."

She nodded, "Visions of the other tribe, correct?"

I looked around again, hoping no one was listening. My eyes instantly locked with a cold gaze. Cole's father, Paco Dyami, was staring at Enola and I. Usually, he regarded me with civility, but I didn't think he had ever truly approved of me. Generally, Paco Dyami was detached and impossible to read, but as I looked into his dark blue eyes, Cole's eyes, I saw fear and confusion.

I finally tore my eyes away from him and back to Enola, "Yes."

She started nodding, her grip on me tightening, "We need to interpret these dreams. I can usually read my own very well, but I do not understand them. Will you help me Adeline? It is very important we find the meanings."

She looked at me like a small, lost child. How was I supposed to help? My dreams terrified me and I buried them deep inside, closing them off so I wouldn't have to think of them again. To bring them back and analyze them . . . that sounded like torture.

I was going to answer her when familiar arms pulled me away.

"That's enough," Cole commanded as he unhinged Enola's grip on me. "Chenoa, take Enola back to her home please."

His voice was demanding and strong, but I could hear the flicker of fear behind his façade. He was just as terrified by Enola's appearance as I was.

"Of course," Chenoa obeyed as she gently took a confused Enola by the arm and led her away.

As we walked away I could still hear Enola helplessly ask, "Where's Adeline? I need to talk to her. We have so much to do. Please."

Even though Cole's safe and comforting arms held me close as we walked away, the deep seed of fear that Enola planted inside of me was growing, taking root. Somehow, my nightmares had found their way to my reality.

THREE

My heart was pounding loudly. I thought for sure Cole could hear it as he continued to kiss me, fervently, adoringly. Several moments passed before we broke apart, gasping for air.

I blushed, my eyes darting nervously from Cole as he continued to look straight into my eyes. Only Cole could look at me like that. Like I was exceptional, extraordinary, worthy.

He gently tucked my hair behind my ear before kissing me again. Only a peck: one, two, three times. He still managed to take my breath away. We were in his family's barn, hiding in one of the empty stalls. The festival was probably over by now and someone was most likely looking for us, especially after my encounter with Enola, but I honestly didn't care. I lived for these moments with Cole. The moments where I felt like a normal teenager whose only worries were what I was going to wear to my sister's wedding or what movie Cole and I would go see. The moments when Cole was just a boy and I was just a girl and we were both falling more hopelessly in love with each other with every passing moment.

He leaned his forehead against mine, pulling me closer,

enveloping me in his arms. I could feel his heart beating.

Those moments were fleeting, because outside of them was a dark world I never knew existed. At least until I met Cole and we were forced to relive an ancient legend.

"What are you thinking about?"

"Nothing," I finally whispered as I buried my head into his chest. "It's just . . . will the Rebels follow me to South Carolina? I'm so worried about Emma and what they would do to her."

"You don't need to worry about them. We'll keep them in the dark about where you'll be. Besides, as far we know they are still trying to regroup and rebuild. I don't think Chandler will be too concerned on where you are at the moment. We are keeping a very close eye on their movements and whereabouts. He won't find you. I promise."

I nodded into his chest, feeling a little bit better. I breathed in his scent deeply, a woodsy barn smell. It was heavenly.

He rested his chin on my head, his hold on me tightening, "Mind telling me what Enola wanted?"

I tensed immediately. I knew it was only a matter of time before Cole would want to know what happened, what was said.

I groaned, burying myself deeper into his embrace, "No."

"Please tell me," he murmured into my hair. "You have no idea how worried I am right now."

"There's nothing for you to worry about." Guilt washed over me, but I couldn't tell Cole about my dreams, figments of my deepest fears.

He chuckled, "With your track record, I have every reason to worry."

I looked up to him, disappointed to find that his smile did not reach his eyes.

"I'm sorry," I whispered. "Really, she is just a confused old woman. She was mainly talking nonsense."

I felt Cole relax as he sighed, relieved, "Okay. That makes me feel better."

"I mean," I continued. "Why does it worry you so much? You

know how she can be."

"Yes, but she is one of the people in the tribe who has a very strong connection with the legends and our past. She might have had something important to say, but you're right. It's nothing to worry about."

Cole leaned in to kiss me again, but suddenly my mind was somewhere else; more specifically, wherever Enola was, waiting for me to come visit her.

Cole held me tightly, his arm snaking around my waist. We were walking to the campfire ceremony Cole's tribe was hosting. It was only the second one of my life and so much had happened since I first learned of Cole's history. I could only imagine how much more I would learn tonight.

"Are you cold?" he asked, already shrugging out of his jacket and placing it around me before holding me by my waist again.

"Thanks," I smiled. There was no point in telling Cole that I didn't need his jacket, He would have insisted.

"There you two are!" Chenoa pushed through the crowd that had already gathered around the campfire. "I've been looking everywhere for you. Where have you been?"

I blushed under her scrutiny, while Cole grinned bashfully. Chenoa looked at us warily, before pulling me out of Cole's grip and leading me to our seats. Cole rolled his eyes in response, but followed faithfully. He knew not to cross Chenoa; she would always get her way.

"We're all sitting over here," Chenoa began. "We've got a seat just for you."

"When you say 'all'?" I questioned, my mind going through each of the Chosen, wincing at two in particular that made it clear my presence was not welcomed.

"Don't worry," She whispered. "They have to come to accept you. Besides, they wouldn't dare say anything in front of Cole."

"They don't have to say anything," I admitted, trying to ignore the stares from the other people of the tribe. Clearly, I was still the topic of conversation for many reasons. "It's the way they look at me. It's obvious."

Chenoa gave my shoulders an encouraging squeeze. I saw them before they saw me. The other Chosen, minus Jacy of course, were sitting closest to the elders. They were impressive and beautiful, frighteningly so. Elan and Dylan were laughing about something, Ava and Olivia were whispering and giggling among themselves, while Ella and Elsu looked on seriously. Neither of them were talking, simply sitting, and looking bored. They were beautiful, even Elsu with his scar that distorted half of his breathtaking face. They looked as if they belonged in a fashion magazine, not around a small campfire.

"Hey Addie!" Dylan smiled, waving us over. I cringed at the nickname. Only Emma ever called me "Addie" and even after I had fervently made my sentiments clear that I loathed it.

"It's Adeline, Dylan," Cole corrected gently as he sat next to his friend. "She prefers Adeline." It still surprised me how well Cole knew every little part of me that most people overlooked, even my own sister.

"Sorry," Elan shoved Dylan's arm. "Dylan is known to be the moron around here."

"Hey!" Dylan yelled, throwing Elan to the ground. "I'm not a moron," and then they began to wrestle. I looked to Cole, but found him laughing with the other Chosen. Apparently, this wasn't considered a big deal. However, Ella and Elsu looked on in disgust and embarrassment. If Cole's father, Paco, hadn't begun the campfire ceremony, I would have thought they were about to leave.

"Welcome, brothers, sisters," his unreadable blue eyes glanced to me, "and guests." I felt Cole tense beside me.

Paco ignored Cole's clear frustration and annoyance, "Tonight, we celebrate a victory of our people. The Chosen have once again defeated the Rebel tribe." Suddenly, a roar of clapping ensued. However, most of the Chosen didn't share in the excitement. They knew this war was far from over. I shifted uncomfortably in my seat next to Cole. He immediately wrapped his arm around me, pulling me closer.

"To mark this momentous occasion," Paco continued as the applause and celebration simmered down, "we will speak of a legend of the third generation of the Chosen. It is the legend of the four elements, an account of how the power of this elite group grew in a time of need."

Paco Dyami sat down next to the current chief, Red Hakan, who cleared his throat before beginning his story.

"It was several decades after Chief Heluka's death," he began, his deep voice reverberating in my mind, already painting the picture, "and civil war between the two tribes had reached its absolute peak. The Chosen were recuperating after a particularly brutal battle. The Delsin at the time, Maska, took the Chosen on a journey of reflection into the Northern Mountains. A few days had passed into their voyage when the answer to his prayers was given.

"Maska was sleeping beside a river with the other Chosen. However, a whisper in the wind awoke the young Delsin. He sat up, confused as to what had woken him.

"Maska quietly left the rest of the sleeping Chosen in pursuit of the whispering. As he continued, the voice became clearer and the whisper turned into a song. He stopped when he came to a waterfall where he saw, what he thought, to be a beautiful angel singing mournfully by the water's side.

"'Who are you?' He asked quietly, feeling guilty for interrupting her song.

"She looked up, tears raining down her face, 'I am Ogin, the power you seek.'"

Suddenly, the blood drained from my face. A numbing sort of sensation took root in the pit of my stomach, spreading to my legs, immobilizing me. Did I hear Mr. Hakan correctly? He did just say that her name was Ogin? My heart began to beat fitfully, banging against my rib cage, threatening to burst as Red Hakan continued.

"Ogin was the name given to the heavenly being several decades before by Chief Heluka. It means 'wild rose' and Heluka named her so for she was his heart; something so beautiful, yet so fragile.

"'What are you doing here?' Maska asked, frightened to see such a beautiful creature crying so. 'What does this mean?'

"Maska feared the final battle between the two tribes was to come soon for the heavenly being's reappearance and reincarnation is the catalyst for a long and bitter war to follow."

Suddenly, every eye turned from Red Hakan to me. My cheeks flared and I tried to escape their intense stares by shrinking into Cole's protective embrace. However, they continued to stare; some angry, others bitter, but mostly, their stares held pity. They felt more sorry for me than they did for themselves. It was like they understood that I never asked to be the heavenly being. They knew I was just as much a victim as they were. At least, most of them understood.

"Ogin replied," Red Hakan gained everyone's attention again, saving me from further embarrassment "'I have not yet been reincarnated. My soul is wanderer, searching and waiting for the proper time when I will be reborn.'

"Maska was amazed and terrified all at once. His ancestors had told him of sprits, but he had never come face to face with one before. However, Ogin was kind. Though sorrowful, she was benevolent.

"'Although I am a wanderer, a soul without a home, I do think I can help you,' She explained to the young Delsin. 'I know you have had trouble these past months. The battles are becoming harder to handle. You are correct in your thinking that the Rebels are growing stronger, but their strength comes from darkness, black magic. I'm here to give you the last bit of my power that keeps me here, in this form.

"Maska stood before the beautiful heavenly being, confused on her meaning. What more power could she possibly give? Ogin walked towards Maska, hands held out. She began whispering to herself, eyes closed as she continued to mumble in a language that was foreign to him.

"Suddenly, Maska felt a change within him. His body shifted uncomfortably as she continued to chant. He felt as if he were on fire, his entire body burning, but there were no flames to be seen. He tried to call out, but his voice had disappeared.

"Then as quickly as the startling pain racked through his body, it disappeared. He fell to his knees in front of Ogin, his breathing labored.

"'What have you done to me?' he asked, looking up to the suddenly fatigued angel.

"'I've saved your life,' she answered simply. Then, before Maska's very eyes, Ogin disappeared into the wind, never to be seen again.

"As soon as Maska regained his strength, he returned to the Chosen, who were all awake and breathing heavily as well. Ogin's gift had extended to all who were Chosen. It wasn't till much later, in the next battle with the Rebel tribe, did Maska and the others realize the priceless gift Ogin had bestowed upon them: control over nature's elements.

"The Delsin have control over all four elements of nature: wind, water, earth, and fire. Each Chosen member has a particular gift according to his or her spirit warrior. Without this gift, the Chosen would not have been able to continue to defeat the Rebel tribe. Without this last sacrifice from the heavenly being, we would all be lost."

Red Hakan paused, glancing towards the eight young Native Americans sitting around me, "That is the legend of how the heavenly being saved our tribe again, even as her soul was wandering."

Silence followed as Red Hakan sat back in his chair, his body relaxing. Different eyes glanced from the Chosen around me, to Cole, and then finally landed on me. I fidgeted under their gaze.

"This is a time of celebration," Paco disturbed the silence, all eyes resting on him, "but we all must realize the hard road that lies before us. Something great, something bigger than what we have ever imagined is coming, and we all," his eyes darted to mine, "must be prepared for what is required of us."

In that moment, when Paco Dyami's blue eyes met mine, I

realized what I must do, what I had to do. I had to become involved, more involved that I ever had been. If Ogin really was the heavenly being and if she was really in my dreams, then I had to figure them out. Only one person could help me: Enola.

I pulled up to the familiar, old cabin warily. I had to sneak away from both Emma and Cole to make this trip. It had only been a few days since the festival and my anxieties and worries had only been intensifying, growing with each passing day. Soon, I would be over two thousand miles away and I would lose my chance to speak with Enola. It had to be done, and done without anyone's knowledge.

I cautiously knocked on the door, unsure of what was waiting for me on the other side. Enola opened the door slowly, looking around before ushering me in quickly.

"Enola?" I gasped as she slammed the door closed, locking it twice. "Is everything alright?"

"Were you followed?" she ignored my questions looking out each window before shutting the curtains.

"No," I answered carefully. "I don't think so. What's wrong?"

She turned to me, her eyes revealing what my heart had known all along before her words, "They are getting stronger."

Terror spread throughout my body like a poison, a virus infecting every part of me. I knew this was possible, but I had foolishly hoped for the best. I have learned that hope can be as deadly as fear.

"I know," I replied sitting at the only table, defeat along with terror overtaking me. "Have you told anyone else about your dreams?"

"No, my loyalty lies not with the Delsin, but with the heavenly being alone," Enola announced resolutely as she sat across from me. I did my best to not roll my eyes. I wasn't exactly comfortable with the thought of being considered something as extraordinary as a heavenly being.

"Tell me your dreams," Enola reached across the table and gently took my hands in hers. She looked so innocent, like a small child asking for a story.

I sighed, "Well, I don't really understand them all," I began.

"You don't have to right now. That comes with time. We will interpret them together," she interrupted excitedly.

So I told her all of my dreams, since the first time I saw Ogin to my latest nightmare of Chandler standing over Cole's dead body. I explained everything, finally finding an outlet for all my horrible nightmares. I felt relief as I could ultimately expound with what my imagination had been torturing me. Enola listened quietly, absorbing all of my words without interrupting, thinking deeply. When I finished she gently squeezed my hands, and then reached across the table to wipe away my tears. I hadn't even realized I was crying.

"These could just be silly dreams, right Enola?" I asked optimistic, wiping away the last of my tears.

She didn't need to say anything. Her eyes revealed everything. I was only kidding myself if I thought these dreams were meaningless.

"So, Cole is in danger?" my voice cracked.

"We are all in danger, my dear," she affirmed.

"What do we do? What do I do? I have to leave for South Carolina in a few days. I can't leave, not when things are about to get bad."

"Would you like to hear my dreams?" Enola changed the subject, allowing me to take refuge in something else besides my thoughts, if only for a few moments.

I nodded, allowing her to begin telling me all of her dreams.

"I have had the same dream, every night for seven nights. I see you on a sandy shore of a vast ocean, waiting for something. You seem so lost, so frightened. Then the rain falls and I can't really see you, but I can see two other figures with you —"

"Cole and Chandler," I told her. I was shocked when she shook her head.

"No, I believe they are your parents."

My heart skipped a few beats, "What?"

She continued, "I hear a bit of the conversation, but the rain is making it very difficult." Enola looked off over my shoulder as if she was actually watching the scene instead of repeating what she dreamed from memory.

"They are telling you how proud of you they are, how much they love you, how much they believe in you."

I shake my head furiously, a new wave of tears blurring my vision, "No."

"Adeline, you always wake up before Chandler tries to kill you, correct?"

Confusion overwhelmed me for a moment. It was so hard to keep up with Enola's thought process, "Yes, but —"

"Yes, my dreams always finish but yours don't because you are not open to them. You are too afraid."

"Of course I'm afraid!" I almost screamed. "I have never been so scared in my whole life! I don't know what to do or if these dreams mean anything!"

She gingerly took my hands in hers, "You need to finish your dream; the one on the beach, and the dream with Ogin. Talk to her, she is waiting for you."

"How do I finish a dream when I don't mean to wake up? Maybe I don't want to finish it."

"You must Adeline. You don't have a choice. You want to protect Cole, yes?"

I nodded my head furiously. It was the only thing I wanted.

"Then take control of your dreams, make them reveal their meanings. You have the power to do so. Trust yourself." Enola persisted in encouraging me.

"When I figure out the meanings? What then?"

She smiled her ancient smile, "Then you will train."

I drove through the reservation, away from the lone cabin in the woods, with a million and more thoughts swirling around in my head. I was supposed to figure out my own dreams and then train? Train for what? I had hoped that going to Enola would answer my questions, not leave me with a hundred more.

I parked in front of the Dyami household, but didn't get out immediately. I still couldn't tell Cole about my dreams or about my visit to Enola's. I had to plan my visit with Enola according to his training time with the Chosen. Only then would no one follow me or notice my absence from my own home. I had told Cole I would come seem him and the ranch after more wedding planning with Emma.

I sat in the jeep for a few more moments, trying to collect my thoughts and put on my façade of the worry-free girlfriend whose only trouble was leaving her boyfriend for her sister's wedding. Tears threatened, but I pushed them back as I walked to the front porch. I was about to knock when Paco Dyami opened the door.

"Hello Adeline," he greeted cordially. "The boys and Chenoa are out back. Come on in!"

It was the second shock, only after my visit with Enola, of the day.

"Alright," I stuttered as I followed Mr. Dyami through the house. He led me outside towards the barn where I could see Cole and Chenoa working with a black stallion. Elsu was unloading feed from a truck, while Chenoa and Cole were trying to break the rearing horse. We were almost half way to the fencing when Mr. Dyami gently took my elbow and stopped walking.

"Before you go off with my boy," he began, "I have a few questions."

"I promise to have him home by curfew," I joked.

He attempted a smile, but I could tell Paco Dyami had something very serious on his mind.

"Can you explain to me why the one woman who never comes to tribal events stormed in on the festival to talk to you?" There was no hint of malice or anger behind Paco Dyami's eyes or in his voice. Only worry, fear, and a haunting like he was looking at a ghost.

"Mr. Dyami," I began.

"Please, call me Paco."

I was shocked again, "Okay, Paco. Well, there is nothing to worry about. It was nothing. She was just confused."

I could tell Paco did not believe me. He only nodded, taking off his hat and wiping the sweat from his forehead.

"If it has something to do with my children, Adeline," he pointed towards Elsu, Chenoa, and Cole, "it is my business to know."

Suddenly, the foggy glass, which I used to look through to view Paco Dyami, cleared. He was not just an elder who believed in the legends of his tribe, but a father who was worried about his children who put themselves in harm's way for me.

"I know," I stuttered, trying to control my sudden change in emotion, "and I would never want any of them to be in danger. Trust me."

Paco looked into my eyes. He nodded and began walking towards the barn again.

"As long as we are clear."

"Crystal," I replied honestly.

He smiled putting an arm around me, "Well, my boy has been asking about you, so we better go shut him up."

I nodded, still confused by Paco Dyami's sudden attitude change towards me. We walked on, closer to the stallion and Cole. Chenoa saw us first and pointed us out to Cole. His smile took my breath away as he ran towards us. We were both laughing as he picked me up and spun me around, kissing me. When he had finally put me down, Paco and the others were nowhere to be seen.

"Where did they go?" I observed.

"To give us privacy," Cole smiled planting another kiss on my lips. "So, how was wedding planning? Is Emma still excited for her big day?"

Guilt washed over me again. I hated lying to Cole, but it was necessary.

"Yeah," I sighed. "She's slowly turning into bridezillla."

Cole laughed, taking my hand, "Well, I want you to meet someone who is slowly trying to kill me too."

Cole led me to the edge of the fence where the beautiful black stallion was galloping and bucking every few moments. He was absolutely stunning and terrifying at the same time.

"This is Sky," Cole introduced. "This is the horse I've been trying to break."

"He's magnificent. How is he doing?"

Cole laughed again, "How does it look?"

I smiled, giving Cole's hand an encouraging squeeze, "You'll train him. I know you can."

"Yeah, it'd help if I could give him more time, but with my other commitments, it's hard."

My heart broke for him. The one thing he loved so much, this ranch, was slowly being taken away from him because of me, because of a stupid legend and me.

"I'm sorry," I breathed. "It's my fault."

"Stop," Cole turned to me. "This is not your fault."

"Before you met me, you were living a normal life. You didn't have to fight, train, or put yourself in danger. You can't do the things you love because you have to protect me. That's not fair!"

I felt myself shaking out of anger. Anger at myself, this legend, and at Chandler and his tribe. Cole took my face into his calloused hands, gradually calming me down.

"Listen to me," his blue eyes bore into mine. "You have got to stop blaming yourself. You've got to realize that there is nothing in this world I love more than you, and I will do whatever it takes to protect you. Nothing else matters to me. I choose you. I want you. Everything else can wait."

Then he kissed me, obliterating any doubt left that had taken hold of my heart. I knew Cole loved me. I saw it in his eyes when he looked at me. I felt it in his arms when he held me. I tasted it on his lips when he kissed me. I heard it when he spoke to me. But, sometimes I couldn't help but wonder if he was forced to love me, like he was forced to become Chosen, to become the Delsin. I always pushed these thoughts away, locked them away deep in my mind. For if they were true, the pain would be too much to handle, too much to bear.

She was staring at me again, ethereal light surrounding her. Her blonde hair fell to her hips, her skin was white as snow, almost translucent, and her gray eyes bore into mine intensely. Usually, I would stand and stare back at her, mesmerized by her beauty, overwhelmed by her splendor and my lack thereof, but Enola's words continued to echo in my head, forcing me forward. *She is waiting for you.*

"Hello," I began awkwardly.

She smiled, encouraging me forward.

"You're Ogin, right?"

"And you're Adeline." Her voice was beautiful, like a symphony.

"Yes," I answered. "Um, what are you doing here?"

She laughed, "I've always been here," she pointed to her chest. "I've always been right here."

"Right," I continued. "Well, I was told to talk to you and that you'd help me."

She nodded, "I'm glad you're finally starting to accept me, Adeline."

"Doesn't really look like I have much of a choice."

Her smile faded, "You always have a choice. I'm just relieved you are making the right one. It was wrong choices, made in greed, which have brought us to where we are now."

"You mean, with the legend and the Chosen," I deduced.

"Yes, and with you and I," she held her hand out to me. "I want to show something."

I hesitated, fear once again taking hold of me, but I was tired of being afraid. I pushed my qualms away, gently placing my hand in hers.

Wind blew all around me and I couldn't see anything. Then suddenly, everything was still. We were in a forest; the sun shone through the trees and their leaves, giving off a green like haze. I turned and saw Ogin walking ahead of me and I rushed to keep up with her.

"Where are we going?" I asked.

"You shall see."

I heard the sound of running water; a waterfall. I knew where we were, but I was confused on why we were there.

We walked up to Cole's waterfall, his one place of solace and safety. I saw two figures by the water's edge. For a moment I thought it was Cole and I, but it wasn't. It was a native man, holding a pale woman in his arms. He was sobbing so loudly, his broken cries tugging painfully at my heart. It wasn't till I noticed the pool of blood that I realized the woman he cradled was dead.

"What is this?" I questioned. I turned to Ogin, surprised to find tears falling helplessly down her face.

"This is my death Adeline," She answered solemnly, "and your birth."

"What?" I was shocked, confused, glancing back to the grieving man and the lifeless body he held so lovingly.

"This is my past, and your present," she continued. "I know you don't want to believe it, but there is a reason why Cole has to protect you. There is a purpose to your life, a purpose to your parents' deaths."

"A purpose to my parents' deaths?" I interrupted. "They died in a car accident."

Ogin smiled sadly, "I'm afraid that's not actually the case."

"Then what happened?" Anger washed through me. I stalked towards her, but suddenly felt myself being pulled backwards, away from the grieving man, from Ogin, from everything.

I woke up with tears still in my eyes.

FOUR

"Come on Adeline! I need you to bring your suitcases to the car!"* Emma yelled from the kitchen. I was sitting on my bed, glaring at my packed suitcases, hating them for taking me away from my home.

"Hey Addie!" Alexia Hamilton walked into my room. "Emma's just about ready to go."

I nodded in response. Alexia left, most likely to continue helping Emma. Alexia Hamilton was my Aunt Cassie's friend who had come to stay with me when Emma had left several weeks ago to cover a story. She was going to stay at our house while we were in South Carolina. We had grown very close, Alexia and I. I had even begged Emma to let me stay with her until closer to the wedding. Of course, Emma shot that idea down.

I eventually took my things to the car, packing them tightly in with Emma's suitcases. I wasn't aware of Cole standing behind me until I felt strong, sure arms wrap around me. I turned around to face him, surprised to find his beautiful face struggling to remain composed. Tears were threatening to spill from his eyes. My heart tugged painfully in response.

"I thought you were training," I assumed, startled to find Cole at my house and not with the Chosen. We had attempted our goodbyes the day before, after dinner with him and Chenoa at their home. We had tried to postpone the actual moment of separation for as long as possible. Even Chenoa offered to let me spend the night with her, but I knew Emma would never go for it and I couldn't keep putting it off. He had walked me to my jeep, tightly holding onto me. He simply kissed me on my cheek and opened my car door, whispering, "I'll see you real soon." I had cried all the way home.

"I had to see you off," his voice cracked.

"Cole . . ."

"I'm really gonna miss you pretty girl," He choked, his voice breaking from emotion.

I held him tightly, allowing tears to finally flow, staining his shirt. We stood for a long time, only holding each other, unaware of the world around us. It wasn't until I heard a deliberate cough did I realize Emma was waiting for me.

"So," he began, eyes clouded. "This is really goodbye."

"Not for long," I countered. "It's more like a 'see you later.'"

"Right."

I felt my face crumble as the tears began anew. Suddenly, Cole's lips crashed onto mine. He kissed me fiercely, quickly. I tasted his desolation and fear as it mixed with my tears. When we pulled away, I was staggered to find tears falling down his face as well.

"I love you," I whispered absolutely.

"And I love you," he held my face, wiping my tears away. "Don't forget me while you're gone."

"Never," I promised.

He nodded leading me to the passenger's side of Emma's jeep. Emma was already sitting in the driver's side, ready to go. Alexia was waving from the porch.

Cole opened the car door and helped me in. He leaned into the car through the window and kissed me twice more. I felt Emma tense in the seat next to me, but I didn't care. I tried to hang on as long as possible to the boy from the Little Shell reservation. It wasn't until we pulled out of the driveway, watching him grow smaller and smaller as the distance between us increased, did I understand that I had to let go of him, at least for now.

It was humid and hot. I was breathing in more water than air as we walked down the street. Emma was busily talking on the phone to Henry as she blindly led us through the small town of Beaufort, South Carolina. If I hadn't been so heartsick, I would have thought it was a beautiful little town; a lot like Great Falls except with an ocean and beaches.

Emma finally got off the phone and we found our new home for the next few weeks. We were staying in a small bed and breakfast inn that overlooked the harbor. It was small and quaint, with a white picket fence and a wrap-around porch with rocking chairs. People were simply rocking and drinking lemonade as we walked in.

"Good afternoon darlin'," a woman greeted me as I walked through the door.

"Hello," I replied shyly, quickly following Emma into the inn.

Emma immediately walked in, quickly talking to the woman behind the front desk and receiving our room assignments. We had two adjoining rooms so we could each have our privacy.

"What do you think Addie?" Emma prattled as she threw open the windows; allowing the water they called air into the cool room. "Isn't this just the cutest little town? I can't believe I'm getting married here!"

I donned the most genuine smile I could muster, "Yeah, Em. It's great!"

Emma playfully fell onto her bed as I walked back into my room closing the door. I immediately took out my phone dialing the one person I needed more than the muggy air I breathed.

"Hello, Dyami residence," a soft, feminine voice answered. It wasn't Chenoa. My heart dropped.

"Who is this?" I demanded, my voice shaking.

"This is Ella," she replied threateningly. "Who is this?"

"Adeline," I whispered. "Is Cole there?"

"Oh, sorry he's busy training. Can I take a message?"

"Just have him call me when he can, okay?"

"Fine." The line went dead. That was my first one on one conversation with Ella and it went worse than any of my own nightmares had imagined. At least I was over two thousand miles away.

But other than the fact that I completely humiliated myself on the phone with Ella, I couldn't believe that Cole had not been near the phone when I called. He was very insistent that the first thing I do when I got to Beaufort safely was to call him immediately. I rubbed my hands together as if the sting from Cole's absence on the phone manifested itself into a physical pain.

A few uneventful days passed in Beaufort which mainly consisted of me sitting in the hotel room, waiting by the phone for Cole to call. Emma would either go on and on about the wedding or insist that I needed to get out and get some fresh air. However the few times that I did venture out, I felt like I was being followed. I'd turn to see but of course there was no one, only my paranoia that was chaining me to the hotel room. Cole had insisted that I was safe, that the Rebels were clueless to my location, but I wasn't so sure.

After a particularly painfully boring day, I had finally decided that my fears were ridiculous and getting outside would hopefully keep me from waiting by the phone like a lost puppy. So, as soon as I could get away from Emma and all of her wedding planning, I grabbed my sketchbook and began exploring the town once more. The main promenade was made up of a few shops and restaurants. There was an old bookstore tucked away down in an alley. I immediately took refuge from the blinding sun and the un-breathable air in the small, old shop. The smell of timeworn books hit me as soon as I walked in, making me feel like I was back at home. I meandered through the different isles, lightly brushing the spines of the books with my fingertips. I stopped abruptly when I came to the Native American section. There were history books, legends, books of origins, and others of the like. The pain in my heart tugged a little.

I pulled out my cellphone debating on whether or not I should call him again. I wanted to hear his voice so badly that I dialed the number, but it went straight to voicemail. He was probably still training, but he could at least take a break and call me. He owed me that much.

"I don't think you'll get good cellphone service in here," A voice shook me out of my thoughts; causing me to drop the aged book I had been flipping through.

I turned suddenly, surprised to find a very tall Native American man standing behind me, leaning against a bookshelf. His skin was dark rich copper, his eyes a true opaque brown, and his long black hair was pulled back. He was divinely muscular, reminding me of Elsu. He continued to stare at me, smirking. He then bent down and picked up the book I had dropped.

"Here," he handed it to me. "I didn't mean to scare you."

I rolled my eyes, "You didn't, but you probably shouldn't sneak up on people. It's rude."

I roughly put the book back and quickly left the bookstore. I let out a sigh of relief and tried to continue my exploration of the small town. The man's presence unnerved me. I suppose being followed wasn't such a ridiculous notion after all.

"I'm Noah by the way," the same voice came up behind me.

I stopped on the sidewalk and turned again, "What?"

"My name," he replied as if it was obvious. "It's Noah Songan."

"Okay . . ." I began walking again. He had no trouble keeping up.

"What's yours?" he prodded.

"Why do you want to know?" The annoyance in my voice threw him off, but didn't shake him.

"Well, clearly you are not a local and technically, neither am I. I just thought we could help each other out," he smiled. I was sure that all the other times he used that smile girls fell at his feet. Unfortunately for Noah, it had no effect on me.

"No thanks," I replied, turning on my heels and walking away.

"Hey, I'm just trying to be friendly," he defended himself while continuing to follow me. "What's your name again?"

Were all people from the South this nosey and insistent?

"I never told you."

"Well, I told you mine," he grinned again.

I stared up at him, debating on whether or not I should entertain this conversation or drop it once and for all. Since I didn't know anyone in Beaufort besides Emma and Henry, making a friend wouldn't be too terrible, would it?

"It's Adeline," I finally answered.

Noah smiled triumphantly in response, "Well, Adeline, where are you headed? To meet up with your boyfriend?"

I recoiled at the personal question, "I was just exploring the city, and my boyfriend is in Montana . . . where I live."

He nodded, "Well, I don't think I would quite call Beaufort a city, but do you mind if I accompany you? I can show you all the sites that actually matter."

I hesitated. I wasn't sure on why this guy wanted to walk with me around Beaufort and I couldn't decide if I was comfortable with the idea.

He noticed my hesitation, "I'm not some psycho, I promise. Just looking for a friend in a new town."

Against my better judgment, I nodded and Noah began showing me around the town. The small painful tug in my chest was quieted, at least for a few hours.

After several hours of walking and talking, Noah and I ended up sitting on a swing overlooking the harbor. I was sketching while he was explaining the history behind the Beaufort harbor. Strangely enough, being with Noah felt natural, like I had known him my whole life and not just for a few hours. As soon as I began to relax, talking became much easier. He kept my mind off other things.

". . . and then the Spanish navy attacked right over there," he pointed. "It was one of the biggest battles this county had seen in a while."

"Well aren't you just a wealth of knowledge," I continued to shade my current drawing, a small child who had been playing on the swings in the back yard of large southern mansion we had stumbled across.

He laughed, "I just really love history."

Silence descended for a few moments.

"What did you mean exactly when you said you weren't technically a local? You seem to know a lot about Beaufort," I mentioned as I took a break from my sketch to look up at Noah.

"I'm actually from the Catawba reservation in Rock Hill. It's about three hours from here," his smirk slowly faded.

"Why aren't you there?" I asked. "What brings you to Beaufort?"

He sighed, "Just felt like a change of scenery, you know? What about you, what brings you here all the way from Montana?"

I tried to hide my grimace, "My sister's wedding."

"Well, don't look so excited," he teased pushing me playfully.

"It's not the wedding," I admitted. "It's just the people I had to leave to come to this wedding."

"Your boyfriend?" he assumed.

I nodded, unable to find my voice. For some reason, explaining all of my issues to a complete stranger didn't seem so crazy or irresponsible. I felt that Noah would possibly understand. He didn't seem to mind and I really needed a friend, or at least someone who was willing to listen.

"Yeah," I finally found my voice. "It's just, we have never been separated like this and I just don't understand why my sister said he couldn't come, you know?"

"And you miss him," Noah concluded. "So much that it hurts, like you're underwater and your body is aching for air, but you can't swim fast enough to the surface. To make it worse, your sister doesn't really understand."

"Exactly . . ." I was shocked at how well Noah understood. "Are you missing someone?" He immediately tensed, his hands turning into tight fists. I tried to drop the subject.

"I'm sorry. I didn't mean to intrude."

"No, it's fair. I'm the one who brought up . . ."

"Cole," I finished for him.

"Cole," he nodded, approving almost. "Well, there was someone, but it didn't exactly work out."

"I'm sorry." I really was. The hint of heartbreak and grief that flashed like lightening in Noah's eyes was a mirror to the pain I had experienced before. I understood.

"Thank you," He nodded. From that point, the conversation stayed relatively safe. That was until Noah snatched my sketchbook from me when I wasn't paying attention.

"Stop!" I yelped. "Give that back!"

"I want to know what you are so busy scribbling over there," he stood, keeping my book just above my reach. I didn't realize how tall he really was.

His cocky smile faded slightly. Blood rushed to my cheeks.

"I know," I reasoned embarrassed. "They are really bad. That's why no one gets to look at them."

"They are not bad," he objected seriously, as if I had offended him. "These are amazing, Adeline."

He continued to flip through the pages, sitting down again.

"Really?" I asked, flabbergasted.

"Yes," he grinned. "I'm assuming that this is Cole." He pulled out several sheets of different sketches of Cole. I hadn't realized how often I used him as my inspiration. Not even Cole had seen my drawings, although he asked me just about every day. He was, unlike Noah, polite enough not to force me to show him and I never usually drew in front of him. I suppose I didn't want him to realize how deep my obsession for him ran.

"You are correct," I snatched my sketches back. "And that is enough."

Noah laughed loudly, "Touchy, touchy."

"It's personal," I muttered softly.

Noah's smile fell somewhat, "I was only messing with you. Your drawings are very good. You have a real talent."

"Truly?"

"Truly," he affirmed.

"Well, thank you," I smiled. "That means a lot."

Comfortable silence descended as we watched the sun dip down into the horizon. Large shrimp boats were heading back into port and the small town was just coming to life as darkness fell.

"I should probably head back," I stood, stretching. "I think my sister has dinner plans for us."

Noah stood as well, "Well, have a good evening Miss Adeline. I hope to see you again."

"Yeah," I agreed genuinely. "I hope so too."

Noah and I parted ways. As I walked down the still unfamiliar streets, a sort of peaceful calm came over me. Because I would be home with Cole soon and life would be normal again. And maybe this wasn't the last time I would see Noah, my new mysterious friend. But while this new feeling of peace was welcomed, I could only hope that this peace wasn't the calm before the storm.

FIVE

The beach was storming violently, the giant waves beating the sand over and over again. The rain was beating heavily down, drenching me from head to toe. I was shaking, but from fear instead of cold. Two figures slowly made their way toward me in the chaos of the storm. I could barely make out their silhouettes, but I quickly came to realize where I was and whom they were. I looked down, mortified to find myself covered in blood. Not my blood, but Cole's. I turned around, horrified to find Cole's mangled body being beaten by the waves. I rushed to his side, pulling his head into my lap.

"Wake up baby," I continued to sob. "Please, open your eyes. Please."

I literally felt my heart break, a raw bleeding hole taking its place. I couldn't breathe, couldn't think, couldn't understand.

"Adeline, dear," A soft voice spoke through the rain, through the searing pain.

I gazed over my shoulder to find my parents standing above me.

"Mom . . . Dad . . ." I whispered. I was so young when they had died, but I had pictures. Pictures I had engraved into my memory and had redrawn on my darkest days.

"Hey there sweet girl," My mother greeted me, her smile just as beautiful as I remembered. The same smile from the picture of their wedding day.

I gently laid Cole's head back onto the sand, placing one kiss on his head, before I stood to face my dead parents.

"What are you doing here?" I mumbled, overwhelmed by all of my different emotions. "What's going on?"

"You know, they're not wrong or ignorant," my father began, "about who you are, where you come from."

"Who's not wrong?" I cried. What was happening?

"Don't fight it sweetheart," my mother added. "Don't fight her and don't fight your destiny."

"My destiny?" I shouted. "What destiny?"

"The one we died to protect," my father answered.

Realization hit me head on, almost knocking the wind out of me.

"You died in a car accident," I tried to reason.

"You were there," my father pressed on, continuing to push me. "What do you remember?"

"Nothing," I countered. "I don't remember anything!"

"Try," my mother insisted. "Just try to remember. It will help you so much."

Suddenly, my mother and father were being pulled away from me. I cried and screamed for them and for Cole's lifeless form at their feet. I kicked and wept till I was finally shaken awake. Through my thick tears I could make out Emma's startled face. It had all been a dream, a horrible nightmare, but for some reason I felt that it was something more. Something Enola had tried to warn me about.

I ate breakfast slowly, chewing each piece thoughtfully. I was trying to break apart and understand my horrible nightmare as Emma sat across from me, watching me warily. After she had woken me up, I sobbed in her arms for several minutes before I could finally gain control of myself and briefly explain that I had a terrible nightmare.

Emma had gently rubbed my back and finally left me to lay awake until it was time to go to breakfast.

"Feeling any better?" Emma's voice finally registered.

I looked up, still dazed and tired from my lack of sleep, "Yeah, a little."

"Well, I hope so because today we meet with the caterers, finalize dress fittings, meet Henry's Aunt Jean for lunch, and hopefully squeeze in some sightseeing if we have time!" Emma started listing things out as she began fiddling with her phone.

"Wait, we're meeting Henry's family?" I realized as I slowly pushed my plate away.

"Just his Aunt Jean," Emma mumbled, mesmerized by something on her phone, "for lunch at one."

Suddenly, my awful nightmare faded away as the idea of meeting someone from Henry's family became more and more real. I felt nauseous.

"Oh," I faintly muttered as I followed Emma out of the small breakfast café.

The rest of the morning passed from specialty shops to fitting rooms where Emma continually shot out orders and I fulfilled her wishes dutifully, but not totally aware of reality. Often, my mind would fade in and out of where I was and back to the nightmare. I had lived my whole life, since I was five, believing my parents' deaths were the result of a drunk driver, a storm, and a poorly built bridge. I didn't remember much from that night. Emma was at a friend's house spending the night and my parents were taking me home from a day at the zoo. Sometimes, I could still remember that day at the zoo. I could remember my mother laughing at the hippo that splashed water at my father. I could still see my father picking me up and putting me on his shoulders so I could look at the elephants over the crowd of people. Sometimes I believed that I made up most of these memories of my parents to give myself something to hang on to. Emma had very real and tangible recollections, while all I had was a rag of a baby blanket and a few photo albums.

Emma had told me about the night of the accident. My parents and I had been driving home in the rain. Apparently, a drunk driver coming in the opposite direction swerved into our lane as we were passing over a bridge. We had hit the water in a matter of moments. I tried to remember anything, but all I could picture in my mind were the images I had created from Emma's description of the events. I knew that someone must have pulled me out of the water. Emma said that an angel had saved me, otherwise I would have drowned like my parents.

What did my parents want me to remember? What about that night was so important for me to figure out?

"Well hello there Emma dear!" The thick southern drawl of a large woman shook me out of my reverie.

"It's so nice to meet you Mrs. Sybil!" Emma exclaimed hugging the older woman.

"Oh, please call me Aunt Jean dear. It's what Henry has called me since he was just a boy," Aunt Jean corrected as she squeezed Emma to her. Aunt Jean's small eyes peered from behind Emma to me. "And this must be your sister Adeline!"

Henry's aunt was a hefty woman with short gray hair, small beetle like eyes, and lips that drew into a tight line like she had smelled something awful. She looked me up and down before pulling me into a tight embrace. She smelled of old perfume and cigarette smoke.

She wasn't technically Henry's aunt either. According to Emma, she was a very close family friend that had helped taken care of Henry when he was much younger. She insisted on everyone calling her "Aunt Jean" to make her feel more a part of the family. Now, I supposed, I was to call her my aunt as well.

"How excited you must be for your sister," her red painted finger nails dug into my arms as she held me out at arm's length, talking down to me. "Weddings are just lovely, aren't they?"

I feigned a smile, "Yes. I'm so happy for Emma and Henry."

Lunch was painful. Aunt Jean continued to complain about everything she could find fault in, from the server's attitude to the flowers outside the window to the lack of selection on the menu.

Relief washed over me when my phone began ringing and I saw that Cole was calling me. I almost jumped out of my seat.

"I'm sorry, but I really need to take this," I stood up quickly, almost knocking over Aunt Jean's iced sweet tea.

"Well, who is so important that you must get up in such a hurry? That's not very ladylike!" Aunt Jean was astounded, however I didn't care.

"I'm sorry," I apologized again. "It's very important."

I walked quickly out of the restaurant to find some privacy before anyone could stop me.

"Hello?" I answered quickly.

"Adeline," he sighed relieved. "I'm so sorry."

"Why haven't you called me back before now?" I whispered as I leaned against the wall behind the small café.

Cole hesitated, "There have been some complications, but nothing to worry about. I just had to take care of a few things. Tell me about Beaufort! How are Emma and all her wedding plans?"

"What do you mean 'complications'?" I ignored his questions. If Cole had been or was in danger, then I needed to know. Immediately. "Is everyone alright?"

Cole breathed heavily, "It's nothing. No need for you to be concerned."

"If it has to do with you, then I will always be concerned," I vowed. "Now, are you going to tell me what's happened or am I going to have to call Chenoa?"

"That won't be necessary," he replied darkly. The change in his tone shook me.

"Cole," I whispered, fear beginning to choke me. "What's going on?"

"They contacted us," Cole admitted bleakly.

I felt the blood drain from my face. I struggled at finding my voice.

"What did they say?" my voice cracked.

He hesitated again, "War is coming Adeline. It's only a matter of when. So, I guess it's good you're there, away from Montana."

I felt as if a semi-truck had hit me. All of my hopes and fears had collided into me like a meteor, slowly breaking me apart. My breath caught short and I struggled to regain composure.

"What?" Tears stung the back of my eyes. "I need to come home. I shouldn't have left you and the tribe like this."

"Stop," he demanded lovingly. "Stop this. You know it's better you're with Emma. Besides, what would you do besides worry here? I at least have peace of mind that you're out of danger for the most part."

"The most part?" Fear echoed through my voice.

He sighed again, "You are completely safe. They won't come near you."

Cole immediately dropped any talk of the Rebels or the Chosen. Our conversation remained on neutral topics such as Emma's wedding, and the plane ride over to South Carolina. When I mentioned my new friend Noah, Cole's voice tensed becoming tighter and guarded.

"I made a friend I think," I continued to answer his questions, hoping our conversation would drift back to the Chosen and what was happening in Montana. "He's really nice. He is actually Native American. He lives in Rock Hill on the Catawba reservation. His name is Noah and . . ."

"What?" Cole's usual gentle, silk like voice quickly turned harsh and angry. The sudden change overwhelmed me for a moment. I never thought Cole to be the jealous type, but was it possible that he could think I would so quickly be unfaithful with someone else?

"Is something wrong?" I questioned innocently. "Noah is just a guy I met in a book store. I probably will never see him again. There is nothing to be upset about Cole . . ."

I could feel Cole's entire demeanor and body tensing through the phone as I continued to try to make him understand. My voice finally trailed off and there was only stressed silence on the other end of the phone.

"Cole?"

"I have to go. I love you. Be safe." The line went dead before I could tell Cole I loved him too.

I walked slowly back into the small café, too upset and confused to even acknowledge the glares of disapproval from both Henry and Aunt Jean. I don't remember how the rest of the lunch with Aunt Jean went or ended. My mind was about two thousand miles away and my heart was on the verge of breaking. The thought that Cole could think I would even consider being with anyone else almost choked me. Usually Cole never hid things from me either. We told each other everything. He was my best friend.

"What happened back there?" Emma's furious voice stung, causing me to come back to reality. We were walking away from the café, back towards the small inn when Emma began to yell at me.

"What?"

"Don't 'what' me! You were so rude back there!" Emma fumed. "I can't believe you just got up to answer your phone and then you came back and didn't say more than two words to sweet Aunt Jean! What has gotten into you?"

Emma's beautiful face was hard and intent. Her hazel eyes, my eyes, our father's eyes, were cold. Suddenly, I realized that I didn't know my sister anymore. The old Emma would not be talking to me like this. In fact, she would have hated Aunt Jean. She would have compared her to our own Aunt Cassie. The Emma Jasely I knew was gone, changed.

Then again, I had changed too. I wasn't going to let my older sister continue to rule over me anymore. A year ago, I would have done anything for her, been anything for her. I wanted to be her. Now, every day I had begun to resent her a little more. I wasn't jealous, I was hurt. The old Emma Jasely would have asked what was wrong, not what was wrong with me. I didn't like this Emma at all.

"What's wrong with me?" I finally answered her, matching her threatening tone. She jumped back in surprise. "I think the better question is what is wrong with you?"

Her mouth fell open in surprise. The new Emma wasn't used to the new Adeline. I had to leave before I said something I would regret.

"I'm going for a walk," I called back to her, storming off before the situation became any more heated. I walked down the street in the opposite direction of the inn. I wasn't sure of where I was heading till I came to the harbor. I found a vacant swing and took refuge there. The sun was still high in the sky, casting shadows all along the ground. I closed my eyes and let the smell of the ocean air and the sounds of the water lapping completely take over my senses.

"Beautiful day, isn't it?" A familiar voice broke through my serene reverie. I opened my eyes to find Noah standing there, his eyes seeming sad.

"Yeah," I agreed. "You want to sit down?"

He sat, sighing. He gazed out into the distance, passed the harbor, deep into the horizon of the ocean, like he was searching for something.

"So," he startled me as he came out of his trance. "How's the wedding planning coming?"

I frowned, "Henry's family hates me. Well, one of them does at least."

"Why is that?" he probed, his eyes drifting from the harbor back to me.

"I'm not very good at making friends. You know, making people like me," I admitted.

"Well, I like you and this is the only the second time we've talked," he joked. "I'd say your batting average is pretty good when you look at those numbers."

He playfully pushed my shoulder with his, "Besides, who cares if they like you? It's Emma they need to approve of, right?"

I nodded, "I guess you're right."

"I'm always right."

"Modest, much?" I rolled my eyes.

He laughed for a few moments. Then, gradually his smile fell into a frown. He glanced over to me, noticing my analysis of him.

"So," he began, erasing any remnants of sadness that had just graced his face. "How is lover boy? Cole, was it?"

My mind ran over the phone conversation again. I cringed and

Noah noticed.

"Honeymoon's over already, huh?" he smirked.

"You could say that," I sighed. "I don't know. It's just really complicated."

"I get complicated," Noah replied gently, trying to encourage the words out of me. Then I looked to this stranger of a man, someone I did not know at all, and realized that I wanted to tell him everything. I wanted someone who could help me try to understand this crazy world I was forced to live in.

"This reaches a new level of complicated," I admitted. "Crazy even. You'd probably have me committed."

Noah's laughter bellowed across the bay. I joined in, but I believed Noah did not understand just how true my words rang.

"Try me," he replied when he finally calmed down. When he noticed my severe hesitation, he looked out towards the horizon again. "What if I told you about just how much of complicated and crazy I understand about relationships? Then you can decide if I'm worth telling?"

I was surprised at Noah's willingness to tell me anything about himself, but I couldn't feign my curiosity about the man from the Rock Hill Reservation. I nodded, allowing him to begin.

"Well, I should probably begin by saying that I didn't come to Beaufort this time around just for vacation and it's definitely not the first time I've been here," he began.

"You see, there was this girl," he swallowed hard, painfully. "She's an elementary school teacher from Beaufort. I'll never forget the first time I saw her. She was bringing her class on a field trip to the reservation and I was the tour guide. I never usually do stuff like that on rez. My sister does the tourist stuff, but she was sick that day so she asked me to do it. Funny how that one day, that one phone call from my sister, changed my life, huh?

"Well anyway, there I was, waiting on this class full of kids and their teacher to show up. They were at least twenty minutes late and I was already pretty irritated that day. She's always late, no matter where she is going."

Every time Noah described the smallest detail about this girl, his face would light up, but just as quickly as his smile shone it disappeared. It was like writing on the sand when a wave crashes against it, erasing any remains that the sand had been disturbed in the first place.

"The minute she walked in, the second I laid eyes on her, I knew I was falling, deep into something I didn't even know I could fall into . . .

"She had beautiful red, chestnut curly hair that she was trying to tame back into a bun. Her eyes were this sea foam green that darted from one child to the next. She was constantly counting and recounting all of her kids. She was a mess to anyone else, but to me she was perfection."

He paused for a long moment, his eyes glistening with tears of a painful past.

"What's her name?" I encouraged, taking his hand in mine.

He glanced back at me, almost surprised to find himself talking to someone, "Cailen. Her name is Cailen."

"What happened?" I queried tenderly "To you and Cailen?"

He sighed heavily as if he was trying to release the ache of his past with each word, with each breath, "We fell hopelessly and foolishly in love. We fell hard, but, just as hard as we fell we landed broken and shattered on the threshold of reality."

Noah glanced over to my shocked face. His hand reached out to my face, brushing away tears I didn't even know I was crying.

"Now, you are not the one who should be crying," he reprimanded gently. "Well, long story short, my past came back to haunt me, quite literally. We were engaged, but when I wasn't the normal guy she thought I was, she left me."

"Why?" I inquired carefully. "If she loved you, then she should have loved all of you, even the you from the past . . ." and then suddenly, realization hit me like lightening.

"What do you mean by not being 'normal'?" I asked, my voice raw from holding in tears.

Noah opened his mouth to answer me when his cellphone

started to ring.

"Excuse me for just a moment," he apologized as he stood and walked a few feet from me, while answering his phone.

Listening to Noah's story gave me hope. Hope that there was someone else on this planet that might actually understand what I was going through. It also instilled a new kind of fear. Fear that there was someone else on this earth that understood just exactly what I was going through, what I went through.

Was it possible that Cailen had gone through exactly what I had gone through with Cole, but instead rejected any possibility of the reality of tribal legends?

Then again, Noah never had said that he was a part of some Catawba legend. I was only making assumptions based off of very loose details of someone else's life. I had no evidence to prove that my theory was even remotely true. But if it was, what did that mean for me? What did it mean for the Chosen? More enemies?

Noah stood above me, catching my attention as he placed his cellphone back in his pocket, "It looks like I have to go now."

His voice trailed off as his eyes focused on something behind me. His copper skin paled as he forced his eyes to look back to me.

"I'll see you later Adeline," he nodded to me and then left quickly.

I stood and watched him until I couldn't see him anymore. I turned around to try to find what seemed to frighten Noah, a tall and well-built man, so much. I scanned the surroundings, but didn't see anything terrifying. There were some tourists eating at a local restaurant, a family playing soccer, and a few kids on the playground. I was just about to head back to my hotel when I saw a flash of red out of the corner of my eye; dark red, curly hair. Cailen.

SIX

At least, I thought it was Cailen. She was lying on a towel under a tree while reading a book and drinking coffee. Her curly red hair spilled over her shoulders, almost masking her face. I stood stunned and unable to move, like Noah. She was incredibly beautiful but by the way she seemed to hold herself she didn't believe it, or maybe wasn't aware.

I was about to leave, pretending I never saw the girl with the red, curly hair when a voice literally stopped me in my tracks.

Go to her Adeline . . .

I whipped my head around, trying to find the owner of the familiar voice, but no one was near me. I was sure the voice came from inside me.

Go talk to her . . .

Again the voice commanded; a soft, gentle yet demanding voice. Ogin.

"Where are you?" I whispered furiously. "What are you doing?"

It was one thing for this creepy angel to stalk me in my dreams, but to try to take over my reality was crossing the line. I was even thinking about having *myself* committed.

Go . . . her voice softly faded into the depths of my mind. Her message was clear, but why would she talk to me now, here, while I was still awake?

Confused and overwhelmed, my eyes glanced back to the redhead who was innocently reading, minding her own business. And here I was contemplating disturbing a perfect stranger because a voice inside my head told me to.

As strange as it seemed, as it was, I was compelled to talk to this girl. I wanted to know what happened, why she couldn't handle Noah's past. This could not, however, be the same Cailen, just one of the few girls in the world with curly red hair. My mind was trying to make it see something, believe something that wasn't there.

I didn't believe that she wasn't Cailen, not for a second. I didn't doubt it was her during the long walk towards her, but that didn't erase my absolute fear of a girl I didn't even know. I don't just walk up to people and start a conversation. Yet, I felt like I didn't have a choice.

I was a few feet away from her when she saw me approaching. She dog leafed a page in her book, and then glanced up to me revealing her sea foam green eyes.

"Cailen?" I asked as she stood up to get a better look at me.

"Yes," she was hesitant, of course. "Can I help you?"

"Sorry," I shook my head, embarrassed. "I'm Adeline Jasely."

She nodded, trying to place my name and face. Clearly, she had no idea who I was.

"Do we know each other?" She asked, doubtful again. I didn't look like a crazed serial killer, so I knew she would talk to me for a little longer.

"We have a mutual friend," I began. "I'm kind of worried about him, so I was hoping you could answer some questions I have."

"A mutual friend?" she repeated, her right eyebrow rose in suspicion.

"Noah," I began to answer when I realized just how stupid this was. I actually listened to a voice in my head that told me to go talk to a complete stranger.

Before I could continue mentally beating myself up, Cailen immediately shook her head, wearing a puzzled, yet concerned expression, "No, I don't think I know a Noah."

Now it was my turn to be confused, "What?"

She continued to shake her head, "I'm sorry. I don't know a Noah. Maybe you have the wrong person?"

"Are you sure?" I continued, unable to believe that this girl would lie about an ex-fiancé so candidly. "Noah from Rock Hill? He lives on the Catawba reservation."

Cailen stood thoughtfully, trying to recall any memories of a Noah from Rock Hill. But she shook her head again, "I'm sorry Adeline. I have no idea who you are talking about."

"Oh," I finally accepted the fact that this Cailen was in fact a complete stranger and I was officially losing my mind. "Well, I'm sorry to have bothered you."

"Don't worry about it," she replied gracefully. "It was nice to have met you."

"Yeah, you too," I began walking away, unable to understand what just happened.

"Adeline," Cailen called to me. I turned around to find her sitting on her blanket again, her book in her hands. "I do hope your friend is okay."

I nodded, "Me too."

I dreamed again that night. I was on the beach with the violent storm swirling around me, shaking me to my core. I, once again, found a mangled body lying several feet away from me. The waves continued to beat against the sand and the lifeless form, spreading the pool of blood back into the sea. I ran towards it, assuming it was Cole, but fell back shocked when I realized it was Cailen. Her skin paled, her red hair brighter for it had absorbed her own blood. I tried to scream, but no noise escaped my lips. I merely sat, mouth open, stunned. Who would have done this? Why would someone hurt her?

"Cailen!" I heard him before I saw him. I looked up to find

Noah running towards Cailen's form. He fell helplessly at her side, grief stricken sobs racking through his body. He looked so broken, so battered. I reached over to try and console him, to let him know someone cared, but when I tried to comfort Noah, he slapped my hand away as if I were a venomous snake. He looked to me with anger, malice, betrayal.

"This is your fault!" he bellowed. "You did this!"

I couldn't breathe, couldn't see, and couldn't understand. I did this? I shook my head furiously. I lifted my hands in defense, but found a blooded knife in my left hand. I looked down to my clothes to find them soaked in blood. Cailen's blood.

"No," I whispered. "No . . . I didn't . . . I didn't mean to . . ."

I looked up to find revenge swimming in Noah's usually gentle brown eyes. He lifted his hand to hit me, but the blow never came. Instead, I suddenly found myself by a bridge. There was no storm or beach. Trees lined the rural road and below the bridge was a rough current of a river. I looked frantically around for Noah and Cailen, but it was only me on the bridge.

"Hello again Adeline," A voice broke through my panic. I looked across the bridge to find Ogin, standing in her usual ethereal splendor. Instead of standing and staring, I ran towards her, drawn to her light. I fell into the comfort and safety of her arms, sobbing into her shoulder. She gently rubbed my back, embracing me tightly.

"What — what happened?" I blubbered, the images of Cailen's lifeless body and the bloody knife in my hand still too raw and fresh in my mind.

"Shh," she cooed. "You're safe now."

"What happened?" I stepped back, more confident in my voice. "Did I really . . . kill her?"

Ogin gently shook her head, releasing my doubts and allowing waves of relief to wash over me, "No Adeline. That was just a dream, but a strong possibility of the future if you don't accept what is to come."

I shook my head feverishly, "I would never kill someone!"

"No, you might not," she agreed, "but your inaction and

passivity will be just as deadly as any knife Adeline."

"Inaction of what?" I yelled. "What is so important for me to accept?"

"Your purpose. You have to accept who you are and your future, then the Chosen will be triumphant. They need you."

I shook my head, "They don't need me. I'm nothing."

"Why do you think the Rebels want you so badly Adeline?" she uttered furiously, yet gently. "You are powerful, but you have to believe in yourself first."

I stepped back, shocked by her outrage, "I don't know how."

"You have to accept your past before you can embrace your future."

Ogin smiled sadly, walking to the edge of the bridge, staring down into the depths below, "Do you know where we are Adeline?"

I looked around again. The surroundings did seem familiar, but it was a distant memory, a memory that was buried deep within me. Something that happened long ago, and I had a feeling it was a memory I had no desire to revisit.

I shook my head; my eyes remained on the angel before me.

"This is where your parents lost their lives twelve years ago. This is where your life was almost taken away. Do you remember?"

I glanced down to the river mesmerized by the currents when, abruptly, different visions and scenes began flooding my brain. I suddenly remembered my mother looking to me in the back seat, smiling at me. I remembered the bright lights of a car that swerved into our lane, my father and mother's shocked expressions, the horrific sounds of metal on metal, bones breaking, the crash of a car hitting the water's surface, the burning sensation in my lungs, the lack of air, the panic, everything. Then I remembered the large rough hands of a man pulling me out of my car seat. I remembered him giving me CPR, begging me to open my eyes, to breathe, to live. I remembered coughing up water and seeing the most beautiful, panicked, blue eyes. I remembered hope.

I was brought back to the present moment with Ogin, who was smiling triumphantly. I licked my dry lips and looked to the angel for answers. Then I realized, I didn't need her to give me any answers. I had been carrying them with me all along. For twelve years I had been carrying a burden, but a gift at the same time. I carried the burden of my parents' deaths, but also the knowledge of something much greater than I had ever imagined.

"You understand," she said. It wasn't a question.

"I believe so," I replied, a calm surrounding me. "Someone did save me that night."

She nodded for me to continue.

"He had blue eyes," I continued to recall. "He pulled me out of the car, out of the river . . ."

Just before I woke up, just as I locked eyes with Ogin, it hit me. Paco Dyami had saved my life.

"So, Addie, do you prefer the lilacs or the tulips for the center pieces?" Emma asked as we made a third round in the flower shop. The florist was busy taking notes, bending over backwards to help Emma in any way. I wasn't paying attention to the different flower arrangements or to anything in particular in the small flower shop. My mind was trying to wrap around my encounter with Cailen, a woman who could have been either lying to my face or telling the truth. I was sure that was the woman that Noah saw right before he left so suddenly. Then again, can I actually trust this man who on all accounts was still a stranger to me? Should I be trying to help him? Cole's reaction to my meeting Noah threw me off as well. And Cole still hadn't returned my phone calls. Although, he was training to fight another tribe of Native Americans who were actively trying to kill me and destroy everything I hold dear.

Then there was my awful nightmare, a dream that seemed so real. I was shocked to wake up and find myself in my hotel room. I sat up in bed, unable to find sleep again. I mulled the dream over and over again in my head, but nothing in my horrible dream could have shocked me as much as the possibility of Paco Dyami being my personal hero. He actually saved me the night my parents died.

If that were true, why hadn't he come forward? Why had he

never told me?

I looked up to find Emma looking at me strangely. Oh, right. I was supposed to choose between the lilacs and the tulips.

"Oh, I really like these Em," I pointed out a beautiful blue flower that caught my eye.

"Those are morning glories," the florist informed us. "Those won't do for a wedding. You'll want something less fragile."

We moved on from one section of flowers to the next and I merely agreed with whatever Emma wanted. As we left, I realized that I had no idea what Emma had picked as flower arrangements.

"Okay," Emma mumbled, "now on to the bakery to pick out the cake, and then dinner with Henry's parents."

"Henry's parents?" I panicked. Had Emma mentioned meeting Henry's parents before?

Emma rolled her eyes frustrated, "Yes, Adeline. I told you this last night, but you were too busy trying to call that boyfriend of yours to listen."

"Oh, I'm sorry," I apologized. "I've just been kind of distracted lately."

"Kind of?" she almost yelled. "Adeline, you're my maid of honor and I really need you to focus on this wedding with me? If there is something wrong, then please tell me! I am here for you, but I can't take this anymore."

I knew not caring about this wedding was wrong, but it was hard to really focus on something as trivial as cake toppers when I knew Cole was in danger of losing his life each second I was away from him. Could I have explained that to Emma? Would she have understood?

"Is there something wrong Adeline?"

As I looked into her eyes, I saw that it would be impossible to tell her. She didn't deserve that. This was my burden and I was determined to carry it alone.

"No, Em. I'm just missing Mom and Dad. Wishing they could be here for you," I admitted. It was true. I was missing our parents, especially since my bizarre dream.

Emma smiled sadly, "Me too." She hugged me tightly and I tried to let go of the supernatural, focusing my attention on the reality of my sister's normal wedding.

As soon as we were finished with the wedding tasks for the day, I grabbed my sketchbook and walked along the bayside looking for inspiration. Once again, as I placed my pencil to my paper, a recreation of Cole peered at me from the page. It had been a few days since our last phone conversation. I physically ached for him, but I understood that he had important things to do. But he was doing them without me and that was what bothered me the most.

"We've got to stop running into each other like this," a familiar voice interrupted my sketching. "If I didn't know any better, I'd say you're stalking me."

Noah plopped himself next to me on the shady grass under a tree. It was the same place I had met Cailen. Of course, I wasn't about to tell Noah that.

"I could say the same thing about you," I countered, raising my eyebrows. "How do you always find me here?"

"Because you are painfully predictable Adeline Jasely," he shook his head, "and there is literally nowhere else for someone to go in Beaufort. This view is as good as it gets here."

I followed his gaze to the horizon where the cloudless blue sky met the rough, dark blue of the ocean.

"Then why do you stay here?" I asked. "In Beaufort?"

His eyes found mine again, "I told you why."

"Then why won't you talk to her?" I blurted out. Suddenly, an overwhelming sensation of urgency came over me. I needed to tell Noah that he shouldn't give up on Cailen. To tell him that there was always hope. "I'm sure if you explained everything, she would understand. She seems understanding . . ."

"How the hell would you know if she 'seems understanding'? " he demanded, betrayal flashing in his eyes like lightening.

I felt the blood drain from my face. I closed my eyes, trying to collect my thoughts and figure out how I was going to explain myself.

"Adeline?" he began warningly, his voice tight.

"I may have run into Cailen," I started.

He groaned, his voice angry, "You ran into her?"

"Okay, so I went up to a girl that looked like Cailen the other day. She matched your description and I thought . . . I just wanted to help you."

Noah's eyes looked at me accusingly, just as they had in my awful nightmare. His mouth formed a thin line as he contemplated his response.

"But don't worry," I tried to calm him. "She didn't even know who I was talking about when I mentioned your name. It must have been another girl named Cailen. I was mistaken."

He sighed heavily, his brown eyes distant. He finally shook his head, "I didn't sign up for this."

"Sign up for what?"

"Sign up for a therapy session Adeline!" he hissed. "I divulge a little bit from my past and you think you have total access to my life, but when I try to ask you about your life you shut down."

"I do not shut down!" I defended, "and what about my life could you possibly want to know about? I'm not interesting."

He rolled his eyes, "You're impossible, you know that?"

"I've been told."

Silence descended as Noah's angry façade slowly melted into understanding, or at least tolerance.

"So, since you have completely barged your way into my life, I believe you owe me," Noah finally spoke again, his usual smirk once again spread across his face.

I knew what he meant the moment he started smiling again. He wanted to understand me the way I wanted to understand him.

"How should I begin paying back my debt?" I laughed, but on the inside I dreaded telling Noah anything. What if I was wrong about him? What if I told him about Cole and this mess of a life I had to live in and he actually wouldn't understand?

"Maybe you could begin by explaining how you got that pretty little brace on your ankle?" he nodded to my foot. "It's hard to believe that you were actually dumb enough to fall off of Chenoa's balcony so I know there must be more to that story."

I smiled remembering me telling Noah the story of how I broke my ankle when we had first met. He had constantly picked on my limp. I thought telling him the truth would finally get him to shut up. But the truth was that the Rebel tribe, who were currently trying to figure out how to defeat the Chosen and steal my "power", attacked me. It wasn't how crazy the truth sounded that caused my breathing to stop, the smile to fade, and fear to take a tight grip on my heart. It wasn't the vision of Chandler Phalcon attacking me that terrified me. It was the fact that when I had told Noah about how I broke my ankle, I never once mentioned Chenoa being the owner of the balcony that I supposedly fell from.

I stood abruptly; my wide eyes never leaving Noah's confused face.

"What?" he stood slowly as well, noticing my unexpected change in demeanor. "Is something wrong Adeline?"

"How do you know Chenoa?" I demanded.

His body tensed, "You told me."

I shook my head fiercely, "No, I didn't."

We stood for a long time staring at each other. I contemplated on whether running away would be a good idea. The problem was that he knew which hotel I was staying at. He also probably knew a lot more about my life and could easily find me if he really wanted to. I was also the proud owner of an ankle brace that made me break a sweat walking, so I wouldn't get very far.

Noah, or whoever this stranger I had so stupidly let into my life, sighed, running his hand through his long hair, "Cole wasn't exaggerating when he said you'd be stubborn."

"How do you know Cole? What are you talking about?" I took a couple of steps backwards.

"Calm down," He held his hands up like he was surrendering. "I can explain everything, but it will take some time and you are going to need to trust me."

"And why should I trust you?" I spat.

He sighed heavily, his natural warm brown eyes turning despondent, "Because you don't have a choice."

SEVEN

I wasn't sure if it was what Noah said or how he said it that made me stay, but I did. We walked along the bayside till Noah felt we had adequate privacy before he finally told me the truth, the whole truth.

We sat down at a small picnic table overlooking the harbor when I said, "Okay, start talking."

He laughed loudly, trying to ease the tension that was now sitting between us, "Come on Adeline. I'm not the bad guy here. I'm not the one you should be mad at."

"No?"

"No. You've got a whole tribe of people you should be more concerned about than little ole me," His humor evaporated as the terrifying truth finally set in. So, he did know about the Rebels.

"Do you work for them?" I demanded, my voice cracking. I was horrified at the prospect of Noah, someone I thought I could trust, working for Chandler.

He shook his head, "No. On the contrary, my tribe is in alliance with Cole's. He's the one who called me. The truth is you are the reason for my stay in Beaufort. I was told to watch you carefully and protect you if need be."

Shock and realization washed over me, but I still didn't completely trust Noah.

"What about Cailen? Was she another lie?"

His face distorted into an angry grimace, "No, everything I said about her is true. She is the only reason I visit this town so often, but you are the reason for this particular stay."

I nodded, believing him for the moment, "Why would Cole feel the need to call you to come protect me?"

He smirked, "I don't know if you've noticed, but this war is much bigger than what you have been led to believe. It would be irresponsible for the Delsin to leave you unprotected. He would have sent one of the Chosen, but as you are aware they still need to train."

"So you know about the Chosen?" I clarified as I slowly became more and more aware of the fact that this war, this supernatural world, was much bigger than Great Falls. I should have known that it would follow me wherever I went.

He smiled knowingly, "I know a lot."

"Are you . . . special?" I wasn't sure how to phrase my question. "I mean, you had said you weren't normal, so I'm just wondering."

"What sort of monster am I?" he finished for me.

I nodded nervously.

"My tribe and I," he began carefully, thinking through each word, "are different. We are called the 'river people'. We're good at fishing, swimming, anything that has to do with the water. Our ancestors were fierce warriors and in order to combat other enemy tribes we evolved and developed special skills."

"Special skills?" I repeated warily.

Noah smiled sadly, his eyes gazing out to the ocean, "There is a reason why I have such an affinity to the ocean, to any body of water really."

He continued, "We can hold our breath under water for hours at a time, our bodies can handle the rough currents, deep dives, and frigid temperatures. We can get from one place to another much faster swimming than any other mode of transportation."

"So basically you're a mermaid?" I finally realized as I tried to desperately fight back a smile.

He rolled his eyes, "Now you're laughing at me, and no, we are not like Ariel. We're much more terrifying."

It was my turn to roll my eyes, "Right, I'm shaking as we speak."

"You should be," he replied solemnly. "If a normal human or one of the Chosen were to fall in our waters, they wouldn't make it out alive."

Noah's threat wiped my grin off my face, "You could hurt Cole?"

"Birds don't know how to swim," he mumbled quietly, instilling dread inside me. "If they came too close to the water and I could reach them, I could easily hold them under. No problem. But I suppose that's why we are allies now. We protect them from water and they protect us from land and sky. We have a mutual understanding."

"Is this why Cailen left?" I changed the subject quietly. Maybe this side of Noah, this version of the man she loved, was what frightened her.

Noah's knowing smirk faded as glimmers of past heart ache clouded his eyes, "Yes. I told her, finally, that the legends of my tribe were true. Of course, she didn't believe me so I thought if I showed her she would believe it and accept it and we could get married without any secrets . . ." His voice faded as tears began to choke him.

"You showed her?"

"Our appearances do alter when we enter the water. I suppose she couldn't handle it," he attempted a smile, but it crumbled away quickly. "I guess she couldn't handle the monster I am."

I swiftly changed the subject, "Why didn't Cole tell me about you? He seemed really angry when I mentioned the fact that we had met." I felt betrayed. If he had known, why did he sound so furious on the phone?

"Yeah, apparently he didn't want you actually noticing my existence. Chenoa explained to me that Cole's orders were really for me to watch from a distance and make sure no one tried to harm you. Guess he was a little surprised when you mentioned my name."

"Why did you make your existence known to me?" I muttered sharply.

He glanced over my shoulder, taking in our surroundings, "I don't like to follow rules."

"Clearly," I agreed. "So, what do we do now?"

"I'm sorry?"

"Well, now that I know you know everything, what do we do now?" I explained. Now that I knew for sure where Noah stood, I could now start to try to figure out my place in this crazy war and do my best to help.

"You stay out of trouble and help your sister with her wedding and I'll make sure no one hurts you. That's what we will do," he answered as matter of fact. There was no other option in his eyes.

"I just thought," I began, but quickly dismissed the notion. There was no way he would either believe me or agree to it.

"Thought what?" he questioned, concern clouding his eyes.

"I just thought that you could maybe help me," I tried again to explain. "You see I've been having strange dreams, maybe you could even call them visions. Recently, these visions have been coming to me when I'm still awake. Well, I'll hear her voice."

"Whose voice?" Noah interrupted me, his eyes wide in interest.

"The woman, angel rather, that I dream about. She talks to me and warns me sometimes. I don't know. This is all crazy. You don't have to listen. I'm just losing my mind."

Noah gently took my hands in his. I looked into his eyes and found genuine concern and support, "What's her name Adeline?"

"Ogin," I mumbled embarrassed. I actually had a name for the voice in my head.

His eyes widened in shock and his body tensed. He swallowed hard, his Adam's apple bobbing up and down. Then, suddenly, he looked at me differently. It was like I was hope in tangible form. He looked at me as if I was something he had been waiting a very long time for.

"I can't believe it . . ." he mumbled, his wide eyes taking me in as if this were the first time he had ever seen me.

"Can't believe what?" I whispered, unsure of what just occurred.

"You are her," he said simply. I didn't need Noah to explain what his beliefs were in that moment. The way he was talking to me, treating me as if I was a valuable treasure that he had found was proof enough. Actions speak louder than words and I knew what Noah was saying. He believed I was the reincarnation. I was the heavenly being. I was their salvation.

"Her being the heavenly being," I clarified out loud. I had to hear it. I had to hear my voice say what many others believed and were trying to convince me of.

He started talking rapidly, excitedly, "You're the one who gave us our skills, our abilities. You have saved countless tribes, countless lives, and now you're here again and you're going to restore order and peace. Finally, we won't have to live in fear and . . ." he went on and on. He sounded like a small child that had found a treasure or figured out how to play and win a game. I zoned out as I let his words wash over me.

Now, the possibility of Ogin being a part of me seemed more and more plausible. Instead of feeling relief at finally coming to terms with the truth, or the very strong possibility of Ogin being reincarnated through me, intense pressure weighed heavily on me. How was I supposed to save countless lives? How was I supposed to help the Chosen? I could barely keep myself alive. I always needed someone else to protect me, to watch over me.

"I need your help," I interrupted Noah's rant of excitement.

"Anything," he immediately vowed, not thinking twice.

"If I really am who you say I am then I want to fight," I began. Noah immediately shook his head frantically.

"No, you can't fight. At least not now," he said resolutely.

"Noah, people I love are at risk here because of me. Why not?" I asked before continuing, "Ogin keeps telling me that now is my time to embrace my future, my destiny. Well, here I am. Like you said, I don't have a choice."

"So what do you need me to do?" he asked after a long moment of silence. I had just found my first ally.

"I need you to train me," I replied determinedly. "I need you to help me figure out what Ogin wants me to do, what these visions she keeps sending me mean. I want to know how to fight. If Chandler finds me again, I want to be ready to fight back."

Noah opened his mouth to deny me when I whispered, stopping him, "I'm the one he attacked, Noah. I'm the one who is afraid to close my eyes when I go to sleep because I see him in my dreams. I'm the one who has to fight my own battles. I have to defeat my own demons. I can't just keep relying on others to fight this war for me."

I didn't realize I was crying till I noticed my shaking voice was raw from the fresh wave of tears. I was tired of living in fear of the Rebels. I was tired of having to be protected constantly. I wanted to be able to protect Cole for once. I wanted to help carry the burden he had been forced to carry alone.

Noah nodded, giving my hand an encouraging squeeze, "When do we start?"

I smiled, relieved that finally someone was willing to help me become stronger. This wasn't just the Chosen's war. This was my war too, and I was determined to fight or die trying.

Reality of Emma's upcoming wedding turned out to be just as frightening, if not more so, than the supernatural part of my life at that moment. I was meeting the people who brought Henry into this world. Emma had met them once before, but that was prior to her engagement. I had never met them and I, clearly, was nervous; I swore everyone in the restaurant could hear my frantically beating heart. It was sort of ironic. I was willing to learn how to fight in order to defeat a tribe full of angry men, thirsty for revenge, but meeting my sister's future in-laws terrified me. I needed therapy.

I saw Mr. and Mrs. Lawrence before they saw me. Henry's mother was wearing a tight fitted blue tweed skirt with matching jacket. Her hair was pulled up tightly, pulling at her aged skin. Her makeup was two shades too light for her skin tone and she wore an expression very similar to Aunt Jean's: displeasure.

Mr. Lawrence wore a navy suit a size too small, causing the buttons to threaten popping off at any moment. His hair, or what was left of it, was smoothed back with gel. He and his wife shared similar expressions of despondency, and soon they were to be Emma's in-laws.

"Mama! Daddy!" Henry stood quickly, kissing his mother on both of her cheeks and then shaking his father's hand. "You have met my Emma already, but this here is her sister, Adeline."

At the same moment they glanced to me, evaluating me from my shoes to my hair. I blushed under their intense scrutiny.

"It's nice to finally meet you Adeline," Mrs. Lawrence very daintily shook my hand.

"Henry has told us so much about you," Mr. Lawrence smiled faintly.

We sat immediately and silence descended as each person looked over the menus. Thankfully, Mrs. Lawrence started asking Emma about the wedding plans, impressed that Emma could throw a wedding together in such a short time. Henry and his father began talking football and I was left alone with my thoughts. I glanced around the extravagant restaurant, my eyes darting from one couple to the next. The tug in my heart painfully pulled. I missed Cole. I missed the sound of his voice, the feel of his arms when he held me. I missed feeling safe. I missed knowing that whenever I was with him no one could hurt me, that he wouldn't let them. I missed everything about him.

"So, Adeline," Henry's mother startled me. "Do you have a special someone?"

I nodded, "Yes, actually. His name is Cole. He lives in Great Falls too."

They nodded for me to continue, "Cole?"

"Cole Dyami," I answered. "He lives on the Little Shell reservation. He is Chippewa . . ." but my voice trailed to a stop when I saw the disgusted looks on both Mr. and Mrs. Lawrence.

"Oh, no, no my dear. That simply won't do," Mrs. Lawrence shook her head.

"I'm sorry?" I questioned, looking to Emma for help.

"Emma, you're allowing your sister to date an Indian?" Mr. Lawrence glanced to Emma disapprovingly.

"Well," Emma tried to defend herself when Henry interrupted.

"Now Daddy, there is nothing to worry about," Henry calmed both of his parents down. "You know once the wedding is over, we are all moving down here permanently so this little relationship will come to an end."

Both Emma and I yelled at the same time, "What?"

I saw only red. My whole world was being ripped to pieces in front of me. The only consolation, the only benefit to this wedding in Beaufort was the knowledge that I would be returning home to Cole as soon as it was over. Emma never said anything about moving here, about living here forever.

I changed my mind on what I had told Ogin in my dream the night before. I was probably very capable of killing someone at the moment.

"Excuse me?" Emma's fury transferred to Henry.

"Babe, we've talked about this," Henry was not fazed. "We agreed to move down here once the wedding was over so we could start our life together as a family."

"I'd said I would think about it," Emma's anger was bringing unwanted attention from the other patrons. "I can't just uproot Adeline from everything she knows and loves like that."

"Dear, maybe we should talk about this at a more appropriate venue," Mrs. Lawrence was becoming more embarrassed by the second.

"No!" Emma shocked everyone. "Let's talk now. Why do we need to live here?"

"Well, to start fresh in our new married lives," Henry answered uncomfortably, "and to separate Adeline from that Indian."

Before I could reach across the table and strangle Henry with my bare hands, Emma slapped Henry across the face. Silence erupted across the restaurant as everyone stopped and stared at our table.

"How dare you?" she whispered. She turned to Henry's awestruck parents, "and shame on you. You don't even know that boy and you already judge him from where he comes from. Well, I'm here to tell you that Cole Dyami is a fine young man who loves my sister. I couldn't pick out a better person for her, and if you can't accept my sister and I as we are, and the other people we love, then I don't know if we can join this family."

Emma stood, straightening out her dress and looked to me, "Ready Addie?"

I smiled, tears stinging my eyes, "Yeah."

Emma and I left the restaurant as Henry and his family sat dumbstruck. I had never been more proud of my sister.

But my pride for my sister melted to sympathy as we walked back into our hotel. Emma's strong façade faded as the tears rolled down her face like rain. We sat up in her bed, with her head in my lap, as I did my best to comfort her.

"Everything is gonna be okay Em," I tried to soothe.

"Am I stupid?" she sobbed.

"No. I think you're incredibly brave," I countered.

"I'm stupid," she reasoned. "I mean, I told the truth, but I'm still stupid."

"So, you meant everything? About Cole and I?" My heart leapt in response.

I was just as shocked as Henry's family when Emma had revealed how she really felt about Cole. I was happy to find that she had accepted him, loved him too.

"Of course," she blew her nose. "I never say anything unless I mean it."

"That's true," I laughed.

"I'm sorry by the way."

"For what?" I questioned, making her sit up.

She looked at me, licking her lips nervously before beginning, "For not telling you about Henry wanting to move here."

I nodded, "It's fine, Em."

"Well," She continued, her voice thick with tears, "I guess I'm gonna need to go book our flights back home." The tears overcame her again and I held her as she cried for a very long time. We fell asleep like that, in each other's arms. Just like when we were little.

PART TWO

Above all, be the heroine of your life, not the victim.

Norah Ephron

EIGHT

The sun's bright rays woke me from a deep, dreamless sleep. It was the first time in several nights that I had not dreamed. I felt strangely rested; an overwhelming sense of peace washed over me. However, this newfound peace was short lived when I found the note from Emma saying Henry called and she agreed to meet him for breakfast.

I took a long shower, allowing the scalding water to numb away my tense muscles. I dressed quickly, grabbing an apple from the complimentary fruit basket as I headed out the door. I was about half way to the bay where I was going to meet Noah for our first training session when my phone rang. I was stunned and thrilled to find Cole was calling me. However, the memory of our last conversation still stung me as I remembered how irate he had sounded.

"Hello?" I asked guardedly.

"Adeline." and just like that, the sound of his voice erased any doubt I had. All the little voices in my head that insisted Cole had finally realized I wasn't worth the wait, worth the fight, were silenced . . . at least for the remainder of our phone conversation.

"Cole." His name was sweet water in a dry, barren land. "I miss you."

"I miss you too," he whispered, his voice, though quiet, washed over me like cool rain. I hadn't realized how being apart from Cole hurt me physically as much as it did emotionally and mentally.

"How is everyone?" I asked carefully as I found a quiet spot to sit outside of a small coffee shop. I couldn't directly ask about the Chosen for fear of being overheard by the many people who walked in and out of the shops and down the busy street.

"Good," he replied proudly yet exhaustedly. "We just finished training."

"You just finished?" I glanced down to my clock, horrified to find the time. "Cole, you stayed up all night training?"

"We really needed it. Besides, training in the dark is good for us. It gives us an edge." I could hear the fatigue and tiredness in his voice with each word.

"Cole, you need to sleep. Call me later," it physically hurt me to end the conversation, but he clearly needed rest.

"No, I'm fine," he insisted. "Besides, from what I hear, I owe you quite the explanation."

"I know that you told Noah to watch out for me," I uttered quietly, "and I know that the reason you were so upset the last time we talked was because you didn't want me to know about him. Why didn't you just tell me Cole? I would have understood."

Cole sighed heavily, "I know, but I didn't want you to worry."

"Worry? I'm always worried Cole; everyday, all day," I wearily admitted. "It's non-stop."

"I'm sorry," his already tired voice seemed strained. "I just wanted to make sure you were protected without you being apprehensive. I was only worried on how much Noah was going to tell you."

"How do you know him?" I asked quietly. I had been curious to understand how Cole knew anyone outside of his own tribe. He never mentioned anyone, before now, that would be involved with the impending war.

"I don't really know him, but Paco does. He has traveled to the

Rock Hill reservation before and he knew they would be the best to keep an eye on you. He mentioned Noah and how he often travels to Beaufort, so I called him and asked for a favor. I didn't want him bothering you. I wanted you to only worry about the wedding, not what was going on back here," Cole explained, his tired voice becoming more and more slurred by exhaustion as he spoke.

"Cole, you need to go sleep. I'm fine and I love you."

"I'll call you later," He yawned. "I love you."

The line went dead, but I didn't immediately leave to meet Noah. I sat thoughtfully at my table as I considered my next conversation with Cole. Would I tell him Noah was going to train me? Or at least help me learn to fight?

I had not completely decided on what to do or say to Cole when I noticed a bit of red hair out of the corner of my eye. I looked to my right and noticed Cailen walking out of the coffee shop. She was walking towards me when she suddenly noticed me, and immediately turned sharply around and began walking in the opposite direction. Why would she avoid me?

I got up and followed her; I was still unsure on exactly why I was following this girl who was still just a stranger to me. I felt a pull, like it was absolutely necessary that I speak to her again. I trusted my instinct and followed her. When I was close enough, I made my presence known.

"Cailen?"

She stopped, turning around slowly, apprehension clearly written across her beautiful features.

"Hey," she greeted me half-heartedly. "I'm sorry, I've forgotten your name."

"Adeline," I replied awkwardly. I wasn't really sure on what exactly I was going to say to her at this point. "How are you?"

She nodded anxiously, "I'm fine. How about you?"

"I'm good," uncomfortable silence followed where the two of us merely stood staring at one another.

"How is your friend? Noah?" She finally spoke again. I was surprised to find she remembered Noah's name, a man whom she claimed she had no connection with, and not mine.

"He's okay," I replied honestly. Now that Noah truly believed I was Ogin's reincarnation, his outlook on the future increased greatly. He was really looking forward to training and preparing for battle simply because he knew that it would keep him busy. However, no amount of passed time or distractions can keep the nightmares of heartbreak away. I knew that. He would learn it too.

Her expression relaxed a bit, "That's good." She seemed to really hope that my words rang true, that Noah was doing okay.

"Why did you lie to me?" I asked quietly, shocking Cailen as she took a tentative step away from me.

"Excuse me?" she tried to feign a smile, but I saw past it. I supposed I knew she had been lying all along. I didn't know if it was my gut feeling, my instinct that screamed she knew Noah, or the way her eyes had lit up when she said his name.

"You know Noah, don't you? So, why did you lie to me about it?" I asked honestly. Cailen stood stunned, mouth open trying to find the words.

"I . . ." she tried to defend herself, to prove to me that I was wrong and that she was right, but no excuse came to her mind. Instead, thick tears clouded her green eyes as a shudder of grief rippled through her body.

"It's okay," I stepped toward her, giving her arm an encouraging squeeze. "You can tell me. I understand."

"I don't know you," she accused, yanking her arm away, "and you don't understand."

"You'd be surprised," I countered gently, "but I get why you don't trust me. Maybe we could have lunch sometime and talk?"

But Cailen began backing away while shaking her head more furiously and resolutely, "No, I don't think that would be a good idea. I have to go. I'm late."

She walked away briskly, placing as much distance between us as possible.

I wasn't surprised to find Noah waiting for me at our usual spot on the bay, wearing his typical smirk.

"You're late," he grinned. "What took you so long?"

"I just lost track of time," I lied. "So, should we start now?"

I was surprised and a little annoyed when Noah started laughing, "Whoa, whoa, slow down. We have to find suitable training grounds first."

I looked around the small park that sat before the bay, "Why can't this work?"

He rolled his eyes as he pointed to the other people in the area, "Too many witnesses."

"Do you plan on murdering me?" I joked.

He shook his head playfully, "No, but I do believe I wouldn't be the first to want you dead now would I?"

I glared, "That's not funny."

"Never said it was," he replied coolly as he began leading me away from the harbor and towards the bay's parking lot.

"Where are we going?"

"Somewhere we can train in privacy," he rolled his eyes again. "Do you even listen to me?"

"I meant where are we going that is private?" I rephrased my question as we got into his car.

"You'll see," he smiled. I immediately tensed. I had a feeling I wasn't going to like wherever we were going.

I was, however, pleasantly surprised when we drove up to a beach. It was incredibly beautiful, much more magnificent than what my dreams had come up with. The waves crashed violently against the white sand. The sun hid behind a few clouds in the endless blue sky. The salty ocean air literally took my breath away. Noah had already started walking towards the ocean's edge when he noticed my awestruck expression.

"Are you coming?" he called to me.

Without taking my eyes off of the beauty of the ocean I walked beside him closer to the water's edge, carrying my sandals in my hands, savoring the feel of the sand in between my toes.

"What's with you?" he laughed as he playfully shoved my

shoulder.

"I've never seen the ocean," I admitted, still captivated by the ocean's splendor and enormity. "I mean, besides in movies. Emma has been so busy planning the wedding that we haven't had the chance to actually come."

Noah looked thoughtfully from me to the ocean, "Well, it doesn't get much better than this."

"No," I agreed. "I suppose it doesn't."

"We shouldn't be bothered here," Noah's mind refocused to the reason why we were at the beach as he set down a huge duffle bag he had carried from his car. "So, we should probably get started."

"What is in there?" I asked curiously as he unzipped the large duffle.

"The tools we need to train," he answered as he revealed the different weapons within the bag. My mouth fell open.

"Is all of this really necessary?" I asked as my eyes fell on a particularly frightening spear with a very sharp edge.

"We won't be using all of this," Noah's hands ran over each weapon, looking for something specific. "We will be mainly training your spiritual and mental abilities. Those are going to be your true weapons, but it won't hurt to give you something a bit more tangible."

"It actually might," I contradicted as my head began to spin from the thought of me wielding a sword or knife. I could barely stab the straw into a Capri Sun.

"Here," Noah tried to hand me a large sword. "Try this."

"You're joking, right?" I asked taking a step back.

"Adeline," he reprimanded. "Trust me."

I carefully took the handle in my hand, however once Noah let go, the weight of the heavy weapon was too much and it pulled me to the ground. Of course, Noah fell into a fit of laughter. His amusement did little to help my self-esteem.

"I told you," I had to shout over his enjoyment. "This is stupid."

After a few more moments, Noah finally was able to calm

down.

"So, this won't work," he took the sword back and placed it safely back into his bag. After a few more moments of searching, Noah took something much smaller out of his bag of sharp, pointy things. Before I could refuse this new object Noah carefully placed it in my hand. It was a small silver dagger with turquoise stones embedded in the handle. It was light and seemed to mold into my hand, like it was extension, a part of me that had been missing. It was beautiful.

"I think this is a better fit," Noah smiled knowingly as I caressed the dangerous, yet beautiful weapon.

"Where did you get it?" I asked, "and who actually carries a duffle bag full of weapons?"

"A woman in my tribe made that," Noah answered as he handed me the case for the dagger and picked up another sword. "I don't normally carry such heavy equipment but, considering how many people want you dead, I wanted to make sure all of our bases are covered."

Noah tossed the sword from his right hand to his left hand with no trouble, as if it didn't weigh anything.

"Show off," I mumbled as I turned my dagger over again in my hand.

Noah laughed, but it didn't quite reach his eyes.

"Are you okay?" I questioned as I placed the dagger in its sheath.

"I never imagined that when Cole called me to watch out for you that it would mean war was so close," he admitted. Guilt washed over me suddenly. I had unintentionally dragged more innocent people, like Noah's tribe, into this war.

"I'm so sorry," I immediately apologized. "If you don't want to help me, I understand. I don't mean to drag you and your tribe into this mess."

He looked to me with a new kind of emotion in his eyes – confusion and wonder.

"You don't know, do you?"

"Know what?"

Great, more secrets that someone felt the need to keep from me. I was looking forward to the day when I would finally understand everything people were saying half the time.

"How important you are," he said simply. The sincerity and honesty in his voice threw me.

"I'm not important," I countered. "I'm just Adeline."

Noah shook his head, "Why do you think I dropped everything in Rock Hill to come protect you? Because you're just some girl who has a few enemies? Adeline, you need to understand how precious your life is. If something happens to you, then we are all dead."

"All?" I felt the blood drain from my face.

"This war," Noah began, "is much bigger than just Little Shell and Turtle Mountain. Ogin is the reason my ancestors had the abilities and powers they had to pass down from generation to generation. A lot of people are depending on you and your involvement in this war."

"No pressure," I breathed as I slowly sat down on the sand.

Noah smiled gently while sitting next to me, "Everything is going to be okay."

I glanced to look at his expression. He seemed strangely calm, like he honestly believed I was some savior who was going to solve all of his worries.

"I'm not so sure about that," I whispered pulling my knees to my chest. I felt Noah place a reassuring arm around my shoulders.

"I promise to protect you, to help you, do anything you need of me. You are not alone in this," his voice did not waver. He was giving me his word, his loyalty.

I nodded in response, not trusting my voice. Thick tears clouded my vision as new emotions began to overwhelm me. I should have known all along that it would come to this. I could no longer sit idly by as Cole and countless others risked their lives for me, because they believed me to be something worth protecting. It was my turn to protect them. If I was as powerful as everyone believed me to be then I needed to prove it to not only them, but to myself as well.

I hastily wiped my eyes as I stood up. Noah, confused, stood with me, waiting for me to explain.

I took a deep breath, "Well, let's get started."

He smiled, his eyes creasing, "Yes ma'am."

I was exhausted by the time I made it back to the room. I fell helplessly on my bed, my head throbbing from all of the new information and techniques I had learned today, or at least, attempted to learn.

Noah had done his best to help me try to control my thinking and my breathing, in order to harness my power. Honestly, I just sat on the sand breathing in and out, trying not to fall asleep. Noah tried to remain patient, but I could tell he was getting frustrated. Finally, he tried to physically train me to know how to protect myself if I ever needed to. Of course, I fell several times due to my braced ankle. Only a few more weeks and I would be free of the stupid thing.

In the end, Noah just asked me to retell all of my vision-like dreams in as much detail as I could remember. I left out the dream that included Cailen, fearing his anger and depression that would possibly follow. He nodded the entire time I explained each dream. In the end, he said that it was necessary for me to try to keep remembering what happened the night my parents died.

"Just keep me updated on those visions," Noah had said as we drove back, "and don't fight them so much."

"Fight them?"

"Yeah," he had nodded. "Just let them unfold, then call me and let me know."

"Noah?" I had asked, my gaze faltering from the scenery outside to his face.

"Yeah?"

"Should we tell Cole about this? About you training me?" For some reason I felt like it was wrong to keep anything from him, but I knew if I told him, he probably would become angry with Noah and demand we stop.

Noah had remained silent for a long time, his expression grave. "Noah?"

"No," he finally replied, his voice stern, "No, I don't think that would be a good idea."

I was just about to fall asleep when I heard the door open suddenly. I sat up immediately, surprised to find Emma grinning from ear to ear.

"How was breakfast with Henry?" I asked, already aware of the answer before the words left her mouth.

She jumped onto the bed while pulling me into a tight embrace simultaneously.

"That good, huh?" I assumed while she finally released me, falling back onto the mattress.

"The wedding is still on," she affirmed, visions of lace, cakes, and flowers swimming in her eyes. "Henry apologized and we had a nice long talk about the future and what we wanted out of it. We are not moving here permanently. Once the wedding is over we will move back to Great Falls so you can finish high school."

I smiled, relief washing over me like cool rain, "Thank you, Em."

Emma's dazed expression faded as she pulled my hands into hers, "I want to do what's best for you Addie. You are and have always been my first priority. I promise I won't forget that again."

I nodded, overcome by emotion, "Em, what do you remember from the night of the car accident?"

Emma's face faltered at the sudden change of subject, "Why?"

"I've just been thinking about Mom and Dad a lot," I spoke quickly, afraid I was going to lose my nerve before I received the answers I needed. "I was just wondering if you remember anything particularly interesting from that night?"

"What do you mean?" her face fell into a frown. Emma and I never really talked about the night our parents died. We both weren't comfortable dealing with that part of our pasts quite yet.

"Like, who the drunk driver was? Who pulled me out of the

water?" I questioned.

I already knew who pulled me out. Even though I had no concrete evidence, I knew Paco Dyami had saved my life. Now that I had come to realize that my entire life has been at the center of a tribal legend, I couldn't help but question whether or not the drunk driver wasn't someone who had wanted me dead, even at five years old.

"We've been over this," Emma was beginning to shut down. It was probably too soon to bring it up again. "The police never found the driver and all they could tell me was someone had probably driven by, saw what happened, and jumped in the river to save you. The police found you on the river bank, barely alive." Her voice drifted to a whisper at the end.

I pulled Emma into another embrace, "I'm sorry Em. I didn't mean to upset you."

"It's fine," her voice shook. "Besides, you need to get ready."

"For what?"

"Henry is taking you and I out to dinner. He wants to apologize to you personally for what his parents said last night," Emma replied, trying to maintain her happy façade, as she jumped off the bed and began digging through the drawers looking for something suitable to wear.

Suddenly, exhaustion came over me once more as I began to get ready and prepare for what was to come.

Henry picked us up around dusk. We were a little early for our reservations, so we decided to take a stroll down the main promenade.

"This is the cutest little shop," Emma squealed. "Do you guys mind if I step inside real quick?"

"Of course not darlin'," Henry insisted cheerfully. "Take your time!"

Emma smiled at me expectantly before she rushed into the little boutique. I guessed this was the time when Henry would apologize to me directly; probably attempt to use his southern charm to get into good graces with his bride-to-be's younger sister. He would most likely grovel, beg for forgiveness, even insist on how Cole was a great guy and that his parents were completely out of line in what they had said.

Instead, Henry's puppy love façade fell as a clear look of irritation ran across his face. His eyes, usually glazed over from love for Emma or being completely oblivious to everything around him, were stern, hard, and cold. Everything Henry was not.

He turned to me, rolling his eyes at my surprised expression, "What the hell are you looking at?"

Another blow I wasn't expecting. I was never usually alone with Henry, but whenever the time came, he was his normal awkward self. He was never this mean, never this cruel.

"I don't understand," I stuttered. What had happened to my sister's fiancé?

"Obviously," he spat back. I recoiled at his tone as he stepped toward me, his face inches from mine. He grabbed my arms tightly, stopping the blood flow.

"I'm going to make sure you understand now, Adeline." There was a foreign harshness in his words.

"You're hurting me," I whimpered.

He ignored my struggle, continuing, "You listen to me. I am going to marry that girl in there and there is nothing you can do about it. I will move this family wherever I please. You will be a good little girl and break up with that Indian as soon as I tell you to. You do what I say and no one gets hurt."

My heart was pounding as I looked from Henry's hard brown eyes to the people around me. No one noticed us. I thought about screaming, but Henry's threat stopped me.

"But Emma said . . ." I whispered, but my voice crumbled as Henry's iron clad grip on my arm intensified.

"But Emma said," he quoted me callously. "Your sister doesn't know anything, and she won't know about this little conversation, will she? I'd hate for something to happen to her, leaving you in my primary care. That'd be awful, wouldn't it?"

My breathing became shallow. I didn't understand. Who was this horrible person, someone I thought to love Emma more than breathing, who was threatening to hurt her?

"Are we clear?" he asked lastly, his grip loosening by a fraction.

"Crystal," I replied just as severely. He finally released me, the blood painfully returning to my arms. Emma walked out in that moment, a smile gracing her face. Henry turned to her, his stern face replaced by what I would have thought to be love and adoration. It made me think that my mind had made up everything that had just occurred, but the throbbing pain in my arms was a steady reminder that Henry Lawrence was not to be trusted.

NINE

"You're not focusing," Noah sighed frustrated. I was breathing heavily, sweat falling into my eyes. I wiped my forehead with my arm. We had been training every day for the past week, almost all day. It was getting more difficult to keep it all a secret from Emma.

I stepped back from Noah, still holding the sword Noah was trying to train me to use. I was still only comfortable with my dagger, but he was trying to build up my endurance and strength.

"I have a lot on my mind." Emma's wedding, Henry's threat, my heart aching for Cole, the war that was looming on the horizon.

"I told you, you must clear your mind and focus," Noah explained yet again. I knew what I had to do, but it seemed impossible when my mind was being pulled in a million different directions.

"Have you had anymore dreams?" Noah asked after a long silence. I breathed in the ocean air deeply, my gaze faltering from Noah to the ocean.

"No," I replied miserably. The one connection I had to this craziness, my one source of information, Ogin, seemed to have vanished. She was remaining silent, right when I needed her the most.

Noah smiled, trying to encourage me, "Don't worry. You can't force stuff like this. It just has to happen."

Another long bout of silence before Noah's face turned hard, "Has Henry said anything else to you?"

I had only told Noah about Henry's threat, not Emma or even Cole. For some reason, I couldn't bring myself to hurting Emma like that and I knew the second I told Cole, he would be on the next flight to South Carolina ready to kill Henry. Noah had been furious of course, believing I should tell Emma immediately. She wouldn't believe me. Besides, Henry had threatened to hurt her if I even mentioned it to her. I knew I had to do something, I just didn't know what.

"No," I finally responded. "Not yet, but I am going to dinner tonight with his family." I was already dreading it.

"I thought the rehearsal dinner wasn't until tomorrow night."

"It's not, but Henry's parents wanted to have a dinner at their home with a few of Henry's close relatives," I moaned, slowly sitting down on the sand. My entire body was so sore from all of the training.

Noah nodded sitting down too, his eyes drifting to my bruised arms. I had bruises not because of training with Noah, but from Henry and the night he had threatened me. I noticed them the next morning, telling Emma I must have run into something. When Noah had seen my arms, he was about ready to call in Cole and the rest of the Chosen, but Cole couldn't know.

"How is that ankle doing?" Noah nodded towards my braced foot.

I rolled my eyes, "Taking forever to heal." He looked at me keenly.

"What?" I asked carefully.

"You could heal that, you know?" he smiled.

I scoffed, "Yeah, right."

"I'm serious," he replied, suddenly offended. "If you focused hard enough, you could heal it yourself."

I looked at him doubtfully, "Right, and if I just clap my hands and believe, I can sprout some fairy wings and fly away too?"

Noah's voice went from insulted to despondent, "Why do you doubt yourself so much?"

I looked up to his brown eyes, finding sympathy. He honestly felt sorry for me.

"I don't know."

"Adeline, we don't have a chance if you don't stop doubting who you are and your destiny. You have to realize how strong you are and use it to your advantage. Now, do you trust me?"

I nodded, "Yes."

"Then focus and prove to yourself how powerful you really are," he looked towards my ankle. "Heal yourself."

His undeniable belief and trust in me left me speechless. What if I couldn't amount to all he believed me to be? What if I was only Adeline? Simple Adeline who couldn't even save the people she loves, let alone an entire tribe?

Noah's loyalty and confidence in me were urging me forward. I had to at least try, for his sake.

I glanced down to my swollen ankle. All of our training and work had begun irritating my ankle for a while now. I never said anything, but just tried to ignore it. I took off my shoe and brace, revealing the swollen foot that was still bruised purple and yellow. I felt Noah shudder next to me. It definitely wasn't a pretty sight.

"Now," he began, "focus. Breathe in and out and visualize what you want to happen. You can do this. Take your time."

I closed my eyes, stretching my ankle out, allowing the subtle pain and ache to spread. I breathed deeply, trying to focus. I sat for what felt like several minutes when I heard her voice. Ogin's voice.

"Good. That's it. Focus," she encouraged me. "You can do this, Adeline."

With my eyes still closed, I could see her. She was just the way I remembered: ethereal, light, and everything good. I focused on her, allowing her warmth to penetrate my mind and body. Gradually, the dull pain in my ankle began to loosen. The aching fell away to warmth. I opened my eyes when I heard Noah gasp.

My eyes darted to my ankle, once bruised and swollen, now smooth and without blemish. I had no more pain. I sat, dumbfounded. Noah chuckled at my gaping open mouth. I twisted and pulled at my ankle, shocked to find no pain or aching. It was like my ankle had never been shattered.

"What did I tell you?" he smiled. "It's about time you started believing in yourself."

For the first time in my life I was actually beginning to have faith in who I was. I was starting to believe that maybe I was powerful, special, a heroine, someone who should be feared and revered, someone of which legends are made.

I was walking quickly from the hotel, desperate to make it to dinner before I was deemed too late by Emma and the rest of Henry's family. Emma had already gone to Henry's parents' home, allowing me to meet her there. I was just about to turn the corner onto their street when a familiar voice stopped me.

"Adeline?"

I turned to find Cailen, standing awkwardly beside her car that was parked along the street. She looked nervous, her finger constantly twirling one of her red ringlets. She seemed paranoid as well, frequently glancing around at the few people who were walking by us.

"Cailen?" I finally questioned, beyond surprised to find her looking for me after our last encounter.

"Hi," she breathed shakily. "How are you?"

I nodded, dumbstruck, "Fine, and you?"

"I'm okay," she replied honestly. "I was actually wondering if you had time to talk. I could buy you a cup of coffee?"

A part of me realized I should have said no that I needed to meet my sister and her future in laws for dinner, but that seemed like a lifetime ago. The only thing that genuinely mattered was talking to Cailen. Having dinner with Henry's family was trivial in comparison.

Emma's wedding had become insignificant compared to a lot of things in my life at the moment.

"Yeah, of course," I had agreed, walking with Cailen towards the small coffee shop completely forgetting the time and the pressing engagement I was supposed to be running to.

We sat at a small table in the corner of the coffee shop, Cailen clinging to her mug of hot coffee while my small cup of tea sat alone, untouched. I waited for Cailen to begin, but she seemed so unsure of herself, like she was debating on whether or not meeting with me had been a good idea at all.

"I wanted to speak with you because I needed to tell you that you were right," she finally began, her grip on her coffee mug tightening.

"About what?" I asked, confusion echoing through my voice. My last conversation with Cailen seemed like a lifetime ago. So much had happened since then.

"About Noah," she breathed. "I did know him. I was engaged to him."

Of course I had already known all of this information but I remained silent, allowing Cailen to tell her story.

Tears threatened to spill over, "I loved him, so much. We had planned out our entire lives together. We were going to buy a house on the beach and have a nice, small wedding. We planned on having a lot of children. But it turns out the happily ever after I had been dreaming of wasn't possible."

She sighed, fighting back tears, as I waited patiently for her to continue.

"You see, Noah's not exactly normal. He had showed me . . ." she paused, unsure on how much to tell a complete stranger. "He showed me his true self and at first, it scared me and I wasn't sure if I could handle it, but I loved him and when you love someone you love every part of him or her, even the not so beautiful parts. But then the threats started."

"Threats?" I questioned abruptly, shocked to think that Noah would ever threaten the one person he loves more than anything.

"Not from Noah," she shook her head immediately, "from others like him. People who are . . ." she paused, looking for the right word. "Different."

"What did they say to you?" I asked slowly, my heart pounding as I waited for her response.

"If I stayed with Noah, bad things would happen to my family. At first, it was only phone calls, which I learned to ignore. Then they became more physical, following me home from work, leaving notes inside my house."

"Why didn't you tell Noah?"

"That's the thing Adeline," she whispered fiercely. "Most of their threats were against Noah; that if I didn't leave him, they would kill him." Sobs overcame her as she sat hunched over her mug, hand to her mouth as she tried to control her tears. "I couldn't live with myself if something happened to him. I couldn't do it. I loved him too much. So, I let him go. I told him it was because he was too different, that our worlds were miles apart. I'll never forget the look in his eyes when I handed him the ring back."

"How long ago did this happen?"

"About a year."

My heart broke for Cailen. She did the only thing she thought she could do. If I had been in her place, I probably would have done the same thing. The thought of someone hurting Cole, even now, was unbearable to me. It was unthinkable.

"Do you know the people who were making these threats?" I asked desperately after she had collected herself. "Please Cailen, this is so important."

Cailen's red-rimmed eyes looked up to me. She was about to answer when her eyes focused on something behind me. She inhaled sharply, fear shining in her sea-foam green eyes. I felt the hair on my arms rise.

She suddenly stood, gathering her things quickly, desperate to leave, "I've got to go. I'm sorry I can't help you anymore, Adeline." and like lightening, she was gone. I slowly turned in my chair, glancing around the small coffee shop, looking for whoever caused Cailen to leave in such a rush. I had an eerie feeling that whomever she saw must definitely not be a friend. It was most certainly someone to fear.

My eyes finally rested on a hooded man in another corner of the coffee shop who was reading a newspaper, seemingly unaware of all that was around him. My heart raced, the adrenaline pumped, and fear coursed through my body like poison paralyzing me.

Sitting only a few feet away from me was the object of all of my nightmares and darkest dreams. Chandler Phalcon. He had found me.

TEN

I sat for a few painful moments. I had turned back around, my eyes locked on my now cold cup of tea. I was frozen in my seat, paralyzed by inexplicable fear. I barely breathed, afraid he would hear me. I became ultra aware of every sound from the register, to the blender, to the argument of the couple a few tables to my left, to the older man giving his order, to Chandler's breathing and turning of his newspaper. I dared to make another glance over my shoulder. He had removed his hood, revealing his unkempt long onyx hair. His face seemed tired, overwhelmed, and frustrated.

I turned back around, surprised that he hadn't noticed my presence yet. If I remained quiet, maybe I could leave the coffee shop unnoticed. I stood carefully, trying to not make any noise. I took a few tentative steps to the door, expecting Chandler to appear and stop me. Nothing yet, so I took another step, and another. So close.

I almost fell midstride when my phone began ringing loudly. Without bothering to answer or to look back, I ran out of the coffee shop, sprinting down the street till I thought I was safe. I hid in an alleyway; finally pulling out my phone to find Emma had called me.

Of course, I was about an hour late to dinner. She was most likely livid. Making sure I wasn't being followed, I swiftly made my way to Henry's parents' home.

I was breathing heavily when I came to their front door and rang the doorbell. Mrs. Lawrence answered, her mouth set in a tight line of disapproval.

"So nice of you to finally grace us with your presence, Adeline," Mrs. Lawrence stated as she held the door open for me. I barely took notice of her grand house or her obvious attitude as I walked in, wiping sweat from my forehead. I had bigger issues than some angry, southern woman.

I followed Mrs. Lawrence into the parlor where her guests were already drinking coffee and eating desserts. Emma immediately stood when I walked into the room. She looked like she was about to scold me when her face fell.

"Adeline, you're out of breath," worry took over her other emotions. "Did something happen?"

Henry raised his eyebrow expectantly. It was the first time I had seen him since our last conversation.

I turned my attention back to Emma, "I'm fine. Just ran into a friend and lost track of time. I'm so sorry I'm late."

None of Henry's family said anything, much less looked at me. I was a disappointment already, and they didn't even know me.

"Adeline," Henry's Aunt Jean stood. "Let's take a stroll through Eugenia's garden."

Both Emma and I were surprised by Aunt Jean's offer. She took my arm without waiting to hear if I would object.

"Okay," I mumbled, my eyes locking with Emma who simply shrugged before turning her attention back to Henry and his parents.

Aunt Jean led me through the kitchen and out the French doors to the lovely back yard. There was a small fountain at the center and many different flowers blooming. The sun was just beginning to set. The twilight of the evening was settling in, making the flowers and the garden feel like a new land yet to be discovered. It was beautiful.

Aunt Jean showed me different flowers, naming the species and giving every detail one could possibly imagine. I had tuned her out for the most part, nodding and smiling at all the right moments. It wasn't till we came across the last flower in the garden that I noticed a change in Aunt Jean's demeanor.

"This one is called a morning glory. They say that it blooms only once before dying. During the Victorian period, people said they represented unrequited love because of their short life spans," She paused turning to look at me. "How sad it must be, to love someone only to know they will die soon."

I looked to her questionably. What was she talking about?

She tried to smile, the skin on her face pulling awkwardly, "Wouldn't it have been a shame for that beautiful red headed girl to have died because she couldn't stay away from that Indian?"

My heart stopped and fell to my feet as her words began to sink in.

"How do you know about Cailen and Noah?" I asked, my voice barely above a whisper. I felt like I was dreaming. I must be in some horrible nightmare.

"Oh my dear," she laughed. "I know everything about this town and the people in it. I also know about your predicament in Great Falls. Henry has been very good at keeping me informed."

"Henry?" my stomach turned. "Did Henry tell you he threatened me?" I exclaimed pulling up my sleeves to reveal the bruises. I probably should have tried to heal those, but I couldn't erase the proof of what he had done to me.

She laughed again, staring longingly at the bruised flesh, "Tell me? My dear, I'm the one who told him to relay the message."

I stood, dumbfounded.

"I don't understand." I whispered. Suddenly, nausea and dizziness hit me.

Her smile faded, "Of course you don't. You were too busy with that Indian boy to see what was right in front of you."

"Why are you doing this?" I took a step back. "What do you want?"

She plucked a morning glory off its vine bringing it to her face,

"Wouldn't it be an awful waste for that boy you love to have to die because you are being selfish?"

I continued to walk backwards, fear causing me to retreat. I took tentative steps until I bumped into something similar to a brick wall. I turned around, horrified to find Chandler Phalcon smirking down at me. How did he get here? Did he follow me from the coffee shop?

I jumped backwards, too shocked to scream. My head was swimming again. Nothing was making sense.

"Ah, Chandler dear! You made it," Aunt Jean smiled, still twirling the blue flower in her hand.

"You know him?" I asked alarmed.

"Chandler and I have an agreement," she began, "an understanding, but that is none of your concern."

"It's been so long Adeline," Chandler finally spoke, stepping towards me as I moved away. "I've missed you."

I cringed away, not sure on where I could go, where I could run. I was trapped and my sister was only feet away, inside the house, clearly in danger.

"We have a proposition for you," Aunt Jean continued, "a treaty of sorts."

My eyes wavered from Aunt Jean and back to Chandler, "What kind of treaty?"

"You do exactly what we say," Aunt Jean continued, "and none of the Chosen are harmed. There doesn't have to be a brutal war. You can end it all."

My eyes widened when she mentioned the Chosen. Then again, if she knew Chandler, I'm sure she was aware of everything that was occurring.

"What do you want from me?" I asked, my lips tight. I was trying to remember all of the defense moves Noah had been teaching me over the past week, but the only ones I knew well had to do with my dagger. And it was tucked away in my bag, currently sitting in the Lawrence's parlor.

"First, I want you to tell Cole your relationship is over, that you and Emma have decided to move down here permanently to escape the life he has forced you to live," Aunt Jean started.

I shook my head furiously, "No."

Chandler took a step towards me, "If you don't, we will kill him."

Suddenly, a vision of Cole's lifeless body flashed before me. This is what my dreams had been warning me. Coming here had separated Cole and I in a way that I would never be able to take back.

Tears began to pour down my cheeks at the thought of what I must do. I had to protect him, the Chosen, the tribe. I had to do whatever I could to keep Cole alive, to keep him breathing.

I slowly, dejectedly nodded. Both Chandler and Aunt Jean beamed in response.

"Then, after the rehearsal dinner tomorrow night you will meet us at this address," Chandler handed me a newspaper clipping of a real-estate ad for a warehouse outside of town, while Aunt Jean continued speaking, "More information will be provided at this venue. Adeline, if you don't complete our first request before tomorrow night, it will most definitely not end well for Cole or the others. And I would just hate for something terrible to happen to that pretty sister of yours the day before her wedding, wouldn't you?"

I numbly held the newspaper clipping as my new reality set in.

Footsteps crunched along the pebbled path until Henry made his presence known, "Emma is asking for her." his voice was gruff, cold, void of emotion.

"You're in on this too?" I asked unfeelingly. At this point, nothing surprised me too much.

He smirked, glancing towards me, "Someone had to keep a good eye on you for the Rebels, darlin'."

"Well," Aunt Jean commanded attention. "We will see you tomorrow night after the dinner. Henry will be sure you make it."

Aunt Jean nodded to Chandler who then walked away, disappearing through the back gate and into the marshy woods.

"Now, let's get back inside before it gets any darker. I just hate the dark, don't you Henry?" Aunt Jean began talking flippantly again, as if she hadn't threatened everything I had held dear. I followed them into the house, numbly aware of the fact that not only did any hope for winning this war disappear but that if all went according to Chandler's plan I had less than twenty four hours to live.

ELEVEN

Emma never asked me to elaborate on why I had been so late to dinner. She never once criticized my outfit, my lack of conversation once I had come back in with Aunt Jean and Henry, or my silence as we walked home. She knew something was wrong and when she asked, my reply was simple.

"I've decided to break up with Cole." The words were spoken softly, dully. Emma merely sat on her bed, looking up to me, her mouth falling slightly open. Before she could ask for a reason, I shut and locked the door that joined our rooms, and she never knocked. Somehow, she understood that talking would not help this time.

I sat on my bed, pulling out my phone. Cole had left me a voicemail. I felt hot tears sting my eyes as I prepared to do the impossible; end my life with Cole.

I dialed my voicemail, deciding to hear his voice one last time, hopefully happy and satisfied. Maybe years from now he would look back on what I was about to do and know I did it because I loved him.

I immediately fell into a fit of tears when his voice echoed in my ears:

"Hey Adeline. It's me. You're probably out with Emma, looking at cakes and stuff, but I just wanted to talk to you." He was silent for a moment, only breathing.

"I really miss you babe. I'm trying not to think about it, but you've been the only thing on my mind. I just can't wait to see you, to hold you in my arms again." He paused again. I could tell he was overcome by emotion, just as I was at that moment.

"I love you Adeline. I'll see you real soon. Call me when you can."

I cried for a long time, listening to the voicemail over and over again. After about an hour, I sat on the floor, next to my bed, my hands shaking as I realized what I had to do, what needed to be done. I dialed Cole's number, trying to figure out what I was going to say. I had to be convincing, otherwise he would know something's wrong and wouldn't believe me.

I was relieved when his voicemail recording began. He must be training. I took a deep breath, allowing the words, the lies, to flow.

"Hey Cole. It's me. Um, I need to tell you something." I swallowed hard, trying to steady my voice.

"Em and I really love it here, in Beaufort. In fact, we've decided to move down here permanently." I paused again, readying myself to give the final blow.

"Cole, I like it here because for once, since we've met, I've felt normal again like there is nothing to fear anymore. I feel free. So, I think it would be best for both of us if we took a break. You're busy with your tribe and I'm busy building my life down here. I just think it would be best, you know? I won't be in the way anymore and you can focus on the things that matter, and I can too."

I breathed in again, wiping away a few tears that fell without my permission, "Please don't call again Cole. Goodbye."

I hung up and allowed myself to cry until I didn't have any more tears to shed and suddenly, in that moment of utter despair and heartbreak, I realized I now understood Cailen. This must have been exactly what she felt when she handed her engagement ring and dreams back to Noah. However, I was luckier than Cailen in a way. I wouldn't have to live very long with my decision. This time tomorrow, I would most likely be dead. For some reason, I wasn't scared. I was ready to end this, ready to die for the people I loved because it meant keeping them safe.

I fell asleep, hoping I would dream of Cole one last time.

I did dream, but it wasn't about Cole like I had hoped. Instead, Ogin appeared to me again, the first time in a long time. We were on the bridge where my parents lost their lives and I almost lost mine. She stood, arms crossed, staring at me disapprovingly like a mother would.

"What?" I whispered, depressed that my last time sleeping would be spent talking to Ogin instead of dreaming of Cole.

"Why are you giving up?" she demanded, her usual sweet face now furious, enraged.

I took a step back, "I can't fight them Ogin, not when they've threatened everyone I love. I have to do this. I have to protect them the only way I know how."

"Protect them? Is that what you call what you did to Cole? Is that the reason you shattered his heart? Because you were protecting him?" she asked, her words stabbing me. "Do you know how many people would give absolutely anything to find their soul mates? And you just threw yours away, like he was trash."

"That's not true!" I screamed at her, anger overwhelming me. "I have to do this. There isn't another option."

"You're a coward!" she yelled back. "You plan on throwing away all of the hard work Noah has done training you. You're just going to give them what they want without even fighting back. If that's true Adeline, then it probably would have been best if you had drowned all those years ago."

I was shocked by her words, hurt that she would even utter them or even mean them.

"You can't mean that," I whispered, my eyes wavering to the river below the bridge, the rough current making me nauseous.

"I wouldn't," she countered. "If you would be the woman I know you are. You can fight this Adeline. You can beat them but you have to at least try."

My eyes wavered from the river back to the heavenly being. She was literally shaking from rage. Her fists were so tight that the tendons were clearly visible through her translucent skin. Her gray eyes were tearing from frustration and anger. She really believed in me.

I took a few steps toward her, all of my previous fear and apprehension melting away. Suddenly, truth was beginning to dawn on me. If Ogin was a part of me then her power was also a part of me, an extension of who I was. It was Ogin who had helped heal my ankle. It was Ogin who had saved me the night Chandler and the others had kidnapped and attacked me, and now I was beginning to see that it was Ogin who had also helped save me the night my parents died.

"I'm really you, aren't I?" my voice was barely above a whisper. I sounded like a small child.

Ogin's rage gradually faded away. Her face relaxed, her glare dissolving into a small smile. Her eyes reflected what I suppose I had always known, but was too afraid to admit to myself.

"We are one and the same," she affirmed.

I gulped. "That means I have your powers too."

"Adeline, you have always had your own abilities and strengths. It has just taken a long time for you to accept yourself and what is to come."

Then, in an instant of clarity, I became enraged at myself. How could I even think of giving up now? Of giving the Rebels what they want? Ogin was right. I had to fight. I would do whatever it takes to protect the ones I love, but by fighting back, not laying down in submission.

"How do I beat these guys?" I asked, my voice and mind determined.

She smiled her ancient smile, "You already know the answer to that."

Then, I awoke in my bed at the hotel in Beaufort, South Carolina. I sat up while turning the bedside light on. I didn't fall back asleep but it wasn't out of fear or dread like it should have been, like it would have been for the *old* Adeline. I stayed awake the remainder of the night forming my plan.

I was resolute, determined, unwavering. Today was not going to be my last.

The banquet hall of the rehearsal dinner was spacious and warm. The flowers were arranged just so and the candlelight gave the room a certain romantic ambiance. Of course, I was hardly paying any attention to the flower arrangements or even to the food I was eating. Most of the guests remained oblivious of my presence except for Henry and Aunt Jean. They were watching me like hawks.

I did my best to avoid Emma. Even that morning, she had tried to talk to me about Cole and our breakup. Naturally, I didn't actually tell her the true reason for my decision. I bypassed most of her questions and it was surprisingly easy. Even at her own rehearsal dinner, she was too busy with other relatives and friends to be able to worry about me completely.

The small tug in my heart pulled painfully when I noticed I had over twenty missed calls and over ten voicemails; all from Cole. I didn't listen to any of his voicemails because I knew that once I did, all of my resolve from the night before would melt away like snow.

Cole wasn't stupid. I knew he must have realized something was wrong. While I had every intention of calling him back and explaining it was a complete misunderstanding, I couldn't just yet. Firstly, Henry, his crazy aunt, and Chandler would possibly figure it out and put Cole in even more danger. Secondly, Cole would most likely insist on flying down here to talk to me, and that was too dangerous to ever happen.

I knew Cole had most likely told Noah about my call because soon after Cole's calls stopped, his began with his ever-insistent text messages. I finally had to shut my phone off to keep my mind from thinking about how worried Cole and Noah were. I knew that, if I asked, they would appear at my side, ready to fight my battles.

This was my battle. I had to fight and prove to myself that I was the heavenly being reincarnated, that I was powerful. Not only was I worth protecting, but I could protect those around me too. Of course, I was still trying to figure out exactly how I would fight off Chandler and the other Rebels. Yet, I was strangely calm and not as worried as I thought I'd be. When the time came, I knew I would be able to come through. I just had to have faith in myself.

I was careful not to make my newfound belief in myself or my unbreakable will to live too obvious. I needed Chandler to continue to think that I was a scared little girl. They had to remain oblivious to my courage.

It was becoming increasingly difficult to watch Henry with my sister. It was bad enough watching them together before I knew Henry had been a traitor all along, but now I had to physically restrain myself from running across the dance floor and ripping Henry's head off. The way he was holding Emma, kissing her, whispering in her ear made me physically nauseous because it was all a lie. Every date, every glance, every kiss, and every moment Emma and Henry had been together had been a lie. The whole time during their relationship, Henry had been trying to get to me. He had been watching me for so long. I had been too stupid to notice.

Now, as I watched my sister the night before her wedding, I wondered if Henry would be cruel enough to actually marry her. Would he really drag her into a lifelong commitment only to most likely disappear after the death of her only sister? Either way, it would break Emma. It had the potential to destroy her. For that, I was going to make Henry pay.

"Beautiful, isn't it?" An aged voice brought me out of my reverie. "I just love weddings. I can't wait to see what the reception will look like tomorrow."

I waited a moment before turning to Aunt Jean, " I'm assuming I probably won't get to see it." I was nonchalant, relaxed. Simply curious.

She slowly smiled, "Unfortunately."

Silence descended between us as we continued to watch Emma and Henry dancing and laughing.

"Emma told Henry about your breakup with your boyfriend last night," she feigned sympathy and surprise. "She said she heard you cry yourself to sleep."

I gritted my teeth as she laughed callously, "Good girl." She then glanced at her watch, tsking at the time.

"It's about time for us to leave my dear."

"Let me say goodbye to Emma," I replied quickly, hoping she wouldn't deny my request. She stared at me long and hard.

"You have five minutes." I didn't even hesitate as I made my way across the hall to Emma who was no longer in Henry's arms, but chatting with some distant relatives.

"Hey Em," I pulled on her arm gently. "Can I talk with you for a sec?"

She nodded, grateful to be pulled away, "Of course."

We walked to the second story balcony of the reception hall that overlooked the bay. The ocean air invigorated me, giving me the strength to do what I had to.

"How are you?" she asked before I could say anything. I heard the meaning behind her words. She was still worried about Cole and me.

"A little tired actually," I lied. "I was going to ask if it'd be okay if Henry took me back to the hotel?" If this did end badly, I wanted Emma to know who had been the last person to see me alive.

She seemed a little surprised, "Sure, that's fine."

We were quiet for a time and I had to struggle against telling Emma to leave Henry now, that he was a horrible man who was using her, but doing that would only place her in more danger. If I did not make it through this night, I wouldn't find it too hard to believe that Henry and Chandler would hurt Emma. Ignorance was her only safety, her only protection.

I pulled Emma into a tight embrace, memorizing the smell of her hair, the feel of her arms around me, and this very moment. She was surprised, but embraced me with equal fervor.

Before she released me, she whispered, "When I get back, we'll talk about you and Cole. I don't want you to think that I don't care."

I held back the tears, "I love you, Em."

She smiled, "I love you too, Addie."

I quickly retreated from the safety of my sister's arms; too afraid my emotions would give me away. I walked away swiftly towards Aunt Jean and Henry, never turning back. They were waiting by the doors. I bravely, maybe even foolishly, walked to my destiny. What that was exactly, I still wasn't sure.

TWELVE

The car ride to the location from the newspaper clipping was long and uncomfortable. Neither Henry nor his aunt spoke the entire time. I was quiet, looking out the window, doing my best not to seem at ease. They still needed to believe that I was unable to fight back, that I was still unaware of what I was capable of, which was still true in a way.

The sun had already set as we walked in to the large abandoned building. It looked like it had still been under construction when investors must have dropped it. The darkness was overwhelming as Henry roughly led me into the cold building. There wasn't a door, only a wide opening. The place smelled of saw dust and mold. Henry let go of me as he went to switch the lights on. I walked away from Aunt Jean and Henry, trying to take in my surroundings, but the darkness was overpowering. Suddenly, a single bright light directly overhead shined. Apparently, there was at least one source of electricity still useable.

"It's so nice to see you Adeline. It has been far too long since we last spoke." I turned quickly to face the owner of the voice.

Standing about a yard away was Chandler Phalcon. He was taller than what I remembered, but he looked tired. His eyes were hard and cold, but fatigued. He seemed weaker.

I glanced around, noticing Henry and Aunt Jean were standing between the only exit and me, but there was no one else.

"Where is the rest of your tribe?" I spread my arms around the surrounding area. Last time, Chandler brought what seemed like his entire army to attack me. Now it was just him.

He chuckled, "It would have been too ostentatious for everyone to make this little trip. Your boyfriend would have noticed and I don't think he would have liked it very much."

"Besides," he continued as he took a few steps toward me. "This shouldn't be too difficult."

I breathed deeply, refusing to allow fear to poison me like it did the last time I was alone with him, "What do you want Chandler? To kill me? Then what? It's not going to make you anymore powerful."

He nodded, "Probably not, but it's not me who wants you dead. You see, after we extract whatever abilities you have, I'll leave you to our leader. She's been dying to meet you."

Now I was taken aback. I thought Chandler was the leader. And *she*? It was a woman who led this mission to kill me?

"Who's your leader?" I asked resolutely. I realized now this was the person I was going to have to fight if I planned on leaving this place alive.

"That would be me," Aunt Jean stepped out of the darkness into the light taking a stand next to Chandler.

"What?" I could only whisper. This didn't make any sense.

"Mother, are you sure this is the time?" Chandler became truly concerned as he turned to the fragile old woman. Mother? What was happening? Who was this woman?

"I have waited a very long time for this Chandler," Aunt Jean began pulling something out of her bag before handing it to Chandler. He quickly discarded her bag to the floor, his attention solely focused on her. Aunt Jean, or whoever this person was, had taken out a blue vile and began drinking it quickly. Then, as if she had drunk poison, she fell to the ground with a yelp. Chandler was by her side in a flash. She sounded like a wounded animal, her voice and body suddenly changing, morphing into something else. Before my very eyes, Aunt Jean began to shudder and melt away. Her skin darkened to a rich copper, her short gray hair grew past her shoulders, dark as night. Her wrinkles disappeared into oblivion as the body and face of a young Native woman appeared before me. Several moments after her transformation, the woman stood tall, all remnants of Henry's old, decrepit aunt gone. She was breathing heavily, but looked strong, determined, and beautiful. She reminded me so much of Chenoa.

"Hello Adeline," Her rich voice greeted me. "It's so nice to finally meet you. In my proper form of course."

In my state of disbelief and confusion, I never noticed Henry walking up behind me. In an instant, my head was met with something hard and cold. I hit the floor, blacking out.

I finally awoke, finding myself still lying on the cold concrete floor. The voices were still muffled, but slowly becoming clearer. I remained still and quiet, trying to catch a bit of the conversation before they noticed I was awake.

"Do you think that was wise?" Henry's voice became clear as he stepped over my body. "Don't you think Emma is going to be wondering where my beloved Aunt Jean is at her wedding?"

"Please," she scoffed. "I think she'll be more concerned about her baby sister and it's not as if you were actually going to go through with the wedding. You know that it was just meant to work for our purposes."

I heard the strange woman, who apparently turned out to be Chandler's mother, steps as she made her way towards me. I tried to remain still, eyes shut, but she suddenly pulled me by my hair, dragging me towards Chandler. I screamed in pain as I tried to fight her fingers, but they were strong and had a sure grip on me.

"I know you're awake!" she screamed, insane rage dancing in her eyes like fire. "Now stand up, girl!"

I immediately obeyed unsure of what this woman was capable of if I did not comply.

"Who are you?" I blurted, desperate to buy myself some time before I had to fight anyone. I had to figure out exactly who this woman was and her connection to the Rebels before I attempted anything.

Her expression softened a bit, but the terrifying insanity still glimmered in her dark brown eyes, "Dena."

Dena. The name sounded vaguely familiar, but I couldn't be sure.

"What exactly do you want from me?" I continued to step back as she took steps toward me.

"What do I want?" she smiled again. "It's quite simple. You."

"What about me?" I just had to keep her talking. Talking meant I had more time to think, time to react.

"You see Adeline," Dena began, pulling Chandler forward with her. "I want you to save my son."

"Save him?" I questioned, astounded. "From what?"

"From this," she stated simply, pulling up Chandler's long sleeves to reveal his horrible new appearance. He was terribly scarred and marked; most of his skin was in dark patches, contrasting to his usual copper complexion, looking like he was decaying. I took a step back in disgust.

"You see Adeline," Dena continued while pushing Chandler's hair back and running her fingers over the deteriorating skin. His eyes fell from his mother's gaze, almost as if he was ashamed. "Since our warriors were never Chosen, we are forced to steal the bodies of the forms we wish to use. However, we are cursed because of it. Our souls cannot handle the change from one form to another; therefore our bodies begin to breakdown, making shifting harder and harder. We tried an ancient ritual of wearing masks in order to hide our souls from the effects of the curse. If the curse can't know which soul to hurt, then we are safe, but as you can see," she pointed to Chandler's skin, "it has failed us."

She paused before continuing, "You know how difficult this is for a mother? To have two of your children Chosen while the youngest is left to suffer?"

My breathing stopped, fear suddenly transforming into a cold understanding, "Two of your children are Chosen?"

She smiled, "Chandler has two half siblings from Little Shell. You've probably met them. They share a close relation with that disgusting half-breed who leads them."

"Chenoa and Elsu are your children? You're the one that left Paco all those years ago?" My head was becoming dizzy from all of this information.

She nodded a matter-of-factly, "Paco and I didn't share the same views on our tribe's ancient histories."

"Meaning he wanted peace and you wanted power," I assumed. I was proven correct when she nodded approvingly.

"You see Adeline," she continued, leaving Chandler and coming closer to me. This time I didn't move, but allowed her to come towards me. "I wanted to find you, desperately. He wanted to let it go, let the past remain in the past, stop the Chosen at his generation. That's why he agreed to marry me; a sort of peace offering. He married a woman from the Turtle Mountain Tribe, hoping to end this civil war. If we promised to stop searching for the same power, the Chosen would disband and allow their gifts and abilities to evaporate."

"But you couldn't live like that, could you?" I reasoned. She nodded energetically. Her attention was completely absorbed on me. I carefully moved my hands to behind my back where I slowly reached into my back pocket to retrieve my dagger. I had to keep her talking, keep her distracted. "You couldn't let power like that go to waste."

"Exactly!" she screamed gleefully.

"That's why you kidnapped Cole's mother? That's why you killed her, because you thought she was the reincarnation, the key to your power," I continued.

She laughed horribly, insanely, "No! I killed her because I wanted to, because she was his happiness!"

Suddenly, I couldn't hold myself back anymore. It all happened very quickly. Without giving her a moment to think, I pulled back my dagger and stabbed her in her shoulder, twisting it till I felt warm red liquid pour out onto my hands and her laughter turned to screams of horror. Then, I felt myself being hit as if by a truck. Chandler had thrown himself at me, pinning me down while screaming in my face.

"You are," Dena's voice was labored. She slowly and painfully pulled the dagger out. "a stupid girl." She walked over to where Chandler was holding me down, bending over to look at me. Drops of her blood fell onto my face, making my stomach churn. She held the dagger gracefully, seeming to ignore the giant wound that was bleeding rapidly.

"I think," she breathed, "I'm going to make you pay for that."

She held the dagger up then reached down grabbing my face. She was about to carve into my skin when Chandler was suddenly hit and slumped over. Dena turned just in time to be knocked out as well. Standing above me, with a crowbar, was Henry.

"What are you doing?" I asked as he held his hand out to help me up. He helped me stand then reached down recovering my dagger.

He handed it to me before answering, "Despite what you may think, I couldn't just stand here and watch her murder you in cold blood. You are the sister of the woman I love after all."

I was flabbergasted. So Henry really did love Emma.

"You have a funny way of showing your love," I spat back as he led me out of the building.

"Listen, I'll be happy to explain everything, but right now we need to get out of here. They might wake up soon, and who knows what Dena has planned," Henry led me to his car. "She might have others coming."

"Wouldn't you know?" I demanded. Just because he saved me this once didn't mean I automatically trusted him.

"She doesn't tell me everything. I was just her informant," he replied while putting the car in drive and speeding down the empty highway.

"How did that happen exactly?" I would love to know when Henry decided to be one of the reasons I almost died at least three times in my life now.

He sighed, "It's a long story that I'll tell you when I'm not currently trying to save your life."

I let it drop for now, but I was determined to have him to tell me the truth, "Where are we going anyway?"

"I'm not sure," he said truthfully. "I just had to get us away from there."

"What about Emma?" I asked. His face crumbled at the mention of her name.

"They shouldn't bother her. After all, Dena still believes that the only reason I was with her was to get information on you."

"Isn't that true?"

"No," he sighed. "I mean, that's how it started, but as I continued our relationship, my feelings for Emma became more real. I really do love her Adeline. Honest."

"Then why didn't you stop working for them?" I exclaimed. "You could have stopped it all!"

"She would have killed me," he replied solemnly, "and probably Emma too. She had no problem taking care of your parents."

Silence descended as truth hit me like a tidal wave. Fragments of grief and reality cut me like glass.

"What?"

Henry closed his eyes for a moment, "I'm so sorry, Adeline."

"What happened that night Henry?" My voice didn't even sound like mine anymore. It was like I was watching all that was happening as someone else, like I wasn't the one whose world was being ripped apart and then sewn back together in new awkward patches. It was like I didn't even know who I was anymore or where I came from. The pieces of my life were morphing into this new truth where everything revolved around a Chippewa legend.

He swallowed before answering, "It was after Dena had been searching for a while. She was frustrated and running out of soldiers and resources. She returned to Little Shell and attempted to talk to

Paco for some sort of agreement. While she was there she heard a rumor about a possible birth of the reincarnation of the heavenly being. It was her first real lead since Cole's mother. Of course, Paco denied your existence fervently. He didn't know for sure if it was true, but he understood what Dena was capable of."

Henry paused before continuing, "Dena didn't believe him. So, the day your parents died, she followed you to the zoo and while you and your parents were driving back home. It was Dena who hit your parents' car on that bridge."

His words echoed inside my head, beating heartbreaking truth into me. Then a subtle wave of guilt began to wash over me. It was my fault my parents were dead.

Tears fell down my face, my voice cracking, "If she wanted my power, then why did she try to kill me? Why did she kill my parents?"

"That's what's messed up about the whole situation," he continued. "It was a test."

"A test?"

"She was trying to see what Paco would do. If he let you die, then you weren't the reincarnation. If he saved you, then she had her answer," he responded, and in an instant it all made sense. Dena and her quest for power had made my sister and I orphans, had ripped Cole away from his mother. She had to be stopped, destroyed if necessary.

"We have to stop her," I mumbled gravely after several minutes of silence.

"We?" Henry scoffed.

"I don't think she's exactly going to welcome you back with open arms after you knocked her upside the head," I proclaimed, fixating my anger back to Henry.

"Listen, as soon I know you and Emma are safe, I have to go into hiding." He was still the coward I had always thought him to be.

"Are you serious?" I screamed. "You're not going to fight back?"

"I fought back!" he countered, "Back there when I risked everything to save your life!"

I was quiet for a moment, unable to properly process all that Henry was saying. He was actually willing to break Emma like that – just disappear and leave me to pick up the pieces.

He glanced over to me, his voice soft, "I know it's gonna be hard, but this is how it has to be."

He paused for a moment before asking, "Promise me something? You owe me."

"I owe you?" he was unbelievable.

He rolled his eyes, "Yes, you do."

I didn't answer for a moment, fuming in my seat.

"Take care of Emma for me. Please."

His eyes were begging for me to understand. For a moment, I saw the love he had for her, the love that I thought wasn't real. The kind of love I saw in Cole's eyes whenever he looked at me. If anything was true, it was that Henry loved Emma, deeply, wholeheartedly, and I believed him.

Before I could reply, our car was hit while we were crossing a bridge. All was chaos, the world spinning out of control as Henry lost control of the car and it flipped over the side of the bridge into the ocean water. The force of the car hitting the water was powerful, almost knocking me out. I looked to Henry, but he was already unconscious and bleeding profusely from his head. Before I could react, the force of the ocean water and the rough currents began gushing through the open windows and filling the car quickly. I tried to undo my seatbelt but found it stuck. I was breathing quickly, yet trying not to panic.

The water level was rising steadily and I was running out of time. I pulled my knife out of my back pocket and began cutting at the seatbelt, but before I could completely cut myself free, water had completely flooded the cab of the car. There was no air left to breath, only burning salt water. Visions of my parents' final moments flooded my mind. My lungs burned desperately, about to burst from the lack of air. I was slowly beginning to black out.

My hand that had been clinging tightly to the knife for dear life, slowly relaxed and it fell into the oblivion. Salt water began to fill my lungs as I continued to thrash about, the will to live dictating my movements. As the submerged car began to sink deeper and deeper, a slow realization crept up on me. A cold poison managed to dig deep inside of me, spreading throughout my body like a disease.

This was death. No visions of white light, no memories of my life flashing before my eyes, nothing like that; just the cold fear and panic of what was to come. The icy rushing ocean water that surrounded me, the pitch-blackness of its immeasurable depth before me, and the undeniable truth that I was dying too young.

PART THREE

Death must be so beautiful. To lie in the soft brown earth, with the grasses waving above one's head, and listen to silence. To have no yesterday, and no to-morrow. To forget time, to forgive life, to be at peace.

Sylvia Plath, *The Bell Jar*

THIRTEEN

The gentle hum of a machine slowly made its way into my consciousness. My eyes slowly opened, but closed quickly when meeting the bright fluorescent lights above me. My nose wrinkled at the scent of bleach and sickness. I tried to swallow, but my throat was a dry desert.

"Adeline," his hoarse, cracked voice whispered passionately. My eyes shot open at the sound.

"Cole," I tried to speak, but no noise came out of my parched mouth.

"I'm right here, baby," his tear stained face came into view. He was holding my right hand tightly, squeezing it repeatedly. "I'm right here." His deep blue eyes began watering again.

I turned my head toward him, his beautiful crumbled face, the only thing I could see, "What are you doing here?" my voice was hardly loud enough.

The distant memory of my last phone call with Cole came slowly. I had broken up with him to save him. He shouldn't have been there. He could have been killed.

"You have to leave," I began again, voice cracking. "I told you not to come."

Cole ignored me, reaching to the bedside table for a cup. He lifted my head gingerly, tipping the cup to my dry, cracked lips. Cold, much needed, water filled my mouth. I drank generously, my throat throbbing from the action but I ignored the pain. The water was sweet and delicious, wetting my desert like mouth.

When I had my fill, he laid my head back on the pillow, placing the cup on the table again, his eyes returning to me.

"You're a horrible liar Adeline Jasely," a small smile tugged at the corner of his lips. "I didn't believe one word you said to me on that message."

Tears threatened to fall, "I'm trying to protect you."

He tried to smile again, but it fell away, "I'm not the one who needs protecting. That's my job, and I failed you again."

I shook my head vehemently, "No. Don't ever say that."

He shook his head, not believing me, "But I love you. That counts for something, right?"

"It counts for everything," my voice cracked again.

He leaned in, pressing a kiss to my forehead. A few of his tears fell onto my cheeks, sliding down my face.

"I'm sorry," he whispered, broken.

"Don't be sorry," I countered. "You did nothing."

"Exactly," he agreed, "and I should have done everything to protect you."

I tried not to roll my eyes at his belief. There was no way I was going to be able to convince him otherwise. At least not today.

"Where am I?" I finally asked glancing from Cole's broken face to the room I was in. It was all white, with a few chairs and two paintings on the wall. It depressed me a little.

He spoke slowly, "You're in the hospital Adeline. There was an accident."

My eyes met his again, "What kind of accident?"

The memories were foggy, distant, like a dream from long ago that I was desperately trying to remember, but at the same time didn't want to relive.

He cleared his throat, "You were in a car accident," he paused, "with Henry."

The memories flooded back to me in broken fragments: a dark cold building, the insane rage in a woman's eye, the sound of a car flipping into the ocean, the horrible burning sensation in my lungs, the blackness that swallowed me.

The heart monitor that I was hooked to, began beeping loudly and uncontrollably. Tears streamed down my face and breathing became labored.

"Baby, calm down," Cole pleaded as he caressed my face gently. "You're safe now. I'm here and you're safe."

He then kissed my face, showering me with light butterfly kisses; first my forehead, then my eyelids, my nose, my cheeks, my jawline, then finally my lips. The moment his lips met mine, my heart slowed and I was instantly calmed. He broke away, kissing my forehead one last time.

I breathed slowly, my lips still burning from his kiss. I glanced from our intertwined hands to his face.

"How am I alive?" I spoke softly, simply. I didn't remember anyone pulling me out of the water this time. I should have died.

Cole swallowed before answering, "When you left me that message and I couldn't reach you, I knew something was wrong. So, I called Noah. He probably would have found you sooner, before you went to meet with Chandler, but I made him wait for me."

He paused, guilt and misery swimming in his eyes.

"When I finally arrived in Beaufort, we couldn't find you at your hotel, but we found Emma. She was worried because Henry was supposed to have taken you back to the hotel hours before, but neither of you were to be found. I searched by air and Noah went by sea. He saw the car flip off the bridge."

Cole paused again, fighting his intense emotions, "He saved your life."

I nodded, squeezing Cole's hand, "It's okay."

Cole nodded fiercely, biting his lower lip, "I know. You're safe and that's all that matters now."

"Where's Noah?" I asked after a long silence.

"Down at the cafeteria. He's been here waiting with me."

"How long have I been out?"

"A couple of days," he shrugged. It didn't look like he slept for any part of that time.

"I missed the wedding," I laughed quietly. "I'm surprised Emma is not in here, yelling at me for her having to change plans."

Cole didn't laugh. I searched his disturbed blue eyes, unsettled to find something else there; something horrible that he was keeping from me.

"Cole?" I questioned, my anxiety rising with every second he remained silent.

He wouldn't meet my eyes for several heart wrenching moments.

"Cole," I repeated, desperate for whatever truth he was hiding. "Where is Emma?"

He swallowed before answering, "She's making arrangements."

When he didn't elaborate, I added, "Other wedding arrangements, right? She's making other wedding arrangements."

Cole's silence was deafening. The heart monitor steadily increased, beeping faster.

Cole shook his head solemnly, "She's making funeral arrangements, for Henry."

Death must be nice. To close one's eyes and never return to a world of pain and heartache. To finally bid farewell to the harsh reality of this earth that bore us, fed us, nurtured us, then very quickly starved us, beat us, and finally destroyed us, welcoming us to return to the ground from which we came. Death: an eternal sleep where one can dream and never have to wake.

I watched as the casket was slowly lowered into the ground. The sun was shining brightly, reflecting the tearstained faces of the people who had come to bid a final goodbye to the body of the man who would never wake up. Emma's grip on my arm tightened as she choked back sobs. Her head, hanging in defeat, bobbed up and down from her flowing tears. Her heart, shattered beyond recognition, was bleeding profusely.

Death, though a freedom for those who have passed on, is a prison to those left behind. A dark, hopeless existence where those who cannot follow must wait until it is finally their time for the arms of death to embrace them.

Gradually, people began to scatter, leaving the almost widow, her younger sister, and her almost in-laws who sat strangely still with shocked sober expressions. I looked to the north side of the cemetery to find Cole, Chenoa, and Noah all waiting patiently. I knew, even though the funeral had been for family only, Cole would not let me out of his sight. So, dressed in all black, his onyx hair pushed back, revealing the beautiful broken face of the man I loved, stood my Cole with Chenoa and Noah flanking him.

Chenoa had flown down to South Carolina after I had been released from the hospital, unable to sit idly around in Montana waiting for more tragic news. Her presence was like sweet medicine to a blistering wound. Her voice, her smile, even her smell calmed me, and made me feel safe. It almost made me forget the tragedy that now consumed my life.

They wanted to know what had happened with Chandler that night. All three of them, Chenoa, Cole, and Noah, had waited for me to reveal what I knew. I had tried several times to explain, but each time I found that the words choked me and an excruciating numbing pain took hold of me; it was grief.

It was only after Cole had finally calmed my grieving heart, that ached for my older sister, could I explain to him what exactly happened the night Henry died. I had told him everything from Chandler's current condition to Henry's role in this war, and in my life. I made sure Cole understood that he wasn't a bad person, that he had saved my life, and that he was a good man, someone who didn't deserve to die.

I didn't tell Cole yet about Dena being the leader, about Chandler being the half-brother to Chenoa and Elsu. It wasn't time yet, I had reasoned. Chenoa and Elsu were to remain oblivious, as to the whereabouts of their mother. I couldn't tell them yet.

Now, as I sat with my grieving sister with the blazing South Carolina sun burning our backs, none of it mattered anymore. This war had gone too far, had touched too many innocent lives. Never did I imagine my own sister being directly affected by the devastations of war, like Jacy had been.

Anger, along with sorrow, boiled within me threatening to burst. I could no longer keep tiptoeing around this war hoping it would disappear and go away. This war between these two tribes was no longer objective. Dena had made it painfully personal. She had knocked on my door and threatened to tear down everything I held dear. It was time for me to answer the call. It was time for me to fight this war, my war.

She sat on the edge of the bed, pulling the oversized man's shirt closer to her petite frame. I carefully made my way into her hotel room, surprised to find she was still unpacked. Her clothes lay carelessly on the floor along with the used tissues. Her face was gaunt and pale, lacking its usual joy. Her hazel eyes were dull, red rimmed from her last sobbing spell.

"Emma?" I called quietly. Her head slightly turned from gazing out the window to me. "Our flight leaves in two hours. Do you need some help packing?"

She didn't respond but looked back out the window. I began to pick up the random articles of clothing that were strewn about the room. I opened the closet to dig out her suitcase but stopped dead in my tracks when I came face to face with Emma's greatest dream and ultimate disappointment; it was her beautiful, white wedding dress.

"It's a beautiful dress, isn't it?" her lifeless voice cracked. I turned around quickly, shocked to find Emma standing behind me, fresh tears already sliding down her cheeks.

"I've been thinking," she whispered, her eyes still lingering on the dress that had symbolized future dreams, but now represented broken hopes. "I think I want to stay in Beaufort a little while longer, with his parents." she paused, blinking away more tears. "I just feel that the second I leave this town and go back home, without him, it's like he's really gone."

Her eyes finally rested on me, "Do you understand?"

I nodded, closing the distance between us and pulling her to me, "Yeah Em. I understand."

She let me embrace her a while longer before shrugging out of my arms, returning to the bed, and staring out the window, "I'll see you later Adeline."

I choked back tears, not sure what to do. Could I really leave my broken sister? Did I have a choice? There was a war brewing, a final battle looming on the horizon, and maybe putting as much distance between my sister and myself would protect her. Maybe it was best for her to fight her own internal battles while I fought mine, separated.

"Em, I can stay too if you need me too," I began, but she shook her head.

"No," she replied. "I need to be alone and sort things out with his family."

"Okay," I began turning the knob to leave. "I love you, Em."

Several moments passed and I thought she wouldn't respond but, finally, hanging her head with her voice shaking, she told me goodbye.

"I love you too Addie."

I closed the door, only to make it a few feet before I heard her heartbreaking sobs echo through the hallway. I felt my own body shudder as I ran down the hall to the stairs, desperate to one day see a smile grace my sister's face again.

As I walked down the stairs, I wiped the tears from my face quickly and roughly, hoping no one would notice. At the bottom of the stairs was the only person who could possibly understand, who could possibly heal me.

"Cole," my voice cracked as I fell into his warm embrace.

"Hey there beautiful," he whispered lovingly into my hair. "What's wrong?"

I buried my face into his chest, soaking in his comforting scent, "Emma is staying here with Henry's family. I'm not sure when she is coming home."

I suddenly felt so small, like the child I was when I lost my parents. I felt orphaned and abandoned, yet again.

He held me tightly, his strong arms squeezing warmth and comfort into me, "It's gonna be okay. She'll be okay. It's just gonna take some time."

I nodded as he led me out of the small bed and breakfast. I was shocked when I found Noah waiting patiently outside, but no sign of Chenoa.

"Where's Chenoa?" I turned to Cole.

"She's at the airport, waiting for us," he answered.

"Hey Noah," I waved, turning my attention to the man who had become a brother to me. He smirked, pulling me roughly into one of his bear hugs.

"I'm not letting you leave without giving me a proper goodbye."

Behind his usual candor and humor, I heard a mixture of foreign emotions fighting for supremacy.

"Are you going to cry?" I asked amused.

"Of course not," he denied heatedly. He playfully pushed me out of his arms and we laughed. It was the first time in what felt like weeks since I last laughed, but I stopped abruptly. I shouldn't be laughing. Not when my grieving sister was sitting alone in a dark hotel room, sobbing.

The moment of temporary happiness dissipated and cold silence, in the southern summer heat, was left.

"I suppose I should go now," Noah began, his eyes shifting from me to his feet. Suddenly, the prospect of leaving him sank in and threatened to break me.

I hugged him again fiercely, my voice cracking as I said, "I'm gonna miss you Noah. I'll see you soon, right?"

I felt him swallow hard, "Yeah. You'll see me again." he smiled sadly, "Don't worry about Emma. I'll keep an eye on her. She'll be safe."

Noah's promise to take care of and protect my sister warmed me, lighting a small flicker of hope. At least I wouldn't have to worry too much.

"Thank you," the emotion in my voice was thick making my throat hurt.

"Of course," Noah quickly kissed the top of my head gingerly. "Take care of yourself, kid."

I smiled, nodding, "You too."

Then Cole led me to the rental car, opening the passenger door for me. Cole turned to Noah, surprising me by embracing him.

"Thank you for taking care of her," Cole's eyes fell to me as he thanked Noah. "You have no idea how important she is."

Noah nodded, his brown brotherly eyes resting on me, "I think I do."

Soon, Cole was speeding down the highway, one hand on the wheel, the other intertwined with mine. As we passed the Beaufort city limit sign, the tears I had been holding back fell through my very carefully built façade. I cried for Emma and her devastated heart. I cried for Henry and how he died so young. I cried for Noah and the consequences of this war that had torn apart his life with Cailen. I cried for my parents and my lost childhood, and finally I cried for this new life I was forced to live. I cried for my old life that used to be so simple. Now, I had to grow up and face whatever was waiting for me in Montana. I had no choice.

FOURTEEN

The morning sun woke me from my fitful sleep. I turned over in my bed, wrapping the covers more tightly around my shivering body, but I wasn't cold. I had another nightmare.

I was standing on the bridge where Henry's car had flipped. I looked over the edge, my stomach churning at the dark ocean water that had swallowed my sister's happiness.

"Hello Adeline," her beautiful, bell-like voice rang.

I turned to face Ogin, a smile nowhere to be seen on her glorious face.

"Hi," I greeted meekly. I wasn't exactly in the mood to listen to a lecture from a dead heavenly being. Even being on this bridge in my dreams was threatening to rip me open like it had ripped Emma.

"I'm sorry," she said after a long silence, her gray eyes glancing to the edge of the bridge, "but now do you realize the scope of this war? Do you realize that the Rebel tribe will do whatever it takes, even hurting the ones you love? You can't be the victim anymore, Adeline. It's time to be a warrior now."

Her words cut me deep, but she was right.

"I understand," I replied slowly, my will resolute.

"Are you prepared for more bloodshed?" Ogin continued, her eyes hard. "Are you ready for more lives to be lost before there can be peace?"

I thought for a moment. Was I ready to watch more people I loved die and those left behind to mourn their loss along with me?

"Yes," I responded, determinedly.

She smiled slightly, "Then go, train, and prepare for the hell that has just begun."

I rolled over again, sleep eluding me. My dream with Ogin didn't leave me feeling strong and sure, like I had hoped. I was still the broken girl whose world was being ripped from underneath her feet.

The smell of bacon and pancakes finally drew me from my bed. I slowly made my way to the kitchen, comforted to find Alexia cooking.

"Hey," she greeted gently, her eyes still sad. Alexia was going to stay with me until Emma decided to return home. No one knew for sure when that would be.

"Hi," I mumbled. "Smells good."

"Good," she smiled brightly. "Hope you're hungry."

After breakfast I dressed and waited for Cole. He was coming to pick me up and take me to the Chosen. I hadn't seen any of them in so long.

"So, what movie are you and Cole going to see?" Alexia asked happily as I walked into the kitchen.

"Oh," I stumbled on my words. "I'm not sure. Some romantic comedy, I think."

"That's good," she smiled. "You need to get out, do something fun."

I tried to smile in response, "Yeah."

Thankfully, the doorbell rang and I excused myself to answer it. Cole pulled me closely to him before I had the chance to say anything.

"I missed you," he said roughly, burying his face into my hair.

"Ditto," I mumbled, taking in his musky scent. If I didn't have Cole, I didn't think I'd be able to handle my life at that current moment. Cole was my rock, my one line of sanity in a sea of chaos.

"You two have fun," Alexia yelled from the kitchen. I grimaced in response. Fun was the last thing on my mind.

"Thank you Miss Hamilton," Cole called back to Alexia. "I'll have Adeline home before eleven."

Quickly, before more lies had to be told, Cole led me to his truck and drove me to his home.

"How are you?" he asked quietly, his gentle grip on my hand securing me to reality.

I continued to stare out the window, watching the world whip past us, "I'm okay."

"The others have been asking about you," He began as he turned into the reservation. "They've been worried."

I didn't respond, but allowed silence to fill the truck. Cole was trying, I knew that, but my heart didn't want to build any more façades that proclaimed false happiness and joy. There was nothing to be happy about anymore.

Cole pulled into his driveway and the beautiful brick home came into view. I didn't wait for Cole, but jumped out of his truck on my own. His hand snaked around my waist as he led me through the front door and toward the kitchen. A soft hum of voices filled the air as we walked toward the seven other Chosen members sitting in the Dyami kitchen.

A chilling silence filled the room as Cole and I walked in. I glanced from face to face, surprised to find sadness. It was for me. Even Ella with her usual superior demeanor was somehow diminished, overshadowed by the others.

"Hey Adeline," Chenoa whispered, smiling slightly. I tried to smile, but it fell away too quickly.

Cole quickly gained everyone's attention, "I'm glad you all could come. We have a lot to discuss."

"What is she doing here?" Ella spat, her eyes narrowed in disgust. I guess she didn't feel sorry for me after all.

"She's here because she is ready to be," Dylan surprised everyone by snapping at his beautiful sister. She stared back, mouth hanging open slightly.

Dylan turned his attention toward me, "We support you, Adeline."

Elan stood, bowing his head slightly, "We will fight for you."

"Always," Ava added, sincerity ringing in her voice.

I nodded tightly, smiling gratefully at their kind words. Cole sat me next to him at the long dining room table as he brought the meeting to order.

"So, what's the plan boss?" Dylan questioned, his usual humorous demeanor gone, as the seriousness of the current situation began to sink in. The air felt thicker.

"Well, I think Adeline has more information on the Rebel tribe. I think we should give her our attention," Cole glanced to me, "if you're ready."

My eyes glimpsed from Cole to the seven beautiful people waiting for me to continue. I swallowed hard, trying to find my words.

"Okay," I began weakly. "Well, you all should know that the other tribe has become very weak. It doesn't look good."

Different reactions rippled through the group. Some physically relaxed, some physically tensed.

"But," I continued, "they are more bent on war than ever before. They realize that if they don't attack soon, they will continue to grow weaker and weaker."

Cole and the others nodded, waiting for me to continue.

"Their bodies are slowly disintegrating. They can't handle the transformations that they have forced themselves to do. I've seen Chandler's decaying body." I shuttered at the memory. "They aren't stupid. They realize that they must act quickly."

I glanced around the table before continuing.

"Chandler isn't the leader," I chose my words carefully, but before I could continue, people began speaking all at once, confused and outraged.

"What?" Chenoa whispered.

"Of course he is! Who else would it be?" Elsu murmured angrily.

"I don't understand," Olivia spoke to Ava.

"What do you mean, Adeline?" Cole's deep voice brought me back to him. I looked into his confused blue eyes, trying to decide if now was the time to tell him just who Dena was and what she was capable of. I glanced toward Chenoa and Elsu who, at this moment, might not be able to handle the truth that the one person they were trying to destroy was their mother.

"What I mean is that Chandler is merely a puppet just like the other Rebels. Their leader is Chandler's mother," I spoke softly, leaving out the crucial part about whom this leader really was.

Everyone was silenced, staring in awe and trying to understand what exactly this meant for them.

Cole spoke first, "Who's his mother?"

I licked my lips nervously. I was trying my best to avoid that particular question.

"I'm not sure," I lied, unable to completely overturn Chenoa and Elsu's lives quite yet.

"Well, what do we do?" Elan asked, his attention turning from me to Cole. "We don't even know who Chandler's mother is or where they are now."

"I think they may be trying to recruit other tribes to help them," I spoke softly, surprised by my own revelation as much as the others. Everyone's eyes immediately looked to me.

"What makes you say that?" The blood had drained from Cole's face.

I took a deep breath before beginning, "It's just a theory, but I think Chandler and the Rebels are looking for more help, and stronger numbers. I think they had tried to recruit Noah's tribe, the Catawba tribe in South Carolina."

"You see," I continued, "Noah had been engaged to this girl, Cailen, but she broke up with him out of the blue. I actually spoke to Cailen and she said someone had threatened her, that if she didn't break off the engagement with Noah, then he would be killed."

"So, why does that make you think that Chandler and his tribe are recruiting?" Olivia questioned.

"Well, it would be much easier to have soldiers who weren't emotionally attached," I explained. "Maybe Noah would have been easier to convince if he didn't have anything or anyone holding him back."

"Do you think Noah and his tribe would agree to work with the Rebels?" Dylan asked.

"No," Cole answered quickly. "Noah and his tribe have vowed their complete alliance with us."

"But there are other tribes, Cole," Ella stated simply, an edge of sarcasm seeping into her voice. "Are we going to go knocking on every tribe's door in North America and ask them nicely to not fight against us?"

Cole shook his head, ignoring Ella's sarcasm, "No, we don't have time to recruit anyone and from what Adeline has told us, the Rebels don't have much time either."

Everyone nodded, but the tension in the air was thick. War was coming, and sooner than everyone had thought.

"Do you think the Rebels have actually got other tribes on their side?"

I was surprised to find Elsu addressing his question to me.

"Oh," I stumbled over my words. "I'm not sure. It's possible."

"Chenoa," Cole began. "I need you and Elan to find out if there are any tribes that have agreed to align with Turtle Mountain."

Elan and Chenoa nodded together. Everyone else looked to Cole and I for their instructions.

"We will meet tomorrow in the clearing at sunrise for more training and hopefully we will have more information about the Rebels and their leader," Cole answered. He soon dismissed everyone, but no one left right away. Ava, Olivia, and Chenoa remained clumped together, their heads huddled toward one another as they discussed something seriously. Elan and Dylan remained glued to Cole's side, paying close attention to everything he said and did. Elsu remained far off from the others, his eyes lingering from one Chosen member to the next. I stood awkwardly next to Cole, still feeling unsure and out of place. I knew this was where I belonged. I belonged with the other Chosen, the other people whose worlds had been flipped upside down due to an ancient prophecy. Yet, I still felt unwelcomed, like this war was not mine to fight.

I noticed Ella sneak out the French doors toward the barn outside. I quietly shrugged out of Cole's protective hold and quickly followed Ella. For some reason, I felt a strong pull to her. I needed to try to understand her complete aversion to me, or maybe just try to understand who Ella really was as a person.

She had made her way to the fenced in paddock area where Cole's stallion, Sky, was restlessly running.

Ella stood gracefully next to the pin, her eyes watching the stallion's every move. She was still unaware of my presence as I came to stand behind her.

"He's beautiful, isn't he?" I asked quietly.

She jumped in response, her once gentle expression going hard.

"Yeah, I guess," she finally spoke, her eyes never meeting mine.

Silence descended as we gazed at Sky, his midnight hair glistening in the moonlight. Ella's expression gradually relaxed. Her once scornful appearance had melted into something more sorrowful. Her dark brown eyes mirrored something I had never seen before. Instead of confidence, she exuded insecurity and fear.

"Are you okay Ella?" I spoke softly, almost afraid of spooking her.

She shifted her weight from her right foot to her left before answering, "What do you think, Adeline?"

There was no hint of sarcasm or animosity in her voice. She seemed lost, scared, and unsure of the future that lay before her.

"I think you're tired of keeping people at arms length now that you know we might not all have a lot of time left," I replied honestly, my heart hammering, as I not only revealed the truth to Ella but to myself as well. Life was not a guarantee anymore but merely a chance, a hope that tomorrow the sun would rise once more.

Her head slowly turned to face me. She opened her mouth to speak, but changed her mind, closing it slowly.

I turned back to watch Sky, "You know I'm right."

"Maybe I just don't want to admit that we're actually in danger," her small, quiet voice finally uttered. I looked to her, surprised by what she just admitted. So, I was right all along. Ella was not a confident Native American goddess who feared nothing. She was just another insecure girl, no different than me.

She continued, "I mean, I've always known the risks of being Chosen, but for a long time I never really cared. In the beginning, I loved the power it gave me and how special it made me, but now . . ." her voice trailed off as her cheeks flushed. She had revealed too much.

"Now?" I prompted. I had never spoken to Ella on such candid terms. I wasn't about to let what could be our only real conversation die so quickly.

"Now it's no longer some small part of my life. It isn't something I can easily walk away from anymore. I'm too involved, and now it's not only my life that has been so drastically changed but my brother's too," she paused, her gaze lingering on the house where Dylan and the other Chosen were still conversing in. "There are a lot of lives at stake."

"That's why you hate me so much, isn't it?"

Ella's revelation had finally made sense to me as to why she always avoided me or seemed to hate me so much. It was because of me that Ella's life had suddenly turned so drastically. It was my reborn soul and this legend that scarred me and countless others, Ella included.

She rolled her eyes in frustration, "I don't hate you Adeline. I've never hated you."

She continued when she noticed the complete shock and disbelief etched on my face, "I'm the way I am because it's all I've ever known how to be. It's my defense mechanism I guess. I'm afraid of you Adeline, but I've never hated you."

I stood, mouth open slightly as I tried to fully comprehend what

Ella was telling me. Ella was afraid of me, and I had been afraid of her at the same time.

"Why are you afraid of me?" I whispered, not trusting my voice.

"You're different," she stated simply, "and when the rumors started circulating that you could be *her*, I freaked out a little bit. I loved my life. I knew it so well and I didn't want change. Little did I know, I was Chosen."

"You didn't know?" I asked, stunned. How awful that must have been.

"I mean, my grandfather always bragged that our blood held the magic for shape shifting, but I never really took him seriously. One day Dylan phased and it wasn't too long before I . . ." her voice trailed off into a whisper.

"I'm so sorry," I spoke quietly, desperately trying to keep my emotions at bay.

"Why are you sorry?" she questioned, her sarcastic tone coming back slightly. "It's not your fault that this war is happening. It was coming regardless."

"But I thought that was part of the reason you didn't like me," I continued. "I'm at the heart of this war."

She shook her head, her eyes gently meeting mine, "I hate change, but I never hated you. I keep people far from me as a sort of protection. If this all ends badly . . ." her eyes fell to the ground.

I finished for her, "You mean if we all die."

She nodded, "I just don't want to get attached to you and then lose you, you know?"

Visions of my parents' graves, Henry's coffin, and my broken sister flashed before my eyes.

"Yeah," I finally replied. "I know."

Several moments of silence passed before I asked, "What about Elsu? I always thought you two had it out for me. You're always together."

Her face instantly brightened, a smile forming, "Elsu probably hates you."

As soon as the words left her lips, we both laughed, the sound of our voices mingling together in the night air. The temporary lighthearted moment faded and the laughter suddenly sounded awkward and out of place. Ella stiffened beside me. Our rare moment had ended.

"Well," she began, the sharp edge in her voice rose again. "I've got to go. Got to rest up before training tomorrow. A girl needs her beauty sleep."

I nodded as she turned to walk away, the sound of her footfalls diminishing as my gaze lingered on the beautiful stallion before me.

Ella's unusual candid moment with me had left me with a few answers and many more questions. Apparently, Ella had never hated me. She didn't particularly like me, but she didn't hate me. Liking me in the future and building a friendship seemed possible; highly unlikely in the current state of things, but there was still a chance.

The fact remained that Elsu still hated me and that would probably never change. The creeping fear of truth slowly began to dig deep in the pit of my stomach; the truth that Elsu and Chenoa's mother was the true leader of the Rebels. I knew I shouldn't doubt Elsu, but if this knowledge were revealed to him, would his alliance change? Surely, he would be more comfortable serving his own mother than the half-brother he never truly even liked.

I was so consumed in my thoughts that I never noticed the midnight black stallion that had slowly walked toward me. I glanced up from the ground, startled to find Sky so close to me. He simply stared, his head tilting back and forth as if he was studying me. His eyes met mine for a long moment. The beautiful creature enchanted me. It was like he was trying to talk to me or communicate somehow.

Against my better judgment, I crawled through the opening in the fence that separated me from the beautiful horse. I glanced back toward the house where Ella had disappeared.

Sky softly neighed, capturing my attention once more. I looked to him before taking a tentative step forward. I wasn't sure why I felt drawn to Cole's horse. I was never a big animal person, but there was a small tug within me that was pulling toward the majestic creature.

Likewise, matching my movements, Sky took a step toward me.

Carefully, I closed the gap between us, reaching my hand out to him. His nose gently met my hand, smelling me cautiously. I smiled, breathing very softly as to not scare him. Suddenly, frightening me a little, Sky took a larger step toward me, burying his head into my chest, as if he was trying to embrace me. The scent of hay and horses overwhelmed me, but I quickly reciprocated the embrace, patting his neck.

A sharp intake of breath from behind me alarmed us. We both turned toward the owner of the noise, surprised to find Cole and Paco standing outside the fencing, faces full of wonder.

Cole's eyes were swimming with both awe and fear.

"Adeline," his voice came out shaky, his body tense. "Come here."

He held his hand out, similar to the way I had held mine out to Sky. The look on both Cole and Paco's face let me know that this was not a request, but a command. I paid one last glance to Sky whose eyes showed distrust and fear as he looked from Cole to Paco.

"I'll see you later," I whispered, patting his neck one last time before crawling through the fencing. The moment I had made it to the other side of the fence, Sky's gentle manor evaporated. He began neighing and bucking, thrashing his body around as ears lay back against his head.

Cole's familiar arms wrapped around me pulling me away from the now furious stallion.

"What the hell were you doing?" Cole's voice wasn't angry, but fearful.

"What?" I replied dumbly, stunned by the indescribable fear in his eyes.

"You could have gotten yourself killed," he whispered, his copper face paling. "That horse is not trained. You could have seriously been hurt."

I glimpsed to Paco whose expression was one of astonishment. He seemed speechless.

"I'm sorry," I mumbled weakly. Cole's face softened in response and I knew I had been forgiven when his arms wrapped tightly around me.

"That horse won't even let me near him," Cole continued, his grip around me tightening. "I don't understand." his voice trailed off as he buried his head into my hair, breathing deeply.

I peeked over Cole's broad shoulders to find Paco Dyami. I was surprised, no, more like astounded when I noticed the tears steadily cascading down his aged face. When his eyes met mine, he didn't seem angry or embarrassed. Instead, he nodded sadly, turning to walk away.

"Cole," his voice echoing through the stillness of the night.

Cole looked up to face his father, surprised to find him wiping away his fallen tears. Paco continued, "We're going to need to talk with the elders." He hesitated as his eyes fell on me, "It seems things have changed."

I realized what he meant, what his actions translated for my life. Paco Dyami now firmly believed I was the heavenly being. I saw it in his eyes when he glanced at me. The absolute sadness and fear that seemed to grip him when he saw me with Cole's horse had suddenly dawned on him something that he had never considered before. The Rebels had gotten it right this time. War was inevitable. Lives were going to be lost. There was no way around it.

I wasn't some innocent girl he had saved from a car accident long ago. He had saved someone more incredibly important and precious than that. Somehow this truth didn't help me feel stronger or more confident. Instead, I nestled myself deeper into Cole's embrace, desperate to hide forever in the safety of his arms. But I realized safety wasn't an option anymore.

FIFTEEN

"It's good to see you again Adeline," Enola smiled, crossing her legs Indian style as she sat on the rug before the fire once more. I returned her smile as I sat across from her, the smell of damp wood and forest overwhelming my senses for a few moments.

Coming to see Enola had been on my mind for a while now. It was difficult to come out here without Cole attached to my hip. His protective instincts had increased tenfold since my little stunt with his stallion, Sky. According to Cole, I was a magnet to life threatening situations.

Normally, I would never object to spending as much time with Cole as possible, but at the moment his protecting me was getting in the way of me learning and growing into the person I needed to become. His heart was in the right place, but I needed someone who was willing to tell me the truth and reality of my situation without the fear of scaring me. Enola was just the person to do that.

"It's good to see you too Enola," I answered. "A lot has happened since we last talked."

Enola nodded, "I know."

Of course she did. It didn't surprise me that much. Nothing did anymore.

"You have grown much," she continued, her aged smile faltering a bit, "and for that I am sorry."

"You're sorry? For what?"

"Death has many lessons to teach, but usually the student is much older before she learns the lesson," she explained. "I am sorry for your sister as well."

I cringed at the mention of Emma. I had called her earlier today only to be greeted by the empty shell of who my sister used to be. It was clear she had been sobbing before answering the phone. Her voice had been raw and lifeless. She wasn't getting better. In fact, I feared she was getting worse.

"Me too," I mumbled.

A silence fell as Enola continued to gaze at me. Her eyes looked for more differences, as if the internal transformation I had gone through had manifested itself physically as well.

"You've been training?" she queried, a smile tugging at the corner of her mouth.

I nodded, "Yes. A member of the Catawba tribe in South Carolina has been helping me."

"Noah?" she asked, startling me with how much she knew.

"Yes," I paused. "How did you know?"

She smiled her ancient smile, "You underestimate how much the Chosen know and how much Chenoa actually tells me."

I nodded, unable to break her stare, "How much do you know about Noah?"

"Enough," she replied. "I know how much you care for him."

I titled my head in confusion, "You do?"

"Although Noah was only asked by Cole to protect you if need be, he has developed a special bond with you. You're family in his eyes. You're someone very important; no longer simply a favor he was doing for another tribe," Enola explained. "He asks about you quite often."

"He does?" I asked, emotion saturating my voice. I suddenly

realized how much I missed the little seaside town and my only friend who lived there.

"He telephones Chenoa for updates on the Rebels and to see how you are doing," she continued. "He is also keeping his word when it comes to watching Emma."

Again, the conversation drifted back to Emma. Not my favorite topic.

"She's not getting better," my voice cracked. I fought the tears down, refusing to succumb to them again.

Enola frowned, "She's heartbroken."

"I know," I sniffed, "but isn't she supposed to get better, not worse?"

The only grief I had known was that of being orphaned. Of course I still missed my parents and grieved for them, but I was able to function unlike Emma. I could go through most days without crying. It felt like Emma wasn't even trying to heal. She was allowing her wound to fester, to worsen. Instead of trying to nurture her pain, she was clawing at it, making it bleed.

She sighed, taking my trembling hand in hers, "Imagine being in her shoes. How would you react if Cole was killed?"

My breathing stopped, my lungs refusing to work any longer. I couldn't even a fathom a world where Cole didn't exist. If his heart stopped beating, then mine would as well. I opened my mouth to answer her, but I couldn't form the words. It was unthinkable.

"Exactly," she concluded. My face, revealing the utter shock and horror, must have proved to her that I understood what she meant. "So be patient with her. Let her grieve in her own way. She'll be better one day."

I nodded, trying to believe what Enola was telling me. I couldn't shake the feeling that Emma's "one day" was very, very far away.

"I have a question for you," I changed subjects quickly, pushing the thoughts of Emma to the side for now. "I want to know what exactly happened the night my parents died. I know that their deaths had something to do with this war and I want to know why."

She looked at me questionably, her forehead creased in thought.

"Are you sure?"

Her words frightened me, but I had passed the point of no return long ago. Remaining in the dark in regards to my parents' death and this new life I was living was no longer a possibility. It was time to embrace the person I was and that required knowing who I had been in the past.

"Yes," my voice didn't waver.

She sighed heavily before beginning her story, "It was several years ago, after the Rebels had kidnapped Cole's mother and she had disappeared. The tribe hadn't heard any news from Turtle Mountain and it seemed that talk of the heavenly being had died down. Paco was struggling to take care of three small children, but he was managing. It was easier now that talk of a heavenly being seemed to have ceased."

She paused before continuing, "One day, a small girl, about five years old came to visit the reservation with her classmates. Paco had been helping with the tour when she came to visit.

"For some reason, the child mesmerized him. She walked behind the other children, with a strange air of maturity, and when Paco introduced himself to her, she smiled up at him asking if he would be her friend. Of course, he agreed and she took his hand as he led her through the reservation."

My breath had caught in my throat when Enola looked up at me. She was talking about me. I was the little girl that Paco had met all those years ago, but I didn't remember anything.

I started shaking my head, "I don't remember that day."

She ignored me, continuing her story, "Unfortunately, that day a member of Turtle Mountain had come and noticed the little girl. She raised suspicion and word spread between the two tribes."

"Just because Paco talked to a little girl?" I yelled. "That hardly constitutes slapping a label on her! It hardly constitutes killing her parents!"

Enola shook her head slowly, "Adeline, this little girl wasn't an ordinary child."

Her words made my blood run cold. I felt my hair standing on end.

"What do you mean?" I choked.

"Paco, and others, noticed certain things she would say. Normally one wouldn't think much of what small children say, but she . . . she mentioned some things that most normal children wouldn't know. At least, not children from outside the reservation."

"What did I say Enola?" I had no memory of the field trip to the reservation, of my innocent life as a small child, or my first encounter with Paco Dyami though I didn't doubt that it happened. My life before losing my parents was very distant and the memories were hazy, like a vague dream that I was trying to remember. I was scared of what that former life meant for me now.

"You mentioned an imaginary friend," she spoke simply. "It caught both Paco and the other tribe's attention."

Well, that was definitely not what I was expecting. An imaginary friend seemed so childish, so innocent. Not many adults would pay attention to such trivial things as a child's imaginary friend, but instead of feeling relieved, my heart continued to race. I was still terrified.

"A lot of little kids have imaginary friends," I whispered. "It doesn't mean anything."

She smiled sympathetically before saying the one thing that completely overturned any notion I had previously thought about my life. If I hadn't already believed that my life had drastically shifted, then now it was no longer in question. Six simple words were all it took to hammer the last nail into the coffin of my previous life. There was no longer any doubt.

"Your imaginary friend's name was Ogin."

I was not sure how long I sat in the small cabin, simply trying to remember how to breathe in and out or how to keep the tears at bay. My world had been shaken to its core, overturned by a younger version of myself who, at the age of five, would have readily accepted fairytales and legends to be true.

I honestly should not have been so surprised by the news, but somehow, hearing it from a younger version of myself made it much more real. It wasn't speculation anymore. I was the heavenly being. I was Ogin; she and I were the same.

I was shaken out of my thoughts when I heard a banging at the door. I thought it would come down from the force.

Enola stood slowly, clearly agitated by the intrusion, "Give me a moment."

"Is she in there?" his voice was panicked, a severe edge of horror trickled through his words.

"Cole?" I stood immediately, all notions of who I was crumbling at the prospect of Cole, my Cole, behind that door. The relief washed over me like cool rain. I basked in it, reveling in the fact that in mere moments I would be tucked safely in his arms.

My relief melted away as soon as Enola opened the door and a furious Cole stood before me.

"Why didn't you tell me where you were going?" he yelled, his breathing heavy. He must have phased and flown all over looking for me.

"I'm sorry," I mumbled, shrinking under his intense gaze.

"Sorry?" he repeated, his body shaking violently. "You're sorry?"

When I couldn't respond, he continued, his rage still severe, "I went to your house and when Alexia said she thought you were with me, I panicked. I thought they had somehow gotten around us, that they had taken you, that you were—"

His words abruptly stopped, his face crumbling in pain. He stepped forward pulling me fiercely into his arms, "Don't ever lie to me again."

I nodded, burying my face into the security of his embrace. As I glanced over to Enola who stood quietly by the door I realized that hiding in the warm and sheltered hold of Cole was no longer a possibility for me anymore.

One day, the Rebels would find their way through the Chosen's protection. One day, Cole's arms would not be there to hide me away from the evils of this world. One day, I would have to stand on my own, fight my own battles, and realize my true potential. That one day was coming soon. I couldn't hide anymore.

"Trust me," she giggled as she led me by the hand while her silk scarf shielded my eyes.

"Chenoa," I groaned, feeling my way in heels that were too high and too uncomfortable to be walking in. "What are you doing? Where are you taking me?"

Chenoa had kidnapped me earlier in the day, in order to play Barbie and dress me up as her personal life-sized mannequin. She refused to tell me why. All I knew was that she had a surprise for me outside, but that I wasn't allowed to see it until later; hence the blindfold.

It had been about three days since I saw Enola and not much had progressed. Sleep eluded me each night for fear of my dreams and whom I would see in them. I was also afraid of the nightmares. I didn't think I could take another night of listening to the screams of my sister while watching Henry's final moments over and over again. I shuddered at the thought.

Cole had been attached to me for the past three days as well, only leaving me when I would go to bed. I insisted that he should go train, but he asserted that it wasn't necessary. I think he was just being paranoid, thinking I would walk right into the Turtle Mountain tribe when he wasn't looking. Then again, my track record didn't exactly say any differently.

I hadn't seen him all day today. It was Chenoa who had appeared in my home before I had even woken up. She quickly packed a few things from my closet while telling Alexia that she would bring me back the next day after our impromptu sleepover. I barely had my teeth brushed before she was dragging me out of my house and into her car.

So, now I was being led to who knows where, wearing a dress and heels that were more like toothpicks on a shoe. I was tripping more than actually walking.

"Chenoa," I repeated again sharply. "Tell me what's going on."

"Just a few more steps Adeline," she laughed. "I promise it will be worth it."

I sighed, allowing myself to be led and trying not to think of all the pain my poor feet were enduring. There was a reason I only wore flats.

Chenoa abruptly stopped, shocking me. Her slender hand fell from mine and I was alone. I reached out, but found no one.

"Chenoa?" I questioned, pulling my arms around myself. The air had dropped a few degrees when the sun fell below the horizon.

Startling me, a pair of rough, calloused hands untied my blindfold revealing the copper skinned angel that was Cole Dyami. Without hesitating, I fell into his arms taking in his strong woodsy scent. He laughed gently, enfolding me into him.

"Hello there beautiful," he smiled.

I looked up to, caught off guard when his lips crashed onto mine. Everything either of us could ever say was said when he kissed me. No words were ever needed, just the feel of his lips dancing against mine. I felt my skin rise as his fingers tangled themselves in my hair. My arms wrapped around his neck, pulling him as close as possible.

I wasn't sure how long we stood there, kissing one another. When we finally parted, we were both breathing heavily.

"I love you," I whispered quickly.

He smiled, his blue eyes creasing from happiness, "I love you."

"So," I began again, taking in my surroundings. "Was this your doing?"

He smiled again, "You could say that. Do you like it?"

I looked around, floored by the beautiful white Christmas lights that glowed in the Dyami's barn. In the center of the breezeway was a single table with candles and dinner. I was overwhelmed by all the trouble Cole must have gone to for this.

"I love it," I turned to him, "but why did you do this?"

He shrugged, "I just wanted to do something for you."

I stood on my tiptoes, placing a kiss on his lips, "Thank you."

He wrapped his arms around my torso, pulling me closely, "You're welcome. Are you ready to eat?"

I kissed him once more, savoring the feel of his lips against mine before I answered, "Yes."

We sat down and ate dinner slowly, savoring this rare moment together. Our conversation was light and airy, not heavy, not burdened by our problems. For the moment, our heavy loads waited outside, beyond the present. We would have to deal with them eventually, that wasn't in question, but for now Cole and I were free. It was a limited sort of freedom, the kind you can't bottle and keep forever. It was fleeting, threatening to disappear as soon as one of us stepped outside of our personal bubble, but it was freedom. It was relief from the problems that plagued us for so long, and I was grateful for it.

"What are you thinking about?" Cole questioned, tucking a strand of hair behind my ear, leaving goose bumps wherever his fingers grazed. I looked up from my now empty plate into his beautiful face. Even though we were free for the moment, the effects of our past, our present, and our future weighed heavily on his shoulders. His curly hair had grown even more, though it was pushed back for now. His usually lighthearted blue eyes were tired and lacking his usual warmth. Though his scars from this war weren't physical they were evident, at least to me.

His hands were entangled in mine, but his grip was calloused and rough.

"You look tired," I whispered. I felt a piece of our freedom slip away.

He sighed, "It's been a hard few weeks." His head fell slightly, blue eyes wavering from mine.

I stood and he seemed surprised by my sudden movement. I carefully lowered myself into his lap and he enveloped me in his tired, but strong arms. He breathed in the scent of my hair, holding me tightly against his chest.

"Let's just stay like this forever," he whispered.

Though I wanted to agree with him, I couldn't, "That's not possible." I looked up, but could only see the contour of his jaw. Another piece of our freedom fell away.

He swallowed loudly, "I know." His voice cracked. I turned to get a better view and was shocked to find his eyes watering.

"Cole?" I whispered, fear clutching at my heart. The momentary freedom had completely evaporated. Only gripping fear of the future hung around us, threatening to choke us.

He stood, taking me with him, "Dance with me."

He spoke so simply, so innocently that I didn't even question him. I placed my arms around him, trying to hold us together as he danced with me. His face rested against mine, his arms wrapped around my waist holding me close.

After a few minutes of silence, I whispered in his ear, "There isn't any music."

I meant to sound funny and sarcastic to somehow obtain the freedom we had so easily lost, but my voice came out broken, shattered, and fragile.

He pulled his head away, so he could look into my eyes, "You are my music." He leaned in and captured my lips in the most beautiful and tragic kiss I had ever experienced. I don't honestly remember how long we stood there, desperately trying to comfort one another.

When we finally pulled apart, my voice was slurred, "I love you."

He attempted to smile, but failed. He cradled my face in his calloused hands, his eyes searching for something in mine.

"I need to ask you something."

It was my turn to gulp. For some reason, I didn't think I would like the question and I had even more reason to believe that Cole would hate my answer.

I nodded, turning my head to kiss his palm, "Yes?"

He licked his lips before beginning, "Adeline, I need you to tell me everything that happened the night Henry died. I know that it is so hard for you, but I have this feeling that there is something you aren't telling me . . ." he paused, struggling to keep his composure. "Baby, I need you to tell me everything. You don't have to fight this alone. I'm here."

Words evaporated from my throat. I had spent the last few weeks trying to rid that night from my memory. It seemed too soon, but the frantic emotions swimming in Cole's eyes made me realize that it was time. He needed to know everything.

"Okay," I agreed softly. "I'll tell you."

SIXTEEN

I had told Cole everything. I told him Dena was the true leader, that Chandler was Chenoa and Elsu's half-brother, that Dena had killed my parents all those years ago, and that Paco had been the one to save me from drowning.

After I had explained everything, Cole sat with his eyes unseeing. I tried not to panic. It was a lot of information to process. He only needed time. But as the minutes continued to pass and he said nothing, I began to worry.

"Cole?" I whispered. I sat in his lap once more, taking his face in my hands, forcing him to look at me. His eyes finally adjusted and focused on me.

"Are you mad?" I asked quietly. His face instantly tensed and his eyes went hard.

"I'm furious," he stated, teeth clenched.

I remained speechless as I watched him stand and pace angrily around the breezeway, his fists constantly tightening.

"Cole," I called. He turned to me, the anger momentarily evaporating from his features.

He began shaking his head, getting on his knees before me, "I'm not mad at you Adeline. I'm furious that this is happening, that she is behind it all. I should have seen it. I should have known."

"You couldn't have known. No one could have known."

"I'm the Delsin," he interrupted me. "I should have seen this coming."

"I'm the heavenly being," I countered fiercely. "I, of all people, should have known about this a lot sooner."

The blood drained from his face, his hands fell away from mine. I suddenly realized what I had said, what caused Cole's strange reaction.

"That's the first time," he stated simply, "that I've ever heard you say it."

I bit my lip nervously, "Well, I am."

We stared at each other for a few more moments, the feeling of dread and an unsure future wrapping around us like a cold, wet blanket.

"Yeah," he agreed, taking my face into his hands again. "I guess you are."

I didn't know what I expected to find when I visited Paco. I couldn't really remember what was going through my mind when I pulled up to the barn, the horses sticking their heads out of their small windows to see who had come. I walked slowly and carefully, somehow nervous of what was to come, what he would say, and what I would say.

I heard him before I saw him, his deep, rustic voice bellowing from the small office into the breezeway. He was speaking quickly, almost anxiously. I could feel my heart pounding as I approached the door, his name etched on the dark wood.

I took a deep breath and knocked softly, awaiting his reply.

His rapid talking faltered, before his deep voice broke the silence once more, "Come in."

To say Paco Dyami was surprised to see me is an understatement. When I had walked in, he was furiously scribbling something down, but when his eyes met mine, the pen fell away.

"I'm going to have to call you back," he said briefly into the phone before hanging up. A stifling silence fell over us as we looked to one another. My words seemed to have evaporated. I tried to remember why I was there again.

"Can I help you with something, Adeline?" he finally spoke, startling me.

"Yes," I replied. "Do you have time?"

He nodded half-heartedly, "I can move things around. What can I do for you?"

It seemed odd that Paco was still trying to work the ranch like normal. It seemed a bit insignificant compared to the war we were going to be fighting soon, but I suppose hanging on to the last shred of normalcy was the only way to not go completely crazy. I couldn't judge him for it.

I sat down before beginning, "I need you to answer some questions."

"I thought Enola was the one you went to for answers," he laughed to himself.

I shook my head, "She can't answer these questions."

His smile fell away, "Oh?"

"Why didn't you ever tell me that you were the one who saved me on that bridge?" My memories came rushing back as did my words. I spoke so quickly that I was sure he didn't catch anything that I had said, but he had.

His copper-toned, aged face fell, his eyes at first shocked and then reflecting years of regret.

He shifted in his seat before answering, "It's complicated."

"Don't even," my voice was steady, unwavering. "I am the definition of complicated."

He laughed softly, "I suppose you are."

I waited for him to answer my question, to finally explain why he saved my life all those years ago.

"I saved you," he began, "because it was the right thing to do."

I nodded, waiting for him to continue.

"It was several years after I had lost my wife. I was devastated. I felt betrayed by the legends I had once held so close for so long. My ex-wife, Dena, had returned to the Turtle Mountain Tribe and most likely had something to do with my losing Algoma . . . to almost losing Cole—" his voice broke off and his gaze shifted toward the window.

He breathed deeply before continuing, "You probably don't remember the day we met, but I do." he paused, his lips breaking into a very small smile. "You were only five years old, wearing a red, plaid dress with socks up to your knees. You were different from the other children. You stood out, alone most of the time. You carefully took everything in, asking many questions."

He laughed, covering his mouth with his hand, "You even took my hand and said, 'Mr. Paco, I want you to show me everything.'"

I smiled slightly, amused by a younger version of myself that I could not remember. His laughter faded and his smile evaporated.

"Then you started mentioning things," the change in his tone frightened me; it made me uneasy. "Things little girls from outside the reservation wouldn't know . . . shouldn't know."

I nodded, trembling in my seat for what was to come. This shouldn't be a shock. Enola had already told me all of this.

"Ogin," I whispered.

He nodded, his aged face seeming even more tired than usual, "Yes."

He continued, "You prattled on and on about your imaginary friend, about how she would tell you stories – secrets. It wasn't until you began explaining more and more did I realize you were retelling legends . . . legends of my tribe."

As I sat, listening, strange and hazy memories were slowly coming back, like I was trying to remember someone else's memories. They were foreign and unfamiliar, but they felt like mine.

Vague instances of a younger me, holding the hand of an older Chippewa man bombarded me all at once. He, listening to my jabbering, and I, talking away about things I thought came from an overactive imagination.

"You can see why I started to worry," his voice brought me out of my thoughts, "for my tribe and my family."

I nodded, still trembling form the sudden outpour of almost forgotten memories.

"So, someone from the other tribe heard me?" I figured, not really seeing the father of the man I loved in the small office anymore. "Saw me?"

He coughed in his hands, uncomfortably, shame etching its way across his ancient features, "It wasn't just someone, Adeline."

My head shot up instantly, "Who was it?"

He paused for a long time, "It was Chandler."

It didn't make sense. It wasn't possible.

"How did Chandler know?" I questioned. "He isn't from Little Shell."

"You're right," he nodded, "but he did come to visit sometimes."

"Why?"

"He'd like to visit his friend, Elsu."

Reality, or the one I had mistaken for so long, suddenly shattered around me like glass. The broken and jagged pieces of unknown memories, of truth, were being placed together, forming a terrifying new picture.

"By friend, you mean half-brother," I whispered, though I felt my breath was barely able to form words.

Paco's face fell in confusion, horror, and fear, "You know about that?"

"I know a lot," I stated, somehow numbed by my courage.

He leaned back in his chair, sighing heavily.

"I'm sorry for that," he continued. "I'm sorry for you and my son."

"So," I changed subjects quickly, fearful of my emotions. "You know about Dena working for them?"

He nodded gravely, "Yes."

"Cole does too," I added, thinking repeating this information would somehow comfort me, but it didn't.

He nodded again, accepting that his secrets had finally been let out.

"He needed to know."

"Why didn't you tell him? Do Elsu and Chenoa know too?" I felt the blood drain from my face when I thought of Chenoa and Elsu's mother.

"I didn't tell him because I was trying to protect him. I thought it would be for the best." he hesitated, "and in regards to Chenoa and Elsu, I don't think they know."

"You don't think they know?" I exclaimed, almost yelling. This was vital information. And I still wasn't sure if I trusted Elsu completely.

"I don't think Chenoa is aware of her mother's whereabouts, but Elsu always had a strong connection with Chandler."

"Always?"

"Not so much anymore, but I know he once considered him a brother, when they were much younger. I'm not sure how much information Chandler revealed to Elsu."

"Do you think he would betray us?"

For a moment, I saw the light leave Paco's eyes and I thought he would become angry with me, yelling at me to leave. I was shocked when he reached across the desk and gave my hand a gentle squeeze.

"I trust my son."

Although his ancient blue eyes shone with absolute trust and love for his eldest child, a nagging feeling, a small knot, formed deep within me. Something told me not to trust Elsu Dyami, at least not completely.

I walked out of Paco Dyami's office, my legs a bit wobbly. The bright sun hurt my eyes and I had to squint before they could adjust. I stumbled out of the breezeway, determined to make it to my car without crying.

"Adeline?"

I looked over, shocked and a little overwhelmed to find Elsu

Dyami with a bag of horse feed carelessly lying over his shoulder, as if it didn't weigh fifty pounds. I simply stared, not completely sure on what I should say.

"What are you doing here?" he asked gently, while placing the bag of feed down beside the wall of the barn. His tone surprised me; instead of the usual hatred I felt when he spoke to me, he sounded concerned . . . maybe even worried.

I only stood there, words not able to form in any way.

He took a tentative step toward me, "Are you okay, Adeline?"

I took a step back at the same moment he came toward me.

"Yes," I said quickly. "I'm fine."

He didn't look completely convinced, but I didn't give him a chance to question me. I turned and ran to my car, never looking back.

I threw my open my front door, desperate to run into the safety of my bedroom where I could properly process everything that had just happened, everything that had just been revealed. I was almost to my room, when Alexia appeared in my doorway, the phone in her hand.

"Adeline!" she smiled brightly. "Emma is on the phone. Do you want to talk to her?"

The last thing I could do at the moment was talk to Emma and pretend everything was okay. I didn't think I could possibly attempt to soothe and comfort my grieving sister, but I had no choice as Alexia gently placed the phone in my hand and smiled encouragingly before she left my room. I put the phone to my ear as I closed my door.

"Hey Emma," I started softly. "How are you?"

"Adeline, how do you know Cailen Willows?" Emma spoke quickly, her usual hollow voice now full. I could almost recognize my sister again.

"Who?" I countered. The name sounded vaguely familiar, but so much had happened in such a short amount of time that it was hard to be sure of anything anymore.

"Cailen Willows," she stated again. "She teaches at a local elementary school in Beaufort."

Noah's Cailen suddenly came to mind. How would Emma know about her? Did Noah mention her? Had Emma been talking to Noah?

"Yes," I said slowly. "How do you know her?"

"She came to my room last night," she replied, "looking for you."

My heart fell to my stomach. Why would Cailen come looking for me? The last time I saw her, she was terrified out of her mind. There would be no need for her to talk to me again, unless something had happened.

"Really?" I tried to sound casual. "What did she want?"

"Adeline," her voice suddenly went tight. "Are you in some kind of danger?"

My back slid down my closed door till I was finally seated on the floor, my knees hugged tightly to my chest.

"No, Emma," I countered, my voice suddenly very tense, "of course not."

"Don't lie to me," she spoke heatedly. "I know something is up."

"What did Cailen say to you?" Fear turned my blood ice cold. How much did Emma know? Was it enough to put her life in danger? Was Noah still keeping his promise?

"She wanted to make sure you were okay, that no one had gotten to you. Adeline, what does she mean? Is someone after you?"

Her panic came in waves over me, scaring me even more.

"No, Emma," I lied, "of course not. She must have been mistaken. Everything is fine. Please don't worry about me."

She sighed heavily, "I'm always going to worry about you, kid, especially now—" her voice broke for a moment, "You're all I've got left."

Tears hit the back of my eyes, "Don't say that."

"It's true," she continued, ignoring me. "First mom and dad, and now Henry; I can't afford to lose you too Addie. I've come so close too many times."

I pondered her words for a moment, thinking over them before finally replying, "Em, can you tell me more about the night mom and dad died?" The last time I had asked her, she had dodged the question, only giving me information I already knew. I was hoping she could shed some more light. Or at least somehow let me know how much she knew and if that knowledge could put her in danger.

Silence greeted me on the other end. Her breathing became a bit shallow.

"I don't remember much."

"Don't lie to me, Em," I spoke gently, trying to ease the truth out of her. "I really need to know if you remember anything odd that happened that night, or a few days before or after."

"Before or after?" she asked, her voice a few octaves higher than usual.

I thought through my words before finally uttering, "I don't think the car accident was an accident, Emma."

I was a little more than shocked when Emma agreed with me, "Yeah. I never thought it was either."

"Really?"

"Weird stuff did happen," she talked slowly, as the memories gradually came back to her I assumed. "Stuff I didn't really realize till much later."

"What kind of stuff?"

"This woman came by the house a few days before the accident," she began. "She was from the reservation and wanted to ask mom and dad some questions for a survey or something."

"It seemed a little odd. Her questions were completely random in my opinion," she continued, "like how many kids did they have? How old were we? Our birthdays? Not much about mom and dad honestly. Dad called me into the room. She wanted to meet us."

My heart continued to hammer against my ribcage, painfully.

"And did she?" I forced my voice to come out louder than a whisper. While my memories from the day I met Paco Dyami had resurfaced, I was still finding it difficult to remember much else from my childhood before my parents' deaths.

"Well, she met me," she continued, still oblivious to my ever-consuming fear that now gripped my heart. "You were playing in the back yard. She insisted on meeting you though. She came out and watched you for a little bit, not talking."

Silence ensued before I asked, "Then what happened?"

"Mom and Dad introduced you and you, being the little kid you were, said hello and then introduced your imaginary friend. It was kind of cute," she laughed. I couldn't join in her amusement. I was desperately racking my brain for any hint of a memory, any vision of a Native American woman coming to my home, but nothing came to mind. It almost felt like Emma was making it all up.

"Well, that was until the lady sort of freaked out," Emma's words brought me crashing back into reality.

"Freaked out?" I probed.

"Well, she sort of laughed and then left just like that. Mom and Dad were really confused too," Emma finished, her voice trailing off at the end.

"I don't remember anything from that day," I admitted shamefully. I should remember the last few days of my parents' lives, but only the terrifying moments of their deaths were what had come back to my memory.

"It's not your fault," Emma tried to soothe me. "The doctor had said memory loss was common for small children in traumatic situations. I always hoped you'd never remember anything from that time."

Silence fell over us again. I wasn't sure how long we simply sat there, listening to each other through the receiver.

"Hey Em," I asked suddenly, the sound of my own voice startling me a little.

"Yeah, Addie."

"Do you remember that lady's name by chance?" I whispered quietly.

She thought for a moment before replying, "I believe she said her name was Dena."

Words refused to leave my throat. I sat there, eyes glazed over, trying to comprehend the fact that Dena, the leader of the Rebels, had come into my home and then left, only to plan how to murder my parents.

I wasn't sure if Emma hung up or if I told her goodbye. All I recalled was the beeping of the phone off the hook as it lay in my hand. The growth of something dangerous and foreign began to fester inside of me. It wasn't the fear I had grown so accustomed to. No, it was something much darker, much more sinister. It suddenly flowed through my veins, wrapping itself around my heart, gripping it tightly, and refusing to yield.

My breathing slowly came back. I felt reborn; a new purpose hung around me, marking a new passage in my life. The road I had to take was waiting for me, had been waiting for me for so long, but I had just been too blind, or scared, or both, to properly see it.

Revenge; I had to avenge my parents' deaths. I had to end this war. I had to destroy the Rebels. I had to kill Dena. I had to kill her before she took anyone else I loved.

SEVENTEEN

I woke up the next morning from a restless sleep with a newfound confidence. I shot up out of bed and quickly got dressed. The Chosen were most likely already training. The sun wasn't up yet, so I had a small window of time to get to their training grounds before they would leave and Cole would come looking for me.

I sped down the highway, never slowing until I had made it to my destination. I got out of the jeep when I saw two figures standing out in the middle of the field, still unaware of my presence. It wasn't until I came closer did I notice it was Ava and Dylan.

"Hey Adeline," Dylan greeted me, his voice echoing confusion. "What are you doing here?"

"Is everything okay?" Ava turned toward me, concern swimming in her eyes.

"Where is everyone?" I demanded, ignoring their questions. They took a few steps back, taken aback by my aggressive tone.

Dylan vaguely pointed up, "Training."

"I need to talk to them," I stated simply.

Dylan nodded once, before running toward the left of the field.

Ava and I didn't even flinch when we heard the thunderous explosion of Dylan turning into his eagle form.

"Is everything okay?" she repeated, her eyes locked on mine.

"I have a plan," I replied, my voice even.

"A plan?" she questioned.

"You don't have to follow it if you don't want to," I explained, "but I'm not going to sit around anymore."

She took a step toward me, "Adeline, I don't understand."

I took a step back. I didn't want to be comforted. The hard grip on my heart tightened a bit when Ava's expression turned from confusion to pain. I didn't mean to hurt her, but I refused to be led anymore. It was time my voice was heard.

I heard the Chosen fly above before diving into the forest that lined the field. Cole, leading the rest of the Chosen, came into view, running toward Ava and I. I saw Jacy still flying in the air above me.

"Adeline," Cole breathed as he took a few strides toward me, pulling me to him. I could feel his heart pounding beneath the skin of his bare chest. "What's going on? What's wrong?"

I shrugged out of his grip. The hurt in his eyes was difficult to ignore.

"I have a plan," I replied quietly, voice even.

I looked from Cole to the rest of the Chosen, meeting each of their eyes. I stared a little longer at Elsu; imagining if I kept staring I would know where his loyalties lie. He simply stared back, until his eyes darted from mine to Cole's. He was confused.

"A plan?" Cole asked, making me look at him. "What are you talking about, Adeline?"

"I'm tired of being afraid," I began. "I'm tired of you all trying to shield me from my own battles. This isn't just your war. It's mine too."

They all stood quietly, watching me.

"I want to destroy them for what they've done. Not just for me, but for you. I don't want to be on the defensive anymore. Right now, they are weak. I propose we go after them; we attack them first. I don't want to wait anymore." I looked to Cole, his expression unreadable. "I don't want to be protected anymore. It's time I start protecting you too."

His fists tightened and he shook his head furiously, "You don't know what you're talking about."

"Excuse me?"

Olivia and Dylan shifted uncomfortably.

"Your plan is not well thought out," he said quietly, coming closer to me. He took my hands in his, squeezing them tightly, "and I don't appreciate you coming in the middle of our training just to tell me off."

"I wasn't telling you off," I wanted to yell. "I'm being honest."

"Then be honest with me alone. Not in front of everyone."

"They need to know too," I defended myself. "I should be training with you."

He scoffed and my blood boiled. I ripped my hands out of his grip.

Regret immediately fell over his face, "Adeline, I didn't mean it like that."

"Yeah you did," I nodded, taking a step back. "Noah never treated me like this."

Cole's eyes went cold, "Noah? What do you mean by that?"

"I mean that he actually believed in me. He tried to train me. He tried to help me," Angry, furious tears threated to spill over.

"We do believe in you, Adeline," Chenoa tried to intercede. I pushed her away.

"No!" I yelled. "None of you do!"

I looked to Cole, surprised to find anger and betrayal reflecting in his deep blue eyes.

"You," I spoke to him. "I thought you of all people would understand."

"I'm trying to," he spoke through gritted teeth, "but you're not making sense. We can't just leave Great Falls and go after them. We will wait. They will come."

"Do you think they waited when they killed my parents?" I screamed. "Do you think I can just sit here and wait for them to come? I have to do something!"

"You think I don't know how this feels?" he took a step toward me, his anger simmering just below the surface. "My mother died because of this war. Adeline, of all people, I understand."

I shook my head, "You don't."

Cole began shaking violently and gulped. He turned to Chenoa, whose eyes were watering.

"Chenoa," he began, his voice very tense and controlled, "take Adeline home before either of us says something we will both regret."

Chenoa took a step toward me, but I took a few steps back, "Don't. I can drive myself."

No one here understood. I tried to explain myself but they all refused; even Cole, my Cole.

I wasn't sure what exactly had come over me. This dark rage and anger was impossible to contain. I wanted to do *something*. It seemed everyone around me was content in waiting, but I couldn't anymore.

I turned, my uncontrollable anger and fury led me back to my car and finally back home.

My absolute anger had only dimmed slightly when I had finally arrived home. Alexia was still asleep, unaware of the fact that I had even left. I quietly closed and locked the door before making it to my room. I fell onto my bed, the emotions from the day overwhelming me, leaving me exhausted. I was so tired, mentally and physically, but I couldn't sleep.

I stood and paced my room for a few minutes, unable to slow down enough for my mind to be able to decide what my next course of action would be. Obviously, the Chosen were not going to help me. Not that I could blame them, but it would make it all a bit easier if I had some backup. I considered calling Noah, but he needed to continue to watch and protect Emma. I couldn't ask him to leave.

My backpack sitting next to my closet caught my eye, causing me to stop midstride. Before I could even realize what I was doing, I began packing clothes, toiletries, anything that I thought I would possibly need. It wasn't until I was in Emma's jeep again did I realize where I was heading.

The Greyhound bus stop came into view. I sat in the jeep for a long while, trying to decipher what exactly I was doing. Unaware of my own movements, I walked inside the station to check the times. The next bus for North Dakota was leaving in an hour.

"Adeline, stop!" her voice ordered, its usual kindness missing. She was angry; absolutely furious. It had been a while since I had last heard her.

Before I had time to buy my ticket I ran into the restroom, somehow trying to run from the voice that was incessantly talking now.

"Go home, Adeline. Don't do this. It's not time."

"Shut up!" I screamed into the mirror. Tears finally flowed freely as I realized what I was trying to do. I wanted to kill Dena so much that I was willing to put everything and everyone in danger by leaving right now. I slowly fell to the ground, crying as the voice continued.

"Go home. This is a mistake. You will ruin everything you've worked for."

"How do you know?" I yelled to the empty room, my sobs racking through my body, my own voice echoing back to me. I missed my parents so much.

"Trust me," she said simply.

I wasn't sure how long I sat there, contemplating my next move. If I went home, then I would have to wait for their next move and face the disappointment in Cole's eyes again. I didn't think I could do that.

If I left now, if I went to North Dakota, what would I do exactly? Find Dena and her tribe? Attempt to kill her?

No. As much as I wanted to kill her, I wasn't ready for that. It takes everything you are to take another life no matter how undeserving she was of the life she was given.

So, I sat there in the greyhound bus stop bathroom, the tears never ceasing as Ogin's voice did her best to try to comfort me. Maybe I really was going crazy. Perhaps I had finally lost my mind completely.

"Adeline," his voice echoed in the women's restroom, bouncing off the plastered walls and cold, linoleum floor.

My head shot up, shocked to find Cole suddenly sitting on his knees before me. Guilt and shame washed over me like a tsunami, knocking me breathless. I had hurt him so much. I could see it in his eyes.

"Adeline," he repeated, placing his hands gingerly on my shoulders, afraid that I would snap at him again. "Are you okay?"

I shook my head, "No." Then I fell helplessly into his arms, sobbing into his shoulder. He held me close, trying to comfort me.

"I'm so sorry," I kept sobbing.

"It's fine," he continued to whisper. "Please don't cry."

"I'm awful," I continued.

"I think you're pretty great," he tried to smile. He made me look into his eyes, where there was nothing but forgiveness and love. "I'm sorry too."

"Stop," I shook my head. "I'm horrible and you shouldn't have come for me."

"I will always come for you," he contradicted. "I love you, Adeline."

Surprising me further, he pressed his lips against mine. I melted into him, the tears and Ogin's voice completely ceasing.

"Want to explain to me what you were planning on doing?" Cole asked when we broke apart.

I wiped my eyes, "I was gonna go to North Dakota."

Cole tried not to roll his eyes, "And do what?"

"Kill Dena," I said simply. The look on Cole's face made me backtrack quickly, "I decided not to do that anymore. I was gonna come home."

"Adeline," he sighed heavily, the burden seeming to weigh heavier on his shoulders, "You can't fight this on your own."

"Neither can you," I countered.

He looked up, smiling wearily, "You're right. We are both wrong. So, what now?"

I thought for a moment, "We do this, fight this. Together."

He took my hands in both of his and brought them to his lips, lightly kissing them, "Sounds good to me."

Before we stood to leave, I looked across our intertwined hands into the blue orbs that were his eyes.

"You promise to include me now? During training?"

His eyes met mine, "Yes. I promise."

After a few moments, he laughed, "We have a lot to work on, don't we?"

I knew he meant our relationship and the balance of power that was so fragile. For the most part, Cole had been the one to make decisions. Most of the time I agreed with them, but now it was time to learn to balance one another, to listen to one another.

I nodded as I stood, "Yeah, I guess we do."

Weeks had passed with still no word from the other tribe or Noah. Cole had kept his promise and let me come to his training sessions. Even after the Chosen had left, Cole would train with me alone. I showed him what I had learned so far, which had impressed him.

"Whoa," he said as I almost nipped him with my small dagger. It felt good to use it again. Several weeks ago, it had stayed safely hidden in a drawer by my bed. Now, it never left my side.

He backed away, breathing heavily. Sparring with Cole was now our usual ritual after the Chosen finished their collaborative training. I started to truly feel like his equal.

He smiled, "You're good."

I beamed up at him, relishing his approval, "You think so?"

"Yeah," he nodded, taking another swig from his water bottle. "Noah did a good job training you."

"You still mad about that?" I asked as I took a sip from my own water bottle.

He shook his head, "No, it just took me by surprise." He turned towards me and then, in an instant, had me locked in his arms.

Smiling, he placed a quick kiss on my cheek, "You can't lie to me ever again, Adeline."

I smiled in response, "I promise." I held up three fingers, "Scout's honor."

He laughed as he released me, but only to take my hand once again as he walked me to his truck. We were only feet away from the truck when someone came bursting through the woods: Elsu.

Cole and I halted and waited for Elsu to make his way toward us. Not much had progressed in that area. Cole insisted that Elsu could be trusted, but I still had my doubts. Cole had yet to confront him or Chenoa about their mother. While I felt bad for Chenoa, I didn't want to risk telling Elsu and losing him as an ally forever, if he was even our ally to begin with.

"Elsu," Cole greeted, his grip on my hand tightening.

"Cole," he nodded towards Cole's directions.

His eyes met mine for a moment, "Adeline."

His voice was softer, as if he were trying to convince me. I only nodded in response, my eyes never leaving his.

He turned to Cole again, "The elders have returned with Tyler."

Tyler. I had almost forgotten about the rebel boy who had helped save my life.

"Already?" Cole questioned. "Where is he?"

Elsu replied, "With Paco and the others. He's sworn allegiance with us."

"Are we sure about that?" I asked. "Can we actually trust him?"

Elsu looked to me, "Well, I suppose that's up to you and Cole."

I nodded, and then looked to Cole, "I guess we better go."

"Are you sure?" Cole asked, concern echoing in his voice. "We don't have to do this, at least not today."

"No," I looked from Elsu to Cole again. "I can do this."

Before I knew it, we were standing before the elders. The Chosen and the elders met at the same place where the legend of the heavenly being had been told to me for the first time. It felt like ages had passed since I was last here. A bonfire was already burning, with the elders surrounding it. As Cole, Elsu, and I walked up, the conversations amongst the people already present ceased. I looked around, but I couldn't find Tyler.

"Where is he?" I whispered to Cole.

"They're bringing him now," he replied, still holding my hand as we came to join the circle among the Chosen.

Chenoa came to stand beside me, giving my free hand a gentle squeeze. She had only just forgiven me after my episode from a few weeks ago. I could still sense a bit of despondency when I caught her eye, like she knew I was still keeping things from her. I didn't know how much longer Cole and I could keep the true identity of Dena to ourselves. At some point the whole tribe would need to know, let alone Chenoa and Elsu.

I was shaken out of my thoughts when I caught sight of Tyler, being led by Dylan and Elan. His face was somber and he looked weak, much weaker than the last time I saw him; the night I almost died.

I wasn't sure what I expected when Tyler would finally be released from the elders. I guess I didn't know for sure if I'd even be around the moment when he would officially become Chosen, when the elders would finally accept him into the tribe.

As I looked around the circle of people that surrounded Cole and I, I realized something very important, vital even. Most of the elders glanced from Cole and I, gauging our reactions. I realized that this moment was extremely important because the only way Tyler would be allowed into the tribe was through Cole and me. It wasn't official until Cole and I said it was, and then the pressure began to weigh heavily on my chest as Tyler continued to approach us. Cole could sense my change in demeanor, squeezing my hand slightly. I looked to find concern in his blue eyes.

"Are you okay?" he whispered.

I glanced around before replying, "I didn't realize how important our opinions would be. I'm just a little nervous now."

He nodded, understanding replacing the concern, "It'll be okay. We'll make the right decision."

Just as Tyler finally stood before us, I quietly replied, "I hope so."

Chief Red Hakan stepped up, his voice booming, "Tyler has spent many nights in the wilderness. We have tested his loyalty and believe he has officially turned over to our side. However," Chief Hakan glanced to Cole and me, "it is up to the Delsin to decide if he is worthy of joining the Chosen."

Cole nodded, turning his attention to Tyler, whose weak eyes revealed fear.

"You've spent time out in the mountains?" Cole asked, commanding authority.

"Yes," Tyler nodded.

"And you've been chosen by nature?" Cole continued.

Tyler glanced to me and to the other Chosen, "I believe so."

"You believe so?" Cole countered.

Tyler cleared his voice, speaking more clearly, "Yes. I've been chosen."

There was rumbling among the other Chosen and the elders present. I stepped up, closer to Tyler before Cole could continue, "And your power? Do you still have visions?"

Tyler's eyes widened a bit, "Yeah. You remember?"

"Of course I remember," I nodded, "Have you seen anything we should know about?"

Tyler gulped and I took that as a clue that the answer was yes. It was silent around us; no one moved.

"Tyler," I reached over to him, gently taking his arm in my hand. He was shaking. "You have to trust us and we have to trust you."

He looked from my hand to my eyes, nodding.

"What have you seen?" I whispered again.

He took a step closer to me, almost closing the gap between us. Cole simultaneously stepped with me, growling under his breath. Tyler immediately took a step away, his eyes glancing to the ground.

I turned to Cole, who was currently burning a hole in Tyler's skull.

"Cole," I warned, "it's fine."

Cole glanced to me. He finally nodded and took a step back, but kept a firm grip on my hand.

"Tyler," I took a step toward him again. "You can tell me."

He looked to me again, fear swimming in and out of his eyes, "I saw visions of war."

There was a small, audible gasp from the people around us. It distracted Tyler for a moment.

"And what happened?" I claimed his attention again.

He licked his lips before shaking his head. He took another step back.

"Tyler," I took his hand in mine. "You can trust me."

"I can't trust anyone," he whispered.

I shook my head, "You have to."

He glanced down to our hands. I did too, noticing his was warm and clammy, revealing his nervousness. There was also gentleness in his touch. I could trust him. I did trust him.

I looked up to Tyler's brown eyes and said the three words that he desperately needed to hear, "I trust you."

Tyler wasn't the only one who was shocked by my words. The others around us all began talking at once. Cole came beside us, looking from Tyler to me.

"You do?" they both asked at the same time.

I nodded, my eyes never leaving Tyler's, "I do."

Tyler's fearful expression finally relaxed, his eyes silently expressing the fact that he trusted me too.

"My visions come and go, both when I'm awake and when I'm asleep. While I was in the woods, they came much more insistently," he began to explain. The voices around us were silenced as they hung on his every word.

"I know the feeling," I commented.

His face lit up, "You have visions too?"

"Sort of," I shrugged, "but not like yours."

He smiled slightly, like he had finally found a friend. Cole's grip on my hand tightened a bit.

"Anyway," Tyler continued, "I started having what felt like

nightmares, but then they started coming when I was awake too, like my normal visions."

I nodded, "What happened in these nightmares, Tyler?"

He swallowed hard, a deafening silence hanging in the air, threatening to smother me. For a long moment I didn't think he would respond, but suddenly, the words flowed out of him quickly and like a knife they cut deeply into the life I had been fighting so hard to protect.

"They're coming. They're coming very soon."

EIGHTEEN

Tyler proceeded to tell Cole and me exactly what his visions entailed, and it was exactly as we all feared. The Rebels were preparing and although they were weak, they were steadily gaining strength in numbers. Tyler had said they were growing their army by contacting other tribes and forming alliances, like I had feared. We didn't have much time, not nearly as much time as we thought we did.

Instead of feeling fear, like normal, an overwhelming sense of peace coursed through me. I wasn't sure if it was the acceptance of the very high probability of my death or a renewed confidence in not only the Chosen's abilities, but in mine as well. I had a feeling it was the former rather than the later. I was suddenly very glad that Emma was still in South Carolina, safe from any physical harm. I couldn't even imagine the emotional and mental harm that could possibly destroy her if she came home and I wasn't there.

After Tyler explained his dark visions of rebels fighting the Chosen, Cole allowed him to return home with Elan to rest. Instead of an emergency meeting with the elders and the rest of the Chosen, Cole dismissed everyone deciding that time to rest was what everyone needed.

"What?" Elsu had bellowed, clearly not in agreement with the Delsin. "They could be coming any minute and you want us to rest?"

"Yes," Cole nodded, exhaustion threatening to take him over. He took a step towards Elsu, placing his hand on his shoulder, "I think we all need a night to take this news in and rest."

"But we need to train," Elsu continued.

Cole's face came very close to Elsu's and his voice was tight and authoritative, "I'm not going to train these people into the ground when death might be the only thing coming for them."

That certainly silenced Elsu.

"So that's it?" Elsu questioned, his voice low. "We're all gonna die?"

"Maybe not," I stepped up, silencing the two Dyami boys. "There's still hope."

Elsu rolled his eyes, "Sure." He turned around and left us.

Cole took me home, walking me to the front door just before informing me he wouldn't be coming in.

"You're leaving?" I asked, confused by his actions.

"I have a lot to think about, a lot to plan," he said as he ran his hand through his onyx hair.

I took his hand in mine, "Together, we'll do it all together."

Cole's eyes met mine and in an instant I knew whatever he was about to say I wasn't going to like.

"Cole," I warned him.

"Adeline, I think that maybe you should go back to South Carolina and stay with Emma."

I felt like I had been punched in the stomach and run over by a train simultaneously.

"What?" I choked out.

He sighed, shaking his head, "I don't want you here when . . ." he paused for a long moment, searching for the right words, "when Tyler's vision comes to pass."

"No," I immediately bellowed. "Not when you and the tribe need me. I'm not leaving you."

Tears swam in his eyes, but he fought them. He turned away from me, burying his head in his hands. He finally sat on the steps of my front porch, his head hanging in exhaustion. I sat next to him, pulling his arm closer to me like I was clutching a teddy bear. We sat in silence except for our breathing. I turned to look at him, reaching my hand to run my fingers through his hair. He leaned into my touch.

"Do you ever regret us?" I asked softly.

He turned to me immediately, his eyes narrowed, "Regret us?"

"What I mean is," my eyes wavered from his, searching for the right words, "if we had never met, none of this would be happening. No one would be dead and we wouldn't be worried about a war. I just can't help but think this is entirely my fault, all because I fell in love."

Cole's hands took my face and gently forced me to look into his blue eyes, "I'd rather only live one hour knowing you than a thousand lifetimes having never met you. I have never regretted you and I never will."

He kissed me, obliterating any doubts either of us had. We both had fallen hopelessly and irrevocably in love. And we were both going to die because of that love. And I couldn't regret it. Not even for a moment.

Cole left after a little while, promising to come get me in the morning to strategize with him and the other Chosen. I walked in my home a little surprised to find Alexia sitting in the kitchen, with what looked like a scrapbook of some sort. She was laughing to herself and didn't notice my presence till I had dropped my bag on the kitchen table.

"Oh, hey there Adeline," she smiled, wiping a few tears from her eyes. "I didn't hear you come in."

"Why are you crying?" I asked, suddenly concerned. I came around to look over her shoulder.

"Oh," she sniffed, "it's nothing. I just decided to bring out my old scrapbook. I made it a long time ago . . ." she hesitated. "When I was still married, before I lost my baby."

I was surprised. Alexia was usually very careful with how much she let me know about her life prior to us meeting.

"Can I see it?" I asked gently.

She nodded, "Of course."

She opened it from the beginning, revealing her college days and her early career. We flipped through many pages, laughing and smiling.

"That was the boy I dated in my senior year of college," she laughed as she pointed out a man with greasy, black hair and glasses too large for his face. I laughed with her, feeling strange at how I could laugh with Alexia so candidly. I wanted to enjoy as much as I could, so I tried to memorize this moment, this scene. The way Alexia's face wrinkled when she laughed, the sound of her voice when she talked too quickly, the way she felt like my own mother. I wanted to forever know her like I did in that moment; beautiful, full of life, and happy.

"This," she turned the page, the happiness fading from her eyes, "is the day I met my first husband."

I turned my eyes from Alexia to the old, faded picture glued to the page. She continued to prattle on about how they met on the Little Shell reservation when she had just started her first job. He had been the one to show her around the tribe and the reservation. Later that night, he had asked her to dinner.

"Loving him was as easy as breathing," she commented, her eyes swimming with tears.

It wasn't Alexia's story that had shocked me so, leaving me speechless. It wasn't her obvious heartbreak or the apparent love for him that had not died after all these years. No, it was the undeniable truth that I was staring at a picture of Alexia and her first husband and her only true love: Paco Dyami.

I felt my body shudder and nausea hit me instantly. I put my hand over my mouth, but my eyes never leaving the picture. Surely I was mistaken, but I looked over the man's features and knew I had seen them before, countless times.

"Adeline?" Alexia's concern interrupted my thoughts. "Are you okay, dear?"

I shook my head, desperately trying to find my voice. It came out in a whisper, "What's his name?"

She looked back to the picture, "Paco."

I stood up, pacing my kitchen, debating on whether I should throw up in the sink or try to make it to my bathroom.

"Adeline, what is wrong?" Alexia's voice rose, trying to gain my attention once more.

"But you're name isn't Algoma," I screeched, my voice rasping. The world that I knew was not only being threatened, but it suddenly wasn't a known world anymore. It was foreign.

"Algoma?" she asked, the blood draining from her face. "Where did you hear that name?"

"You know it?" I countered, swallowing hard.

"That's what he called me," she breathed. "That was his nickname for me. I don't understand how you would know it."

I backed away till my back hit the counter behind me. Suddenly, it all made sense; in a sick and twisted sort of way. My eyes studied Alexia's, or Algoma's, features, a little shocked to find how similar she was to Cole. It suddenly made sense that he was her son, but several questions remained: how could she not remember Cole? How did she not recognize him when he would come over? How did he not recognize her?

"Adeline?" her voice was shaking, so she truly had no idea. I licked my lips, searching for words that would not come. What could I say? What could I do?

A silence hung in the air, smothering the both of us. I opened my mouth to speak when the phone rang. We both jumped in surprise. I quickly picked up the phone and answering it in one shallow breath.

"Hello?"

"Adeline?" A deep familiar voice boomed through the receiver. He sounded alarmed, worried, concerned.

"Noah," I breathed, relieved and glancing to Alexia again who was still staring at me, tears in her eyes. "I'm gonna have to call you back."

I hung up before he had a chance to reply.

"Adeline," she said once more, her voice strained. "Can you please explain to me how you know Paco?"

I shook my head, "No, but I know someone who can."

Alexia wordlessly followed me to the jeep. I knew there was only one person who could make sense out of whatever was happening: Enola.

NINETEEN

The small cabin sat quietly in the woods, like it was waiting for us. Alexia said not one word on our way there, but I kept watching her, glancing over every other minute. Her hands were held tightly together in her lap, clutching at the scrapbook. I was waiting for her to recognize where we were heading, but not once did she appear to know where we were going.

We walked up to the door and jumped back in surprise when Enola threw it open, her eyes instantly drawn to Alexia.

"Algoma," she cried out in absolute happiness. She reached her arms out to her, but Alexia stepped back in apprehension, looking to me.

"Adeline, what is happening? Who is this?" she asked warily, looking from Enola to me.

"You don't remember me?" Enola asked, her hands hanging empty by her sides.

Alexia nodded, her eyes clouded with confusion. She looked to me desperately, "How does she know that name?"

I immediately turned to Enola, "We need your help. Alexia is having trouble remembering important things, like Cole."

"Cole?" her voice went sharp, her eyebrows furrowing together in anger. "What does your boyfriend have to do with this?"

"Why don't you come in?" Enola recovered from the sting of Alexia's rejection, shuffling us into the small cabin.

"What is going on here?" Alexia's usually kind voice was slowly turning angrier and angrier. "I want answers."

Don't we all? I wanted to mutter, but held it in.

"Alexia," Enola began calmly. "Why don't you sit with us? I promise to explain everything."

For a moment I thought Alexia was going to refuse, but she finally complied and sat down across from Enola. I sat on the left of Alexia and to the right of Enola, forming a small triangle.

"How did you," Alexia glanced to me then back to Enola, "and you know I used to go by 'Algoma'?"

Enola sighed before beginning, "I knew you back then before you left Paco."

Alexia immediately shook her head, "No, he left me, after we lost our baby."

"What was your child's name?" Enola countered, arching her left eyebrow.

Tears clouded her eyes, "We never got a chance to name him."

"You had a name picked out, didn't you?" Enola pointed a knowing finger at her.

Alexia bit her lips and glanced in my direction, "I don't understand how my unborn child has anything to do with this."

"Oh my dear," Enola smiled sadly, "he has everything do with this."

Alexia sat speechless, her mouth hanging open slightly.

"You don't remember much from those last few months of pregnancy do you? Of your last few months of marriage to Paco?" Enola asked gently, her voice echoing throughout the cabin softly.

Alexia shook her head, "The doctors said a hazy memory is quite common after extensive surgery."

Enola nodded, "What hospital was that again? The doctor's

name?"

Alexia opened her mouth in answer, but the answer was caught in her throat. She closed her mouth, trying to remember something that never actually happened.

"Can't think of it because it never actually happened," Enola spoke softly.

Realization slowly crept up on Alexia and covered her in a truth she never thought possible.

"I don't understand," she stated simply. "I lost my baby and my husband. I had to leave Great Falls." The way she said it sounded distorted and unnatural coming from her voice, almost as if those phrases had been repeated and repeated in her subconscious until she finally believed them, until she had the words engraved on her brain.

"That's what you were told to say if anyone asked," Enola whispered. "Your son is alive and well, but he and Paco still believe you to be dead."

Alexia's head shot up at that revelation, "Who would trick us like that? I think you're lying to me. There is no way my baby lived. I saw his corpse. I held my dead baby. Don't you think I'd know if my baby were alive?"

Her anger did not seem to faze Enola, "If you hadn't been drugged and then brainwashed to believe those lies, then yes. I'd think you'd be extremely capable to know where your child is."

Alexia began to tremble furiously, yelling, "You have no idea what you are talking about!"

Enola sighed as she stood, walking over to her teakettle and preparing to make us tea, "Would you like some tea to calm your nerves?"

"No, I would not," angry tears threatened to overtake her. "I want you to tell me how you know all of this about my life. I want to know why you think my baby is alive and why Paco would think I am dead."

Enola shrugged, continuing to prepare drinks, "The rebel tribe believed you to be the reincarnation, kidnapped you, tested their theory, then when they realized they were incorrect they erased your memory. After you gave birth, they took your child to Paco, leaving you to pick up the fragments of your life with many of your memories altered or erased altogether."

Both Alexia and I sat completely speechless, unable to fully process all of the information that had been so casually thrown in our faces. I almost slapped myself in frustration at Enola's directness. There was no way that Alexia would leave completely sure, with a firm grip on reality. Maybe taking her to Enola was a mistake. I had, unintentionally, placed Alexia in much danger. At least in her ignorance, she was safe.

I glanced to Alexia, who sat strangely still, not speaking. Enola came to sit back in front of Alexia and I with a single cup of tea in her aged hands, "Here," she forced it into Alexia's grip. "Drink this. It will make you feel better. Calm you down."

After several seconds, Alexia finally took a sip from the cup. I thought it was strange and kind of rude that Enola did not offer me a cup or even maker herself one.

"Who's the rebel tribe?" Alexia asked, finally finding her voice and reason. "What reincarnation? Why didn't Paco try to talk to m— " but her voice abruptly stopped when she lost consciousness, the cup falling from her hand as she slumped over, her eyes closed.

Now I knew why Enola didn't make a cup for herself or me.

"What did you just do?" I asked panicked, checking Alexia's vitals. "Did you poison her?"

"She is not dead," Enola spoke calmly, "but there was no way her fragile mind could handle the truth, at least not now."

"Well, what do we do now?" I asked exasperated. "She's gonna wake up with the same questions and I don't exactly know how to answer them."

Enola shook her head, "No, she will wake up having no memory of this day. You need to take her home and act as if nothing has happened." Enola took the scrapbook that lay carelessly by Alexia. " I will keep this. No need for her to go through it again and start making connections like today."

"Why?" I asked warily, glancing to Alexia's very still body.

"Her very life depends on it," Enola spoke a matter of factly. "If she is made aware again of the Chosen, of Paco, or of Cole, she could be in very real danger of the rebels."

So I was right. Ignorance was protection. If only I was so lucky.

That night, after bringing Alexia home and laying her on Emma's bed, I dreamt of Ogin. Even with all of the chaos that had occurred that day, I fell asleep once my head hit the pillow. It wasn't long until I started dreaming and visions of what Tyler had described to me began flickering in and out of my mind.

I was standing in an open field, the same open field where the Chosen train. I was alone and the dark clouds of a storm were brewing, thunder rippling through the air. The air had grown uncharacteristically cold, my breath easily visible every time I exhaled. The sound of footsteps pounding on the forest floor caused me to look to my right. I was surprised to find Tyler running toward me, his body covered in sweat. He had been running, from what I wasn't sure. He didn't notice my presence until he was only a few yards from me.

"Adeline?" he questioned. He seemed very real, and confused. "Why are you in my dream?"

I took a step back, shocked. He was dreaming too.

"What?" I whispered, not completely sure on why I was dreaming about Tyler, or why he stated he was dreaming too.

His breath was still ragged when he said, "Why are you in my vision? I don't understand."

Neither did I, but I was suddenly aware of something both incredibly powerful and incredibly dangerous. Tyler and I were dreaming together, at the same time. I had no idea what it meant.

"Adeline," her voice softly called to me before I had a chance to address Tyler's question. I turned, not so surprised to find Ogin standing before me, her beautiful face creased in worry.

"Who is that?" Tyler asked coming to stand beside me. His voice wasn't filled with fear, but wonder and awe. He had never seen anyone so beautiful, and neither had I to be honest. I'm sure that was the same reaction I had when I first met Ogin.

"I'm Ogin," she replied delicately, her eyes never leaving mine.

"What does this mean?" I questioned, my hands gesturing to Tyler and the scene around us. The sky continued to thunder above us, threatening rain any moment.

"It means," she began slowly, "that we don't have much time."

"I'm sorry," Tyler interrupted, suddenly frustrated. "What is going on? I've never had this happen before. No one has ever . . ." he paused looking for the right word, "interacted with me in a vision before."

Ogin turned to him, attempting to smile, "You both have a gift and now that you are aware of one another, it will most likely happen more often than not. You both will view visions together and interact with one another."

Tyler and I glanced to each other. I wasn't sure if I was particularly looking forward to sharing visions or any of my own nightmares with Tyler, and I don't think he was too excited by the idea either.

"But who are you?" Tyler asked again. "I've never seen you before."

Ogin looked to me, prompting me to answer. Tyler noticed that Ogin had now focused on me. He turned to me as well, his eyes widening with realization.

"You really are the reincarnation, aren't you?" he asked, his voice soft. His eyes took me again with a new look of reverence. I blushed under his intense gaze.

"That makes you . . ." Tyler immediately turned back to Ogin, his hands shaking.

"A part of her," she finished for him, her eyes still resting on me. "She is powerful on her own."

I shook my head, "I don't feel powerful. I just feel confused. I don't understand what I'm supposed to do."

She smiled knowingly, "That is why you are here with Tyler. You are going to help each other better understand."

"How do you know my name?" Tyler asked suddenly, irritation

seeping through his voice.

"Help each other understand what?" I ignored Tyler, desperate to grasp what Ogin meant.

She sighed before beginning, "You each have the gift of witnessing visions of the past, present, and future, but you are both young and ill equipped to properly understand these visions on your own. You need to help one another try to interpret what you have seen."

"I know what I see," Tyler scoffed. "I don't need help."

Ogin turned to him, "No? You do need the Chosen to trust you, no? Here is your chance, Tyler."

He blushed, embarrassed, under her intense gaze.

"So, how do we help each other?" I asked, ready to finally see what I could do to help Cole and the other Chosen.

"Tyler, do you remember your last visions? About the others coming?" Ogin asked. I felt chills course through me at the mention of the "others."

"Of course," he answered. "What does that have to do with anything?"

Her eyes went cold, "It has to do with everything."

Then she disappeared. I took another deep, cold breath, trying to prepare myself for whatever was to come.

"Where did she go?" Tyler asked, turning around, looking for Ogin.

"She's gone," I replied quietly.

"What happens now?" he questioned just as the sky thundered again, finally releasing the rain that had been waiting to fall. Within seconds we were soaked to the skin, shivering in the cold air.

"Do you remember how your vision began? Where it ended?" I yelled over the sound of the pouring rain.

Tyler nodded, shivering, "I usually would have already woken up, but instead of waking up while running, I found you."

"What's the last thing you remember? There has to be a reason we haven't woken up yet."

"Um," he closed his eyes, thinking. "I just left the battle where .

. ." his voice stopped and his eyes shot open.

"What?" I yelled, moving closer toward him. "You left the battle when what happened?"

He gulped, licking his lips, "I never told you everything that happened in my visions, Adeline."

I felt the blood drain from my face, "What are you talking about?"

I remember Tyler telling Cole and I everything he had seen. He had seen hundreds of Rebels attacking the Chosen and the hard battle that followed. He had said that he always woke up before the actual battle began. He just knew that the Rebels were coming soon, that was all. We still had a chance. We still had hope.

He sighed, about to respond when the sharp cry of someone from within the woods suddenly frightened us. Tyler and I locked eyes and then without a moment's hesitation, we ran towards the constant sobbing. We ran and ran through the pouring rain, no longer aware of the cold numbness that had settled into our bones or the branches that were tearing at our clothes and skin.

We finally halted when we came into another clearing where the remnants of a battle remained. Smoke and the smell of burning flesh made me gag. I scanned over the bloody picture before me, only slightly obscured by the never-ending rain that was coming down harder and harder with every passing moment.

The sound of the sobbing caught my attention once more and I looked across the clearing surprised to find a young woman crouching over a lifeless body. Her sobs were unearthly, like an animal. For some reason I walked towards her, over the dead bodies that were spread across the ground. Tyler followed me, careful not to step on anyone. They were all unrecognizable to me, like they were faceless and therefore easily forgettable. Her cries were not; they echoed inside of me, rattling me to my core.

The only force propelling me forward was not my instinct or my own will, but that of the young girl's unbearable sobs and cries. I felt nauseated by the sound, like her cries were clawing at me from the inside out. The smell of death was wrapping around me, choking me.

The frigid rain made my steps slow, but they were still purposeful. I had to see this girl and whom she was crying for. I was afraid I would see Emma and Henry again. I had nightmares about her and him more and more now.

I stopped, only a few feet away from the grieving girl, shocked by what I saw. I couldn't breathe. I couldn't see. I couldn't even fathom in what alternate universe that this sort of life was possible.

The young girl was me. The young boy who lay lifeless in her arms, all of his blood steadily flowing from him, was Cole. My Cole. My vision began to black in and out as I heard Tyler finally speak, his voice steady, calm, and not surprised.

"This is how my vision ends, every time."

TWENTY

I sat up in my bed, pulling the covers tightly around me, trying to suppress the sobs that were now racking my body. It was a dream. It was a nightmare, nothing more. It didn't mean anything.

Although, it felt like it meant everything. All of my deepest fears were realized in that one vision; the one vision Tyler lied about. I almost jumped when the phone rang. I quickly answered it, clearing my throat, but unable to stop the tears that were steadily falling.

"Adeline?" Tyler answered, his voice nervous. "Are you okay?"

"Yeah," I cleared my throat, attempting to sound strong. "Are you?"

"I'm fine," he sighed. "I'm sorry. I didn't want to tell you the whole vision because I didn't want to scare you. Cole said he was afraid you wouldn't understand . . ."

"Cole knows about your vision?" My blood ran cold and my heart hammered painfully in my chest. He knew about this.

He hesitated, "Yeah. He made me tell him everything last night when he came over to Elan's. He also made me promise not to tell you." He paused again, "I'm really sorry, Adeline."

Cole lied to me. I couldn't shake the terrifying feeling that his reason for not telling me about this possible future was that he wasn't planning on trying to avoid it, or that he felt there was no way around it, like he actually believed that death was the only option for him. I refused to believe that. I refused to live like that.

"Don't lie to me ever again, Tyler," I replied coldly, the tears subsiding for the moment. "If you have any more visions, you must tell me immediately. Do you understand?"

He didn't hesitate, "Completely."

I hung up, but did not attempt to sleep again. There was too much to do and to worry about. I couldn't even think of trying to sleep. I stood and quietly made my way through my dark home. I stopped in front of Emma's door where Alexia was sleeping. My body shivered when I thought about Cole's mother being so close to him, yet so far away. She had slept all through the night and, for her own sake, I hoped Enola was correct in that she would wake up with no memory of the day before.

There was nothing that could wipe my memories away. I was trapped within them, drowning in them. The terrible truths, which I had begged for at one point in time, were now my downfall. They say truth is supposed to set you free, but I felt more bound, more chained than ever before.

Before my tears could overtake me once more, the phone rang shrilling through the early morning air. I ran softly to the phone in the kitchen, desperate to answer it before it awoke Alexia.

"Hello?" I whispered quietly, surprised to find my voice cracking.

"Adeline! Where have you been? I've been trying to contact you," Noah's deep voice bellowed through the receiver.

I had completely forgotten that Noah had called me only hours ago. I gently started to rub my forehead, trying to massage away the migraine that was settling in.

"I'm sorry, Noah," I spoke softly, "things came up."

"Are you okay?" Worry and concern quickly replaced his anger and frustration. Noah could always read me. "Has anything happened?"

I rolled my eyes, suppressing the urge to scream. Everything had happened.

"I'm fine," I reassured him, "just really stressed."

"You and me both," he admitted, sighing heavily.

The tone in his voice made me start. My first thought was Emma.

"What's happening?" I asked him sharply. "Is Emma okay?"

He hesitated longer than I would have liked.

"It's not looking so good down here, Adeline." Of course it wasn't. Why would it?

"What's going on?" I persisted.

He sighed before continuing, "Emma is fine, at least physically. There is talk among the tribes down here about the war that is brewing where you are. They're trying to pick sides. They don't want to be on the losing team, Adeline."

I breathed a sigh of relief knowing Emma was safe. I couldn't shake the feeling that what Noah was telling me about the other tribes wasn't an update, but a warning. I realized that we needed to be more convincing of ourselves. I wasn't going to die, or let those I love sacrifice themselves, without a fight.

"What do you think, Noah?" I asked quietly, watching the first rays of the sun peeking over the trees that lined my back yard. "What side do you think I'm on?"

He didn't hesitate, "You're going to beat this. You're going to be okay. I know it."

For some reason, I couldn't quite convince myself of what I had been so desperately trying to convince Cole and the others of. The future seemed to be sure of only one thing: there would be no winners.

Cole was standing in the clearing, giving some advice to Tyler who had never transformed before, at least not on purpose and in his own control.

Tyler had admitted to phasing only twice before: once when he was still with the Rebels and the other time when he was on his journey in the woods, to prove his loyalty to the elders.

I sat on a blanket not far from where Cole was instructing Tyler, trying to help him gain control of his shape shifting.

"You're overthinking it," Cole explained, his voice strong, but gentle. "You have to let it come naturally. Let your spirit warrior come from within you."

"I'm trying," Tyler complained, throwing his hands in the air in frustration.

Cole smirked, his eyes drifting to mine. I attempted to smile in return, but not sure if it came across right.

I was still upset at Cole for keeping the end of Tyler's vision from me. It seemed like Cole had to know my whereabouts and future, secure in the fact that my life was not going to be over at the end of this war, but I wasn't allowed the same information about him. I had to be kept in the dark, and it wasn't fair.

I had been meaning to confront him about it, but could never find the right time. It had to be done soon. I had been losing sleep; I was afraid that my dreams would not only turn to Cole's death, but also what my life after was supposed to be like. Living without him wouldn't be an option. I didn't think I could do that. I definitely didn't want to try. I had personally seen the effects of grief's hold on Emma. She was still suffering within herself, not allowing herself to heal, but I couldn't blame her. I understood, if only from the possibility of losing Cole. It was unthinkable.

"You okay over there?" Cole called, noticing that I was no longer paying attention. I was reliving Tyler's vision again. Tyler walked up, his eyes wary. He was nervous about when I would finally tell Cole that I knew about his vision. I think Tyler feared Cole's anger and renewed lack of trust more than the battle itself.

I nodded as Cole and Tyler came closer, "I'm fine."

"Are you cold? Do you need my jacket?" Cole asked, his protective instincts kicking into overdrive. I smiled in spite of myself. He was so loyal to me – obsessed with my every need, no matter how minute.

"No, Cole," I replied softly. "I'm fine."

"Well, I'm exhausted," Tyler interrupted, falling down a few feet away from me, stretching his legs out as he folded his arms under his head. "It's been a rough day."

Cole rolled his eyes kicking Tyler's feet, "Poor kid. Get up."

"Just give me some time," Tyler whined. "This phasing stuff is hard. It doesn't come as easily for me."

"Why is that?" I asked before I had time to retract it. It wasn't really my business, but I was still curious. For Cole and the other Chosen, it was as easy as breathing. Cole said he hardly thought about it anymore.

Tyler's happy-go-lucky expression slowly began to fade away, "It's complicated."

"Well, there is obviously a reason you're not letting yourself phase," Cole added, sitting down next to me, causally laying his arm around my waist. I felt chills run up and down my spine. "A bad memory or something is blocking you from properly phasing. Most have trouble phasing in the beginning, but are able to finally master their phases. Some begin to phase randomly – usually after an extreme emotional upheaval. A fight or heated argument is the usual catalyst, at least that's what did it for me."

I had flashbacks to when Cole spoke about his childhood when he took me to his mother's grave. I realize now that Elsu's facial scars were the products of Cole's first phasing when he was merely a boy. I shuddered at the thought.

"Yeah," Tyler's voice brought me back to the present. "I shifted for the first time after a fight."

"With who?" Cole urged, concern reflecting in his blue eyes.

"My dad," his eyes went dark, hinting at a past long ago, but not easily forgotten.

Cole and I waited, allowing Tyler some time before continuing his story.

"My dad drank a lot," Tyler began, as he sat up, his head hanging in shame. "It started after my mom died when I was a kid. He took to the bottle and never stopped. At first, he would just yell a lot when he was drunk but then he became more physical, especially when I wasn't too keen on believing all the legends about our tribe and the Chosen. He would get really mad then."

Tyler paused, closing his eyes as he remembered his past, like he was watching what had happened to him rather than explaining it, "He had just gotten home from the bar. He reeked of whiskey. I had left dinner in the oven for him and gone to bed early. Usually, if he thought I was sleeping he would leave me alone, but this time he came crashing into the house, breaking things as he stumbled his way to my room. I had crawled under my bed when I heard his screams. He eventually found me, cursing the whole time as he dragged me outside of the house. He started beating me again, but this time I didn't think he would stop. He just kept hitting me over and over again . . ."

I leaned in closer to Cole, but also reached out to Tyler. I placed my hand on his shoulder, trying my best to comfort him. He glanced to me, trying to smile, but his smile faded as he continued his story.

"I was so angry, angry at my father, at my tribe, at my mother for leaving me, but mostly angry at my own weakness. I'm not sure what came over me next, but my body started shaking uncontrollably. My dad's voice became a distant sound; I couldn't see him anymore.

"My body was being ripped apart, from the inside out. I screamed, but no sound reached my ears, only the ripping of bone and flesh. There was no way I was going to survive this. I was going to die. I was sure of it.

"My body convulsed again and an explosion ripped me out of my thoughts. I struggled to get my breath back. I tried to stand and move, but found my body was unbelievably heavy. I could barely lift my head. It felt like an elephant was sitting on me.

"I looked for my dad, stunned to find him only a few feet away, smiling like he had seen his son for the first time. It was then I knew that the legends were true, I was Chosen, and that I had finally gained some sort of power. The beatings stopped after that night."

I finally breathed again when Tyler finished his story, giving his shoulder another reassuring squeeze.

"How old were you when you turned for the first time?" Cole's voice broke the silence.

Tyler thought for a moment, "I was ten. That's when my dad brought me into the Rebels' dealings. It's the only life I have ever known."

"Why do you think you haven't phased again since that night?" I asked, my voice sounding very quiet.

He shrugged, "I didn't trust my dad. I just had a bad feeling that if I kept phasing he would bring me to the leader, our chief. I was afraid of what would happen. So, if I do phase, it's never on purpose."

"Well," Cole began as he stood up, forcing Tyler up with him. "That's gonna change today."

Tyler rolled his eyes, "We've been at this for hours. I don't think I can do it today."

Cole nodded his head, "Yes, you can. You need to focus on the night that your father was beating you. Focus on the emotions you just told us about. Use that anger to release your spirit warrior. As you learn to phase more and more, you won't have to think about it. It comes with time."

Tyler took a couple steps back, "I don't really like thinking about that night."

Who could blame him? I would do my best to forever forget something like that. Cole was asking too much.

I stood up, pulling on Cole's hand, "Maybe we should do this another day."

Cole kept staring at Tyler, "No, he can do this."

I didn't argue, but looked toward Tyler who had closed his eyes. His forehead furrowed in concentration. Cole, with a tight grip on my hand, pulled me several feet away from Tyler.

"Are you sure about this?" I whispered to Cole.

He was grinning, "Positive. He's about to do it."

When I looked over at Tyler again, he was violently shaking, his body becoming a blur. I remembered the times when the same had happened to Cole and tried not to shiver.

Tyler's body suddenly became indistinguishable and in a split second an explosion of thunder clapped and Tyler was no longer a teenage boy, but an enormous eagle the size of a bear.

I had to lean into Cole so as to not fall over. Cole was laughing and smiling, proudly. Tyler had done it. He had phased.

Tyler's large and awkward body began to move as he tried to stand on his new feet, his talons digging into the ground. He looked to me and Cole and I swear I could see him smiling. In an instant, he shot up into the air, flying.

"I didn't know he could fly already," I whispered, mesmerized by him.

Cole shrugged, watching Tyler fly, "It's in his blood. After you phase, your animal instincts take over. It should be easier for him from this point on."

I glanced from Tyler to Cole, studying his face. To an outsider he was happy, carefree even, but I knew better. A heavy burden was weighing him down, only allowing him few moments of joy like this one with Tyler. I squeezed his hand, causing him to look to me. His eyes mirrored my concern. For a moment I thought he was finally going to share his burdens with me, but instead he feigned another empty smile, his hand coming up to caress my face.

"Everything's gonna be okay, Adeline. You're safe."

Everything was not okay, and Cole was not safe. That was what really mattered.

TWENTY-ONE

I was walking up to the Dyami barn, the morning air and sun rejuvenating me. My night had not been restful – nightmares constantly kept me on edge and I was unable to fully sleep. Visions of Tyler, Ogin, and Cole's breathless body continued to flash across my mind every time I closed my eyes. I finally gave up and turned all my lights on, waiting for the morning to come.

The still morning was calm, the wind only stroking my skin caused goose bumps. I rubbed my arms, angry at the fact that I forgot a jacket. I continued to walk to the barn when someone came up behind me, his deep voice startling me.

"Adeline? What are you doing here?" Elsu asked confused. I turned around to find his eyebrows furrowed and both his gloved hands holding barbwire and a barbwire cutter. I took several steps back, fear dictating my movements.

He seemed confused again, then looking to his hands, sighed, "I was fixing the fence on the north side of the pasture line. A tree took it down last night."

I only nodded, words unable to form in my dry mouth.

He continued, "Did Cole ask you over?"

I nodded again, wondering where exactly he was. I didn't like being alone with Elsu. I couldn't exactly explain why. Maybe it was the fact that his mother tried to kill me – twice now, but Dena was Chenoa's mother too and I never felt odd around her. I felt guilty, maybe, but never scared.

Elsu was about to say something when I felt familiar and sure arms wrap around me. Cole towered next to me, intimidating. Elsu took another step back.

"Cole," he greeted, his voice cold and void of any real emotion.

"Elsu," Cole replied, matching his tone.

Elsu nodded towards me, "You didn't tell anyone she was coming."

Cole's grip on my waist tightened, "I don't believe I need your permission, now do I?"

Elsu recoiled at Cole's harsh response, as if it were a snake that struck him. He didn't reply, but turned and walked away leaving a trail of dust behind him. Elsu had lost any sort of control over Cole that he had previously. Ever since Cole became the Delsin, the dynamic of their relationship had altered. Elsu had to respect Cole now. He had no choice.

Cole turned to me as we started walking down the breezeway, "Sorry about that." his voice suddenly lacked its previous severity, almost as if he was embarrassed by what just occurred.

"It's fine," I insisted. "He has to respect you."

Cole ran his fingers through his hair, abruptly bringing me out of my thoughts for a moment, "Yeah, but it's not so fun when I know he'd love to rip my head off rather than listen to anything I have to say."

I halted and Cole turned to me confused, "What?"

"You think he'd try to hurt you?"

My words came out in a whisper, afraid of the reality that could suddenly make Elsu not the untrustworthy older brother of the man I love, but the disloyal man who could attempt to take away my soul mate. I'd kill him.

Cole hesitated, scaring me. He licked his lips before responding, "No. I don't think he'd intentionally hurt me."

"Intentionally?" I almost cried out. I didn't care if it was an accident. If Elsu harmed Cole in any way, he would pay. "Cole. His mother is their leader. When he finds out, don't you think he might consider switching allegiance?"

He sighed heavily, "It's no secret that Elsu hates me, but I trust him, Adeline. He is loyal to the Chosen and to this tribe. I don't think he'd try to hurt anyone in Little Shell, ever. When he finds out, I'm sure he and Chenoa will both be shocked, but he will remain loyal. I know him."

The conversation regarding Elsu ended. Cole refused to revisit it. I tried to let it go, but the nagging feeling in the pit of my stomach wouldn't go away. The soft voice in the back of my mind still echoed one thing: Elsu Dyami could not be trusted.

Cole had kept me busy by letting me help around the ranch. We talked while feeding, moving hay, mucking stalls, and brushing the horses that had finished eating. While some girls wouldn't consider this a romantic date by any standard, I relished in it. For a few hours I felt normal, like this was what Cole and I would have done together many times before now. If there had been no legend, no Rebels, no war to fight, we would have been able to focus more on each other. We would have been able to be normal.

"You want to do something fun?" Cole's voice broke me out of my thoughts. At the moment I was brushing Honey in her stall. Her head came to nudge me every now and then, like she was thanking me.

"What? Like this isn't fun?" I asked, stroking Honey between the eyes. "He didn't mean it Honey. Being with you is the only place I'd like to be."

Cole rolled his eyes, while brushing his hair back, "Well, I'm insulted. But I'm serious. You wanna go riding?"

I felt the blood drain from my face. Riding? I loved being around Cole's horses, but not once did it ever cross my mind to actually attempt to ride one.

Cole noticed my hesitation, "I'd be riding with you. All you'd have to do is hold on. I'd take care of everything else."

I hesitated, trying to buy myself some time, "I don't know, Cole."

He smiled, taking my breath away, "Trust me. You can do it."

I smiled slightly, still not completely convinced.

He opened the stall door and brought me into his arms in one motion, "I won't let anything happen to you. I promise."

I nestled into his warm embrace, memorizing his scent: horses, the woods, and summer rain. I finally nodded, trusting Cole like I always have.

Cole had bridled a tall, chestnut Appaloosa with what looked like white socks that started at his hooves, stretching up to just below his knees. I brushed his neck, speaking softly to him.

"Now remember Ritz, I've never done this before so you need to be patient with me."

Cole released his head after placing the bridal on and Ritz turned his head to me, gently nudging my shoulder, like he was trying to reassure me.

Cole began leading Ritz down the breezeway and out of the barn. He stopped and turned toward me, his onyx hair glistening in the sunlight.

"Okay, time to get on," he smiled.

I stopped midstride. There wasn't any saddle, just Cole and bareback Ritz.

"Excuse me?" I asked, fear and anxiety overtaking me again.

Cole rolled his eyes as he walked toward me, taking my hand in his, "Don't freak out. It's fine. It's much more fun without a saddle."

I wasn't so sure. I didn't exactly think that the first time I ever rode a horse would be without a saddle or stirrups. There was nowhere to put my awkward feet.

Cole gripped my hand encouragingly, "Trust me."

I took a deep breath before nodding, "So how do I get on?"

Before I could even finish my question Cole had already lifted me in his arms and easily slid me on Ritz's back with no effort. I sat uncomfortably, not sure where to put my hands – should I grip his mane or the reins than now hung loose.

Before I could decide what to do, Cole had already jumped and swung his leg over Ritz, leaning into my back and taking the reins from my hands. His breath whispered huskily into my ear, "See? Not so bad."

I shivered involuntarily and merely nodded. Cole held the reins in his left hand and slung his right arm around my waist like a human seatbelt. Ritz began walking and I clung to Cole's arm tightly, nausea already threatening to overwhelm me.

Cole chuckled, his breath tickling my cheek, "Relax. We're just walking."

I nodded, my mouth dry and unable to form any coherent words. Ritz continued to walk and, as time went on, I became more and more comfortable with the rhythm and pace. I relaxed into Cole, finally able to breathe fully.

"Finally," Cole laughed again. "I was wondering when you'd relax."

"Shut up," I glared up at his grin. He was smiling, but it didn't quite reach his eyes. He looked from me to the trail in front of us. It was beautiful and serene, but not even the sun and the picturesque scene could fool me.

"Why did you want to take me riding?" I asked, absentmindedly making abstract designs on Cole's bare arm.

"Because it's fun," he answered simply, not meeting my eyes.

"Cole," I said again, tenderly. He glanced to me, his eyes mirroring mine. We were both thinking the same thing: no matter how hard we tried, we would never be able to escape the burdens and chaos that lay heavy on us. Even for a few hours, we knew that we would be weighed down again, like swimming in a rough current. We would obtain a few precious moments of stillness to breathe before another wave came crashing down, forcing us under again.

"Yeah?" he cleared his throat before replying.

I took a deep breath before asking, "Why didn't you tell me

about Tyler's vision?"

Cole shook his head, "I did. Tyler told both of us everything."

I shook my head, my hands gripping his arm afraid he'd disappear.

"No, you didn't. You didn't tell me about the end of Tyler's vision where you . . ." my words trailed off as tears stung the back of my eyes. I tightened my hold on Cole, unable to allow my thoughts to continue what they already knew. Cole was breathless, still, and dead. It was impossible.

"Shh," Cole attempted to soothe me, kissing my cheek. "This is why I didn't tell you. You'd worry."

"I will always worry," I turned to look at him. "I can't live without you."

He nodded, "I know."

Then he kissed me, his lips crashing onto mine, attempting to melt away my worries and concerns. It wasn't that easy. It could never be that easy. It just proved one thing: Cole was fragile. My strong, superhuman, spirit warrior was breakable. And it was possible I would end up like Emma.

He didn't deny Tyler's vision. He didn't attempt to pacify me with words like, "It's impossible" or "Nothing like that would ever happen to me." His urgent and desperate kiss was proof of that. Cole believed he didn't have much time left. He at least thought that our days together were numbered. The thought left me numb.

Living without him was not option. We would either leave the battlefield victorious or neither of us would make it home. It was all or nothing, and it didn't feel like luck was on our side.

TWENTY-TWO

We had made it back to Cole's house late afternoon. Neither of us mentioned Tyler's vision again, however I did mention that Tyler and I could communicate together during my dreams.

"What do you think that means?" I asked Cole as he released Ritz back out into the pasture. He took my hand in his and walked me towards his house.

"I'm not sure," he grimaced. "This hasn't happened before."

Of course not. Everything had to be difficult.

I was nervous while walking into Cole's house again where I knew I'd most likely see Paco. I wanted nothing more than to tell both him and Cole that Algoma, Alexia, was still alive, but I also knew that it would endanger her even more. If we made it through this war, I would tell them. I'd tell Cole his mother was still alive and Paco that his wife thought he had left her and that she was actually at my house, safe. Then again, Alexia would have to be strong enough to remember everything over again. She had woken up the next day after the episode with Enola ignorant and protected. She had no recollection of the day before, and for that I was grateful.

We walked into the kitchen, surprised to find Elsu and Paco in a heated argument with Chenoa steadily working around in the kitchen, trying to ignore them.

"She's hiding something," Elsu persisted, his voice harsh.

"Let it go, Elsu," Paco countered, his voice deep and demanding.

"She's a part of this family now. Get over it," Chenoa added as she glared at her older brother. She glanced toward the open door, her angry expression melting into a forced smile.

"Adeline! Cole! You're just in time. I'm getting dinner ready before we have to go train."

The tension in the room was thick, like smoke filling up the room making it hard to breathe.

Elsu glanced toward me, his eyes narrowed, "Adeline."

I nodded to him, "Elsu."

He stared at me for a moment longer before turning quickly and leaving. The front door slammed behind him.

Paco sighed heavily, wiping his forehead, "Sorry about that. He's not having a great day."

"Why was he talking about Adeline?" Cole demanded. He tried to control his defensive tone, but both Paco and Chenoa still jumped in surprise.

"You know Elsu," Chenoa recovered quickly, "always angry about something."

The conversation immediately drifted onto another safe topic, avoiding any mentions of Elsu or me, but I knew why Elsu was upset and felt the way he did. He knew that I didn't trust him. He understood that there was a part of me that couldn't fully rely on him. I had an intense foreboding feeling that the moment Elsu found out who and where his mother was, he would switch alliances. After all, he hated working under Cole and he hated me just as much if not more.

So I just had to wait and see. See if Elsu would live to be the man that his family claimed him to be. I, however, still had my reservations.

After dinner, I drove home while Cole and the others went to train. He offered to let me come, but I needed some time alone. Time to think, to sit, and try to figure out how to keep everyone I loved alive.

I was taken aback when I noticed an unknown car parked in the driveway next to Alexia's rental. I slowly walked through my door, trying to figure out who would come. My heart raced at the thought of Emma having returned. Instead of carefully walking through the front door, I burst through the entryway rushing my way to the sound of voices in the kitchen. It was not Emma who had come, but someone equally important to me.

"Noah!" I screamed, running into his open arms. I fought back the tears that threatened to fall.

He held me tightly, laughing, "Whoa! I'm not that exciting, kid!"

"I missed you," I said simply, mortified that the tears were falling anyway.

I heard Alexia leave, her soft voice trailing behind her, "I'll give you two some privacy."

After a few moments of hugging and me finally being able to stop my tears, I looked up to Noah, wary of the strange way he kept glancing from me.

"Noah, what are you doing here?" I ultimately asked, my voice a whisper.

He sighed heavily, attempting to speak, but closing his mouth instead.

"Is Emma okay?" I asked, my voice cracking. If anything had happened to Emma, I'd never forgive myself.

He nodded, "She's the same, living with Henry's parents and doing her best. I wouldn't have left if I didn't think she'd be okay."

"Why did you leave?"

His eyes finally met mine and I knew his reasons before he even spoke them aloud.

He looked over my shoulder to be sure that Alexia was out of hearing range, "We know war is coming, Adeline. My tribe and I have come to help the Chosen. I'm not letting you fight this war

227

alone."

I nodded, nausea overwhelming me for a moment, "Your whole tribe?"

There were more lives that could be lost, because of me. The pressure was excruciating, smothering me.

"Not everyone, just the ones who can fight. They should be meeting the Chosen at training right now. Didn't Cole tell you about this?"

Cole knew that almost an entire tribe had come to Montana to put their lives at risk for me, and I didn't know.

"No," I said tightly, my blood boiling. I was shaking, outraged that Cole continued to keep things from me. This had to stop and there was only one way it was going to happen.

"Adeline?" Noah took a step back, noticing my sudden change in mood.

"We're going to the reservation," I stated, pulling Noah by his jacket sleeve.

"We are? Why?" he asked, still oblivious and confused.

"I need to talk to the Delsin."

Noah drove, seeing as I was too irate to see the road properly. The yellow lines were blurring – from both my anger and utter sense of betrayal. I couldn't believe, following this afternoon, that Cole still felt the need to keep things from me, and I refused to let him keep doing just that.

Noah followed my directions silently. He knew when to be quiet, leaving me alone with my thoughts. I wasn't sure what I was going to say to Cole exactly. My thoughts were jumbled. All I knew was that I had to see him, speak to him. I had to convince him to trust me.

We pulled up to a large gathering of both the Chosen and Noah's tribe. I jumped out of the car before Noah had fully put the car in park.

I heard him yell after me as he struggled to keep up, "Adeline, wait!"

Everyone turned to me, both familiar and unfamiliar faces, but I looked passed them for Cole. As I came closer, I could see the blood drain from Cole's face, most likely from concern rather than fear. That would change very soon.

"Adeline," he met me half way. "What's wrong?"

"What's wrong?" I repeated, my voice more high-pitched than usual. "How about the fact that Noah and his tribe are coming to fight with us? Forgot to mention that?"

Cole, sighed relieved, but then ran both of his hands through his hair, "Adeline, please."

"Please what?" I almost screeched. "Why didn't you tell me? You think I can't handle this? I'm not as weak as you think I am!"

"I never said you were weak," he replied dangerously, his tone matching mine in severity. "Don't put words in my mouth."

"I don't need to," I replied, desperate and angry tears stinging my eyes. "I see it in the way you look at me, handle me, like I'm this fragile doll that will break at any moment. I'm not weak. I can handle this."

He shook his head, "I never said you couldn't handle this."

"Yes you have," I countered. "You have by your actions, Cole, and they speak louder than words."

He stood silent with his anger just brimming below the surface, ready to project itself physically. He closed his eyes, the anger slowly melting away. The understanding was evident when he opened his eyes again.

"I'm sorry," he said simply. "I should have told you. I promise from this moment on you will be aware of every decision. I won't hide anything from you."

I wanted to stay angry with him. I wanted to hit him, make him feel the betrayal I felt. I wanted to say some snide remark, turn on my heels, go home, and maybe listen to some indie punk rock music, simmering in my rage for a little bit longer.

But when I saw the sincerity in his eyes, I couldn't deny that I had already forgiven him, maybe even before he asked for it. I could never stay angry with Cole for long because it was a waste of the very valuable and precious time that we possibly had left. Tyler's vision was always on the backburner, threatening our future.

I nodded and pulled his torso into my arms, burying my head into his chest, soaking up his warmth and savoring his heartbeat. He pulled me closer, burying his head into my hair.

"I need you to trust me," I whispered into his chest, pulling him closer to me.

"I do trust you," he sighed into my ear, "always."

I forgot we were in front of several people until Noah's voice broke through the silence.

"Well, this has been sufficiently awkward," he sighed as he walked past Cole and I towards the others. "So, now that is out of the way, can we strategize please?"

Cole and I pulled apart, both of us slightly embarrassed.

"Yes," Cole agreed, pulling me to stand with him in front of the Chosen and Noah's tribe. "First, I want to thank you for coming here, for helping us."

Noah's tribe nodded in response, shifting uncomfortably when their eyes rested on me. Guilt washed over me again – more lives on my shoulders.

I gripped Cole's hand tighter, trying to secure myself to reality in the moment with Cole. We would be fine.

No matter how long or how earnestly I repeated it to myself I found it so difficult to believe that we would all be okay, that this war would end soon, and we all would walk away unscathed. Nothing was certain. The future, even Tyler's visions, remained balanced on a cliff, tipping one way and then the other, and at the moment the wind was blowing our lives the wrong way.

Cole and Noah continued to strategize with one another, looking to Tyler for when he believed the Rebels would come.

"I'm not exactly positive," he said, his voice echoing hesitation, "but they'll be here soon; three or four days at most."

Everyone gasped in shock at how little time we had left. My hand in Cole's began to tremble, but he squeezed it reassuringly. At least one of us was confident, or at least feigned it well.

"Then we better get started," Cole's voice boomed, his confidence overwhelming everyone for a moment. His hand fell from mine as he began to strategize with the Chosen and others from Noah's tribe. Noah came up beside me, bumping my shoulder playfully. I couldn't even look at him.

"What's wrong with you?" he teased, sensing my lack of lightheartedness that we used to share. What point was there to it anyway? Three days, four at the most, then we all might be dead.

Noah took a step closer, placing a reassuring arm around my shoulder, "It's gonna be okay. We're gonna fight this."

I nodded, trying to swallow back the tears that ached to be released. Crying would solve nothing. I had to be strong.

"Listen," Noah's voice became much quieter. "No one knows, besides you, me, and Cole who their leader is."

Guilt, like poison, rippled through me as he continued.

"She wants you," he whispered fiercely. "She could care less about Cole or the Chosen. You just need to distract her, lead her away from the fighting. Dena is their strongest warrior, but she's only coming here to get you. Understand?"

A small smile crept onto my face as I realized what Noah was getting at. I could be useful. I could lead Dena away and the Rebels would fall apart. She was their strength, but she doesn't really want to fight. She wanted me, and in a few days' time she would get what she wanted.

Before I could turn and reply to Noah, another's broken voice entered our private conversation.

"Dena is their leader?" Chenoa spoke softly, betrayal and confusion swimming her brown eyes. "My mother?"

Noah swore under his breath and my heart felt like it was going to fall out of my chest.

I reached out to touch Chenoa, make her understand, "Chenoa."

She recoiled at my touch, as if I slapped her. I took a step back.

"Chenoa," I began again. "Please understand."

"How long?" her voice began to rise and others turned toward us. "How long have you known?"

"Since the night Henry died," I whispered, shame overwhelming me, guilt making it hard to breathe.

Chenoa took several steps back, her eyes moving from me, to Noah, and then finally to Cole who had walked over as Chenoa had begun to yell.

"You! Have you known too?" she screeched, finally succumbing to her tears. "That my mother is their leader?"

Everyone began speaking at once, shocked at this new revelation. Elsu walked up beside his sister and placed his arm around her in a brotherly affection I had never seen him display. His eyes found mine – the deep seeded sense of betrayal rose in me again. Guilt was crushing me, but more for Chenoa. She didn't deserve to find out like this.

"Chenoa," Cole stepped up, walking towards his half siblings. "We were going to tell you."

"When," she yelled, Elsu having to physically retain her, "after she's dead?"

Her words made me recoil as if I had been punched. The heavy feeling in my stomach was spreading, sinking me lower and lower until I finally wished I were dead. I never meant to lie to Chenoa.

"No," Cole shook his head, drawing closer to his siblings, who took a few steps back in response. "I was trying to find the right time. I didn't mean for it to happen like this."

"No, we understand," Elsu spoke finally, his deep voice echoing through the clearing. "You've chosen where your loyalty lies. You chose her and left us in the dark. It's nothing new."

Cole took a stumbling step back before replying, "You don't know what you're talking about."

Elsu took a step forward, leaving Chenoa behind him, coming up to Cole's face, "I know what I see. Your only concern is for her, not for the tribe. You are selfish and you are using us to maintain your perfect little fairy tale—"

Elsu was interrupted when Cole punched him, his inhumane strength, throwing Elsu back twenty feet. The sound of Cole's fist meeting Elsu's face made a horrible cracking noise. Everyone was silent, waiting for Cole or Elsu to make the next move.

"Don't ever talk to me that way again!" Cole bellowed, his voice strong and sure, demanding respect in every word. "Everything I do is for this tribe, for our family. She," he pointed to me, his voice determined, "is a part of our family, and yes, I will do whatever it takes to protect her. I will die if I have to. I'm willing to do that, for everyone standing here."

Everyone was silent, the severity and seriousness of Cole's voice silencing not only our voices, but our thoughts as well. No one could deny the truth behind Cole's words – not even Elsu.

Chenoa's eyes continued to water as she glanced from Cole to Elsu who was slowly sitting up, physically feeling the weight of Cole's words and actions. It was as if she was trying to decide whom to trust.

Us! I wanted to scream, but I remained silent. There would never be enough words to take back what I had kept from her. Her forgiveness and trust would take much effort and time to gain once more. I was afraid we would never be the same. I had lost a friend.

"Now," Cole's voice began again, still strong and demanding, "we are going to train and we are going to fight. You can stay and fight alongside your brothers and sisters, or you can leave."

Cole's statement was directed towards Elsu who had finally found the strength to stand again. He wiped his mouth that had begun bleeding from the force of Cole's fist. He looked up, his brown eyes dark and untrusting. He didn't respond, but quietly turned and walked away. We watched his silhouette disappear into the woods. Chenoa's tears had finally quieted, but my deep seeded mistrust and doubt continued to flare within me and I think Cole finally felt the same as me. He didn't trust Elsu anymore.

TWENTY-THREE

The days were too few and with each hour that passed, the possibility of not only my death, but of those who were so precious to me became more and more real. Like a picture that was out of focus, the reality of our situation became clearer and clearer. Cole tried to make me think positively, but even I could see the lack of hope within his eyes. We were counting the moments, praying for more time. We weren't ready. We were so young. It wasn't fair.

I had come to Cole's house after training the day before the Rebels were supposed to come. I was looking for Chenoa, but when I walked into the kitchen with Cole by my side, she was nowhere to be seen.

Paco walked in when he heard the door open, "If you're looking for Chenoa, she took my truck and left. I'm not sure where she went."

Paco was clearly worried, but quietly left the room before either Cole or I could respond.

"You should go after her," Cole said, his voice tired.

"I'm not sure where she would be," I replied, turning to face him.

He smiled slightly, pushing a stray hair behind my ear, "Yeah, you do."

He dug in his pocket for his keys and handed them to me, "You can take my truck. I'll take you home when you get back."

He kissed my cheek and left me standing alone in the kitchen. I thought about chasing after him, demanding to know why he thought I would know where Chenoa would be, but it suddenly hit me and then I was running outside to Cole's truck.

Chenoa was with Enola, and I needed to see them both.

I walked up to the small cabin carefully, taking in my surroundings. I tried to memorize everything about this place: the way the flowers smelled after a summer rain, the aged, rough surface of the wood of the cabin, and the comforting feeling that bubbled within me every time I walked up to this ancient place. If tomorrow ended badly, I only hoped that Enola would be safe.

The door opened before I had even made it to the front porch. It was not Enola's sweet and aged face that greeted me, but Chenoa's angry grimace.

"What are you doing here?" she asked quickly, her voice furious. "Come to spout out more lies?"

"Chenoa," I walked up the front steps. "I'm so sorry." I had been apologizing for the past few days with nothing said in response. I wasn't expecting her to forgive me so soon, but I hoped. It made me sick to not be able to talk to her anymore. She wouldn't let me.

Enola pushed Chenoa to the side, "Adeline! Come in, come in. I've been expecting you."

"You have?" both Chenoa and I asked at the same time. Chenoa continued to glare at me as Enola pulled me in. I feared Chenoa would leave, but instead she sighed, irritated as she closed the door behind us. She came to sit on the rug before the fire with Enola and I.

At least she hadn't left. That was a start.

"Now, why have you come my dear?" Enola asked, taking my

hand in hers. The feel of her aged skin against mine was comforting – I felt like I was speaking to someone who had become my grandmother, someone I could find comfort in.

Chenoa scooted away from me, her body tense. I tried not to sound as pathetic as I felt, "I came looking for Chenoa."

Chenoa's body tensed even more, her breath quickened, "Why?"

I turned to her, taking my hand from Enola, "You know why! I want to talk to you."

"What else is there to talk about? I think everything's already been said," she replied, her tone neutral.

"You know that's not true," I exclaimed. "I want you to talk to me. I want you to say something."

"What, Adeline?" her voice caused even Enola to lean back in alarm. "What would you like me to say? That I'm sorry my mother is trying to kill us all? That I swear I'm nothing like her? What? Is that what you want?"

Her determined, strong voice broke towards the end, tears she had been trying to keep in finally overwhelmed her. She cried and I looked over to Enola for some clue on what to do.

Enola smiled sympathetically towards me, "Talk to her. She'll listen now."

I licked my lips before beginning, "Chenoa, I'm sorry that you found out the way you did, but please know this changes nothing between us, at least on my end. I trust you and I know that you are nothing like your mother. I can't even imagine how much this must hurt, but please know that Cole and I have always believed in you. I trust you with my own life."

I reached out and took her hand in mine, giving it a squeeze. After several moments of silence, she nodded and silently stood and left, leaving Enola and I alone in the small cabin. I wasn't sure if she forgave me, but at least she listened. It was all I could ask.

"You look so sad," Enola commented, her forehead furrowed in worry.

"You could say that," I agreed, my whole body exhausted,

straining under the weight of what was to come tomorrow. "It's just hard, knowing that there is nothing I can do to change it. The future is already set."

"What do you mean?" Enola asked, confusion replacing her concern.

"Tyler's visions haven't changed," I continued. "Tomorrow is known, and I'm scared." My voice broke at the last word.

"Visions aren't always certain," Enola interrupted me. "They give you an idea of what could happen, but the future can always change. You only have to be strong enough to make it change."

She sighed when I didn't respond.

"I think that you are still underestimating all that you are capable of."

I tried not to scoff, "Enola, everyone I love is in danger of dying tomorrow. I'm even in danger of dying tomorrow."

"So?" she asked, so simply.

"So?" I wanted to scream. "Don't you understand how crucial tomorrow's battle is? This is life and death! Nothing is guaranteed."

She smiled her knowing smile, "Life is never guaranteed, Adeline. Life is a series of beautiful, random, miraculous moments and each should be treasured, for no one knows when the next will come or if it will come. You've lived a thousand lifetimes in your few years on this earth, compared to the many people who live to see old age. You're one of the lucky ones, my dear. So, don't be sad when one moment ends," she took my hand, "because your most precious moment is yet to come."

"How do you know?" I sniffed, wiping tears away. I hadn't even realized I was crying.

"Because there are great plans for you, plans that far exceed any expectations you may have ever had. Have faith, believe, and don't ever give up hope. Hope is all we have to hold on to."

I nodded, taking her hand in both of mine, "I've never said thank you . . . for all you've done for me."

She smiled again; bringing my hands to her lips, she kissed them, "You never needed to, my dear Adeline."

For the first time in months, I felt peace.

TWENTY-FOUR

I'm not really sure how long we waited, standing in the cold, foggy air. They were coming and we were waiting for them, hoping the Rebels would not expect Noah's tribe to have come to help us. We still weren't completely sure on how many tribes had sided with the Rebels, but we were not going down without a fight.

Maybe Enola was right, maybe I could change the future. I had to be strong, just like all the others who were standing around me, putting their lives on the line. I had to try. I had to change Tyler's vision.

I felt Cole's fingers intertwine with mine, squeezing them reassuringly. I glanced up to him, knowing that if today was our last day we were at least going to die together. For some strange reason, that thought comforted me. This was going to be over today, somehow. Whether or not I lived to see the end of this day, at least it will be over. A cold, prickling sensation of relief flooded through me and I basked in it. Relief, even in the form of death, tasted so sweet.

Cole's hand once again squeezed mine. I couldn't give up yet. Tyler's vision had not come to pass. We could still change the future.

I could still have a life to live, with Cole.

Tyler's voice broke through the silence, shattering like glass, "They're almost here."

Several Chosen transformed, taking cover in the forest that surrounded the field we were in. Cole stayed close to me on my right and Noah stood to the left of me.

We were going to try talking first, reasoning with them that this did not have to be the way it would end. I already knew that talking would not work, but it was worth a shot. After all, I didn't want to see another person die like Henry.

The crunching of the ground beneath their feet shook me out of my thoughts. Looking across the field, I saw them. Led by Chandler and Dena, several of the Rebels, maybe thirty, came walking across the field, their eyes set on those of us who were waiting. Cole's hand squeezed a little tighter and I squeezed back. There was no going back now.

"Such a lovely day, isn't it?" Dena asked as she walked closer. Her grin caused my stomach to clench in response.

"Well," she continued, her insane smile plastered across her face, "Why so serious, everyone?"

Cole took a step forward, "This doesn't have to be violent, Dena. We are willing to form a peace treaty."

She laughed loudly, callously, insanely, "You actually think a peace treaty would satisfy me? That it would be enough for all that I've been through? What my tribe has been through?"

No one responded. We knew this would happen. There was no way she was going to back down. We'd have to fight.

Her eyes glanced over all of us, finally resting on mine, "How's that sister of yours, Adeline?"

I didn't even realize I had thrown my body toward her, in absolute rage, until I felt Cole's hands wrap around me, restraining me. I had lunged at her, wanting to make her shut up. However, Cole had pulled me back at the last moment, his iron tight grip wrapped around my waist. Dena laughed insanely in response.

"Not yet," Cole whispered in my ear, fighting to keep me still.

"She mentioned Emma," I argued, seeing nothing, but red.

"Adeline," he whispered, his grip on my waist tightening. "No."

I finally relaxed as Dena's laughter quieted. The air was thick with anticipation, and it slowly dawned on everyone that talking would not settle this – action would, fighting would.

"Now before we continue," Dena began, her voice calm, but untrustworthy. "I want to know how my other children are."

Silence descended and the tension began to suffocate me again, threatening to destroy everything I loved, everything that mattered to me. Elsu tensed from behind Cole and I. Chenoa stepped forward to take my other hand, squeezing it gently. So she had forgiven me. I glanced out of the corner of my eye and she smiled slightly. Relief flooded through me, but was suddenly chilled when I felt Elsu walk past Cole and I, heading toward Dena, toward his mother. Cole's mouth fell open and the little trust I had for Elsu shattered, replaced by bitter anger. Cole trusted him. Chenoa trusted him. We all trusted him.

Dena smiled as she took Elsu in her arms, embracing him tightly. Chandler slapped his back in a brotherly like gesture before Elsu took a few more steps to stand beside Dena.

No one saw this coming, not even Tyler. I had my suspicions, but Cole had been absolutely sure of his half-brother. He had trusted him completely, and he had been betrayed.

"Alright," Dena continued, gloating from her newly won victory. "I believe I'm ready to begin."

We all stood silently, expectantly, waiting for someone to make the first move. I stopped breathing, the anticipation overwhelming my senses for several moments.

Then chaos exploded at once, all around me. Dena and her followers charged at us. Cole was quick and pushed me behind him, transforming at the last second.

Several thunder like explosions rippled around me, making my ears ring for several moments. I tried to remember where I was supposed to be, but disorientation was clouding my thoughts, making it difficult to move and think. It wasn't until I felt someone punch me in the face did I realize I had hesitated too long.

I looked up from my new position after the punch threw me to the ground, shocked to find Dena leaning over me, the scar from where I had slashed her contrasting against her copper skin.

"Hello there dear," she smiled, her voice once again mirroring that of someone who had just escaped an insane asylum. "I've been waiting to repay you for this." she pointed out her scar with the sharp edge of her knife. Adrenaline pumped through me, replacing the oxygen in my lungs with anxiety. I had to take Dena down. She had to pay for what she had done.

Just as she was about to come down on me with her knife, I kicked her legs out from underneath her. She fell back and I had just enough time to get up and start running. I knew she'd follow me. I needed to take Dena far away from the battle, as far as I could. It was what she wanted. She'd do anything to get me.

Just as I had thought, I heard Dena's footfalls as she chased after me, completely forgetting about the battle that was taking place just above us and around us. Noah's tribe was leading many of the Rebels to the river nearby. If they were able to get them close to the water, they wouldn't stand a chance.

I glanced up, sending silent prayers to the Chosen and to Cole specifically. They were all blurs, the Chosen and the transformed Rebels. I wasn't even sure who was winning. I was almost to the forest edge of the field, when someone's heart wrenching screams made my pace slow. I looked over my right shoulder, horrified to find one of the people from Noah's tribe sobbing over the body of someone who had fallen, someone who hadn't made it to the river; our first casualty.

I kept running, forcing the tears, the sharp pang of grief, and the fear deep down within me. I'd deal with it later, if I lived long enough.

I just needed to focus. I had to get Dena further into the woods so I could and deal with her myself. She was on our territory. I had an advantage.

I whipped my head around as I stopped. Dena had followed,

breathing heavily and still holding a firm grip on her knife.

She smiled again, "Why so far away from all the action? Didn't want to watch your boyfriend die?"

"Shut up!" I yelled fumbling in my pant pockets until I finally found my own knife, the one Noah had given me.

She shook her head at me, "Tsk, Tsk. Testy today, aren't we?"

Silence descended between us as we circled each other, waiting for the other to make the next move. The sounds of the battle continued and seemed to be growing louder. I tried not to focus on it, not to think about it.

She picked up on my distraction, "You hear them?"

I remained stoic, refusing to fall for any of her games.

She continued, "Those are the sounds of death," she paused, gazing my reaction. "The deaths of all those you love."

"It doesn't have to be this way, Dena," I whispered, trying to ignore the sting from her words.

"You can stop all of this violence. You can end it," I continued, trying to convince her of some reason, anything that could save our lives.

She took a few steps toward me, her face unreadable, "I am going to end it. I am going to annihilate anyone who has gotten in my way. I am going to destroy the Chosen. I will start with that half-breed Cole. I'll be sure you're there to watch; to see the one person you love most die. I want that to be the last thing you ever see."

As her words rang through the air, echoing inside of my head, my whole world came into focus. My mission, though slightly altered, was clear. There was no other option. Dena had to die. Either she died, or I would lose everything that ever meant anything to me.

Suddenly, my anger overwhelmed me, causing me to forget everything Cole and Noah had taught me in training. I simply lunged and tried to stab her. I missed as she sidestepped me. I stumbled, as my knife met nothing but air. Dena had twisted just in time for her own knife to plunge deeply into my torso. I stumbled several steps back before falling to my knees, dropping my own knife as I took my two hands to the knife that was sticking out of me, the red stickiness of my own blood covering my hands, staining my shirt. The blood flowed out of me steadily, confusing me slightly. There was so much blood.

Dena began fading in and out of my vision. I had to focus. The pain was unbearable, fatal. I had to focus. I couldn't breathe, I couldn't see. I had to focus. Nausea at the sight of my own blood threatened to overtake me. I had to focus. Dena's laughter made my head dizzy. I had to focus. I was going to die here. No. I had to focus.

I carefully, slowly pulled the knife out, placing my left hand over the wound that was overflowing. Dena continued to pace, her eyes wide and wondering. I was curious as to why she wasn't finishing me off. Why was she letting me live?

She believed me to be the heavenly being. She wanted to see magic sprout out of me. I didn't know what she expected. Lightening from the sky, animals coming to my aid, blinding light? She didn't know what would happen for sure. If I could just fool her for a little bit longer, I could end this now; but the throbbing of my blood pumping out of me was making it more and more difficult to form a coherent thought.

I gripped Dena's knife tightly, allowing myself to slump over, feigning death. I held my breath, my left hand holding tightly to my wound. Trying to focus on healing and listening to Dena's movements was difficult.

"Focus, Adeline," Ogin's reassuring voice echoed in my thoughts, calming me and making the extreme pain less apparent. "Let your body do what feels natural."

I closed my eyes, allowing my body to fully relax. As I did so, I felt the muscles reconnect; the blood vessels manage to find their way back together to properly flow blood; the broken skin stitching itself back together; the lightheadedness from the loss of blood disappeared. I had healed myself. I had actually done it! I wasn't going to die, at least not at the current moment.

My celebration remained internal, as I continued to feign death. I could hear Dena's tense pacing as her feet crunched the ground around me.

She screamed in frustration and I had to clench my jaw as she kicked me to the side. Her knife remained in my right hand. I could feel her bend over me, her breath tickling my eyelids. She was so close.

"You can't be dead," she whispered, her voice suddenly void of her usual callousness. "They said you were it. That you'd finally been reincarnated." Her voice broke on the last word. Her hand rested on where she had stabbed me.

I feared she would notice the wound no longer existed, but instead her cold voice mumbled, "What a waste of my time, you stupid, useless girl. I should have drowned you with your parents."

I opened my eyes immediately, surprising Dena.

"You're the stupid one," I spoke softly, "and I feel sorry for you." Before she could move or respond, I took her knife and stabbed her neck. She shrieked, confusion and fear swirling in her eyes. She fell back, holding onto the knife that was now embedded in her body. I searched the floor for a nearby rock on the forest floor. When I found one I took it, determined to take her out of her pain. Dena's screams continued as panic coursed through her. She looked no longer human, but like an animal, confused and disoriented. I fought my tears as I slammed the rock into her head, the place Noah had taught me to hit, and she fell back instantly. Her hand fell from the knife in her neck where the blood continued to flow like a river down her neck to her chest, staining her white shirt a vibrant red. I watched as she finally released her last breath. I staggered backwards, grief, tears, and nausea hitting me all at once.

Dena was dead. I had killed her, and there was no taking it back.

I'm not sure how long I sat there with Dena's body. I don't know what I was waiting for, maybe some sort of punishment for taking a life: God to send a lightning bolt down. That person had been trying to kill me and I know there had been no other option, but I could still feel her blood on my hands.

I uselessly fought the tears that flowed helplessly down my face as I fought with myself. The only other option was to let her kill me. Death was going to take one of us. I walked into this forest with that knowledge, understanding that a price had to be paid.

But no one ever warns you. No one tells you that when you kill someone, a part of you dies with them. You are never the same. The person I was before I killed was a stranger, an old friend that seemed centuries in the past.

I stood slowly, wiping the last tears away. I silently bid Dena and the forest that had witnessed her death farewell. No matter how I tried to reason that there had been no other option, I realized that I'd never be able to forgive myself. I was changed, altered and different from the girl that had woken up that morning. This new person was someone I couldn't accept. At least not now.

I had found my way to the clearing, shocked to find that the fighting had drawn to a close. Without Dena, the Rebels were much weaker, unable to defend themselves as strongly as the Chosen could. Bodies of those fallen lay strewn across the field. I sidestepped several bodies, never looking into their faces. I couldn't. I'd break down.

I walked toward the center of the field where I could see Noah and what was left of his fighters.

His eyes met mine, "Adeline!"

He ran towards me, scooping me in his arms, trying to squeeze life into me.

"Thank God," he kept talking, his voice fatigued, but relieved. "The Rebels started to retreat when they realized they were outnumbered. It turns out not many tribes had actually agreed to help them. Cole and Jacy have been flying, looking for you. Are you okay?"

His eyes widened in shock when he saw the blood stained shirt and my empty eyes.

"What happened, Adeline?" he asked as the other Chosen, who had transformed back to their human forms, came to greet me.

"I killed her."

The words, spoken softly, rang a disfigured sort of truth that threatened to smother me, "I killed Dena."

No one responded. Noah's eyes widened in horror, his grip on my arms tightening. Chenoa and Dylan, battered and bruised, came up from behind Noah. They, too, were shocked at my revelation, tears already coursing down Chenoa's paled cheeks. Another pang of remorse and guilt rippled through me, trying to suffocate me. I didn't just kill Dena, leader of the Rebels. I had killed Chenoa's mother.

My breath came in short gasps as the guilt wrapped around me, blinding me. Noah pulled me into his arms, enfolding me in the comfort of his brotherly embrace.

"It's okay, Adeline," he whispered. "It's all over now. We won. The war's over."

Not even the relief that the end of the torture of this battle could eliminate my guilt. I was drowning in it.

"Looks like Cole and Jacy are back," Dylan's voice whispered despondently. Not even the excitement of winning a battle could lighten his load. We may have won the battle. Dena and her Rebels may have lost, but there were no victors.

I looked up to the sky just in time to see two eagles flying toward us. It wasn't until I heard Chenoa gasp that I noticed a third eagle had joined them. I glanced around and counted six of the Chosen that were standing around.

Then all thoughts of my guilt vanished when I realized Elsu was flying with Cole and Jacy. I felt myself scream, but no noise reached my ears as I saw Elsu begin to attack Cole and Jacy. As they continued to fight in the air, bodies hitting roughly, beaks stabbing at crucial arteries, I heard Elan and Dylan phase, attempting to aid Cole and Jacy, but Elsu was too strong. He had slammed Cole and Jacy into one another, causing them to suddenly lose their equilibrium, and they both began to fall. In mid descent, they both had phased to their human forms, horrifying me as they continued to speed toward the earth again.

Their bodies hit the ground with a sickening, bone breaking noise. I ran to Cole and fell next to his broken and battered body. His collarbone stuck out of his skin disjointedly. The left side of his body twisted unnaturally, bones protruding out of his skin. His legs were broken and fell at unnatural angels. Blood poured out of him, and his once vibrant eyes were glazed over. He should be dead already, but his body was still fighting uselessly. Death was covering him like a blanket. His breaths were numbered.

Chenoa was on the other side of Cole in an instant, glancing from Cole to Jacy. Jacy was now in his human form also, laying only feet away from Cole in a similar condition.

"Cole," I screamed, as I touched his face. His blood began to seep out of him into the ground, staining it a dull red.

"Adeline," he whispered, his dull eyes searching for me.

"I'm right here," I came very close to his face, feeling the shortness of his breath against my eyelids.

His cloudy blue eyes finally found mine, a smile tugging at his dry lips, "I love you."

I shook my head, "You can't leave me." My voice cracked, broken. If he died, then I knew I would too. My heart would not be able to handle this grief. I'd die of it.

"You can heal him," Noah's voice registered from behind me. "You know you can. You have to."

I gulped, glancing behind to find Noah, bruised, but still intact, "I can?"

"You healed yourself," he motioned to my torso. "I have no doubt you can fix him."

Cole's breathing was fast and short, indicating that I had very little time. This fact only intensified my panic. I had to focus.

"What about Jacy?" Ella's voice resonated as I looked over Chenoa's shoulder to the face of a man who had done everything to protect me. I had to save Jacy too. I had to.

But when his eyes met mine, the eyes I had always seen in the face of an eagle, he smiled knowingly, "No. Heal him. I want to go."

Ava and Olivia's cries rebounded through the field.

He was still staring at me, "Let me go."

My broken heart screamed in protest. I had to try to save both of them. Jacy had been there for me so many times, too many to count. I owed him my life. As I saw his breathing begin to slow, I knew he didn't want me to heal him. He wanted to die. He had waited over one hundred and fifty years to finally bid this world goodbye. I'd be doing him a dishonor if I attempted to stifle his one desire.

Tears slid down my face as I whispered, "Thank you."

He smiled his ancient smile, turning from me to look into the sky where I was sure he could already see his wife and daughter waiting for him.

I looked down to Cole who needed my immediate attention. I placed my hands on either side of his face, whispering, "I'm gonna fix you."

I wasn't sure if he heard me, but he smiled, closing his eyes. For a moment, I thought I had already lost him, but the steady rise and fall of his chest proved to me that I still had time. But it was fading quickly. Time was slipping through my fingers.

I closed my eyes, focusing on his broken body, determined to fix him. There was no other option. If he died, so would I. Like this war, there would be no winners.

MORNING GLORY

EPILOGUE

Cole

The air was cold and still, the light of the dawning sun washing over the sky and land like a warm blanket. The morning glory overwhelmed the mourners for a brief instance, blinded by the golden hue of the sun. The steady hum of drums and voices filled the air and the funeral continued in a steady stream of tradition and respect. The sobs of those around me reminded me why I was standing at the Chippewa burial ground.

He deserved much more, but this was all we could do. I think he would understand that.

I turned to my right, my eyes glancing over her face. Her tears hadn't stopped since I had woken up; after she had healed me.

I wrapped my fingers through her hand, squeezing them gently. Eventually, her eyes met mine, the hazel pools reflecting the internal chaos she was suffering. It had been a week since the battle, and she still couldn't talk about it without succumbing to uncontrollable sobs.

I had only woken up five days ago, after she had healed me. My body was whole again, but the emotional pain of having my own brother try to kill me left scars that would never fade.

The final drum echoed through the air and silence ensued, heightening every sob. The entire tribe came to say goodbye to their guardian, Jacy. A good fighter, a brave warrior, and a tired man who was more than ready to move on from this life on to the next. No one blamed him. In fact, most of us envied him.

Adeline and I stood there for a long time, our eyes glued to the newly dug grave, nestled under a tree. It was a very simple gravesite, just the way he would have wanted it.

Several people began to leave, patting my back, apologizing to me, for there was no other family to Jacy. Only the Chosen, we were his family.

Noah and his fiancé, Cailen, stepped towards us to say their goodbyes. Apparently, after Noah left South Carolina to aid my tribe, Cailen realized that even through the danger, Noah was worth it. She had seen how Adeline and I were dedicated to each other through it all and wanted to give it another try with Noah. She had flown in a few days ago, after hearing that a battle had taken place. Realizing Noah was safe, she asked for them to try again. Of course, he had been thrilled and proposed once more.

Their hands still clasped together, Noah reached out to grab my shoulder and give me a reassuring squeeze, "He was good warrior. This was a beautiful ceremony."

I nodded my thanks to both Noah and Cailen. Noah glanced down to Adeline, but even he knew not to disturb her thoughts. She had barely spoken since the day Jacy died.

Eventually, the area was cleared besides Adeline and me. Her quiet expression scared me more than any near death experience. I wanted her to talk to me, to tell me what she went through. I only knew the rough details from Noah. The news was shocking, overwhelming, but I knew that this was possible. Adeline was strong, but not strong enough to handle this load alone.

Yet, when Noah and the other Chosen were counting the dead, they couldn't find Dena's body. Most likely retreating Rebels found her and took her back to their tribe to give her a proper burial, not that she deserved it. I was glad she couldn't be accounted for. It would have destroyed Adeline even more to see her again. I couldn't let that happen.

The most important person on my mind was Adeline. She was being attacked; it was self-defense, but I knew the emotional damage from killing someone would stay with her forever. She'd never escape it. Not until it ate her, destroyed her, but I wouldn't let it. I'd protect her from anything, even herself.

"Cole," her voice croaked, crackling from the raw emotion that threatened to overtake her again.

"Yes?" I exclaimed, turning my complete attention to her. She turned toward me, her eyes glued to our intertwined hands like she was trying to solve something. It was as though, if she stared long enough, she'd be able to make some sort of sense out of everything that had happened.

She finally looked up to me, her eyes mirroring what she must have seen in mine: emptiness and weariness. I took her face in between my hands, trying to bring warmth back into her face.

"I love you," I whispered roughly, frantic to get my point across.

She nodded, not speaking, but at least understanding. It was a start.

I leaned in, capturing her lips in mine. We stood there, above the grave of a fallen comrade, of a friend, desperate to try to heal one another. Healing wouldn't happen overnight, or even in a year.

It would take years for us to finally put ourselves back together, before this internal war would ever be over. Especially when the very real truth that this war with the Rebels still hung in the air like a fog.

About the Author

Allison Blanchard is currently a student at Georgia College and State University in Milledgeville, Georgia where she is pursuing her bachelor degrees in English Creative Writing and French. She is an active sister in Sigma Alpha Omega where she continues to grow as a woman in Christ. She writes every day, drinks too much coffee, and is looking forward to the next adventure her characters will take her.

Learn more about Allison Blanchard and what she is currently working on at allisonblanchardbooks.blogspot.com.

25365714R00144

Made in the USA
Charleston, SC
27 December 2013